T0157640

FORTY DOLLARS

ALLAN HARDIN

iUniverse, Inc.
Bloomington

Forty Dollars

*This is a work of fiction. All of the characters, names, incidents,
organizations, and dialogue in this novel are either the products
of the author's imagination or are used fictitiously.
iUniverse books may be ordered through booksellers or by contacting:*

*iUniverse
1663 Liberty Drive
Bloomington, IN 47403
www.iuniverse.com
1-800-Authors (1-800-288-4677)*

*Because of the dynamic nature of the Internet, any web addresses or links contained in this
book may have changed since publication and may no longer be valid. The views expressed
in this work are solely those of the author and do not necessarily reflect the views of the
publisher, and the publisher hereby disclaims any responsibility for them.*

*Any people depicted in stock imagery provided by Thinkstock are models,
and such images are being used for illustrative purposes only.*

Certain stock imagery © Thinkstock.

*ISBN: 978-1-4697-9500-3 (hc)
ISBN: 978-1-4697-9499-0 (sc)
ISBN: 978-1-4697-9501-0 (e)*

Printed in the United States of America

iUniverse rev. date: 3/8/2012

This one is for my dear friends

Pat and Len

CHAPTER ONE

THE RATTLESNAKE LUNGED; its needle sharp fangs barely scraped the man's right hand as he pulled it out of harm's way with the reflexes of a cat. Having missed its intended target, the snake quickly recoiled into a defensive posture. Its rattle accelerated as its tongue flashed out of its mouth with greater frequency, in rhythmic balance with the movement of its tail. It stared at the man with transfixed eyes, biding its time, waiting for the right opportunity to strike.

Jake Romero, focused and intense, was on his haunches about five feet away from coiled death. He casually shifted his weight from one leg to the other, watching the rattlesnake with matched intensity. He very slowly and deliberately began to raise his left arm. The snake's eyes began to follow the movement. While the reptile's attention was on his left hand, Jake quickly shot out his right arm, aiming for a spot just to the right of the snake. The rattler responded just as quickly with a strike, barely missing Jake's right hand again.

Jake shifted his weight to his left hip and stared at the snake for a few minutes before beginning the routine for the third time. Again, he slowly raised his left arm, and the snake followed it with its eyes, but it had learned to expect some movement from Jake's right hand, so its eyes shifted quickly back to the right and then just as swiftly back to the left, watching Jake's slowly rising left arm. Instead of extending his right arm fully, Jake began the motion but quickly pulled his arm back. The rattler lunged, but there was nothing there. As quick as the snake was, Jake was faster. When it lunged for his right hand, Jake reached in with his left hand and caught the snake behind the head, rendering it harmless.

As he got to his feet with his captured prize, he heard someone behind him say, "Pretty impressive! Tell me where I can find Jake Romero."

Jake turned to look at the speaker. He still held the rattlesnake behind its head with a firm grip of his left hand, while his right hand held the reptile's lower body near the tail to keep it from moving. He eyed the three riders, saying nothing.

"Are you deaf or just plain stupid?" asked the rider in the middle. "I asked you where I could find Jake Romero."

"Who is asking?" Jake replied, never taking his eyes off the man.

At the sound of Jake's voice, a large grey canine that was lying against the warmth of an adobe wall lifted its head and looked around. Some people thought the creature that traveled with Jake was a pure bred wolf because it was about the size of a wolf, but more importantly, it had the coloring. Others were of the opinion it was a breed of dog that just looked a lot like a wolf. Someone once asked Jake what the animal was, and Jake told him he thought it was a wolf. When asked where he got it, Jake said he didn't get it anywhere; the creature had shown up one day and had tagged along with him ever since. When asked what he called the wolf, Jake simply said that he liked to be called '*Azul*', which was Spanish for blue. No one seemed to understand the name, but when Azul looked at you, in a certain light, his eyes did appear to be blue.

The three riders looked like ranch hands from one of the two large outfits or one of the dozens of smaller ranches in the area. The man in the middle, who was doing all the talking, was a tall, very lean man. He wore a large grey Stetson that made him appear even taller. Over top of his red flannel shirt, he wore a tattered sheepskin vest adorned with three braided sets of short leather tassels on each side of the garment, used to tie the sides of the vest together in colder weather. A Schofield .45 pistol was tucked into his belt. He sported a handle bar moustache and a week's worth of whiskers. One couldn't see the color of his eyes because he seemed to be constantly squinting. His left cheek was bulging from the wad of chewing tobacco he was working on.

The man on his right was of average build and height. Over top of his long-johns, he wore a brown suit jacket that was about two sizes too small with the sleeves stopping just above his wrists. Unlike most of his peers who wore wide brimmed Stetsons, he donned a brown derby hat that must have come with the suit jacket. Around his waist, he sported a two pistol rig with the handles turned outward.

The rider on the tall man's left was a thin, almost gaunt looking man of Spanish decent with perhaps some Indian blood in the mix. He had on a cotton shirt that matched his pants which were tucked into a pair of expensive looking Spanish riding boots. His large straw sombrero hung draped across his back. If you looked into his ebony eyes, they looked almost lifeless. Lying across his lap was a short, double barrel, 12-gauge shotgun; his weapon of choice.

The tall man in the middle turned sideways in the saddle and looked at his companion to his right and then shifting his weight, he glanced at his cohort to his left. He moved his attention back to Jake, spit out a large gob of brown liquid, and said, "Didn't know we had to explain ourselves to some goddamn 'Pache." He dismounted and handed the reins to the rider on his left. As he approached Jake, he said, "Last time I ask 'fore I teach you some manners. Where do I find Jake Romero?"

As Tall Man approached, Jake extended his arms, launching the frightened, agitated rattlesnake in his direction. Tall Man's eyes bulged out, his mouth fell open, and he staggered backwards, nearly falling over. As he was stumbling, he still had the wherewithal to pull his pistol and cock it, ready to shoot the snake at his feet. He looked down, but there was no snake. In fact, to his perception, it was nowhere to be found. "What the hell?" he asked of no one in particular.

Tall Man's two companions looked puzzled. They didn't understand what Tall Man was going on about, for they had seen the old man throw the snake ten feet to his left. They saw it hit the ground and crawl away as fast as it could to the safety of a pile of rocks a few feet away.

Jake smiled and said, "I am called Jacob Romero."

Tall Man seemed surprised as he checked out the man in front of him. Jake stood five foot ten with a very solid build. He had no facial hair, and his bronzed skin was set off with a pair of sky-blue eyes. He wore a black headband to keep his shoulder length, dirty blonde, graying-at-the temples hair out of his face. His attire consisted of a dark blue flannel shirt and a pair of soft buckskin britches tucked into a pair of knee high moccasins. From a distance, he looked like an Apache, but up close anyone could see he was definitely a white man.

Tall Man, still a little shaky from the snake incident, said, "We didn't know 'twas you. We was told to look for an ole white man. No 'fence, but you look like you just come off the reservation."

"What do you want of me?" Jake asked with a hint of annoyance in his voice.

Tall Man's thoughts returned to the snake, and he said, "Tell me what you did with that rattler, and maybe we can talk some business."

Ignoring Tall Man's request, Jake asked, "What sort of business?"

By this time, Tall Man's two compadres had dismounted and joined him. When they did, Azul got up, stretched, and sauntered over to stand beside Jake. Tall Man said, "Name's Pat Wilkens. These two yahoos is Jim Clemfeld and Antonio somethin' or other. We just call him Mex."

Wilkens extended his hand for a shake and was taken aback when Jake didn't reciprocate. Jake didn't say anything but simply stood with a look of expectation, waiting for anything else Wilkens might have to say. "Well," continued Pat, "we work for the White Sands Land and Cattle Association, and our boss, name of Mr. Sinclair Thornsbury, wants to hire you for some scoutin' needs doin'."

"What does the job pay?" asked Jake.

"Don' rightly know. I was told to bring you in, so's you two can talk 'bout it," replied Wilkens.

Jake's silence and the recent snake incident seemed to be unnerving Wilkens. He shifted his weight and said, almost in frustration, "You don' say much, do ya?" After a pause, where he was hoping Jake would respond, he continued. "Look, it ain't no skin off my nose, but if'n I was you, I'd at least hear what the man has to say."

"This I can do," replied Jake.

Jake's answer seemed to please Wilkens. He was smiling when he said, "Good. Good. Alright then, get your horse and let's get a goin'. We got a three hour ride, and I'd like to make it 'fore dark."

"No horse," stated Jake.

Wilkens lost his good humor and went on a rant, "Jesus, no horse! Everyone has a goddamn horse! Shithouse mouse, someone get this white 'Pache a goddamn horse!"

The man Wilkens called Jim Clemfeld mounted and galloped a short distance down the street to what passed for a livery. In reality, it was a small adobe hut with several sectioned corrals. There were three horses in one section and a half dozen donkeys in another. A Mexican lad, about ten or eleven years old, stepped out of the hut, and Jim ordered him to quickly saddle one of the horses.

While Clemfeld was getting the horse, Wilkens tried to make small talk. Thinking Jake might be interested in what Thornsbury had to say, he began to elaborate. "We been havin' trouble with rustlers and horse thieves. That ain't out of the ordinary, mind you, 'cause we always have trouble with rustlers and thieves. It comes natural with the territory, like coyotes and cowshit. Lately, though, there's been more cattle and horses missin' than usual. The ranchers what make up the Association is gettin' a little concerned, and then the damn thieves up and stole a bunch of breedin' mares from Mr. Thornsbury. Yes Sir, he really got his hair on fire o'er that one."

Jake interjected, "You sure talk a lot."

Wilkens gave him a long hard stare, shook his head slowly from side to side, and said, "Ya know, when Mr. Thornsbury is through with you I am really gonna enjoy givin' you the whuppin' of your miserable life."

Jake just smiled. There was an awkward silence for what seemed an eternity. The approach of Jim Clemfeld, with saddled horse in tow, broke the tension.

"Mount up! Let's go," bellowed Wilkens.

"I did not say I was going anywhere," countered Jake. "Mr. Thornsbury can talk to me here."

"Oh, you're goin', one way or another; o'er the saddle or sittin' in it. It's up to you," replied Wilkens, as he glanced at the Mexican to his left. Jake followed Wilkens' gaze, and he saw that the Mexican had pulled back both hammers on the shotgun. With a quick glance at Jim Clemfeld, he noticed Jim had also drawn one of his pistols and cocked it.

"This must be important," said Jake as he mounted. "I shall talk with this Mr. Thornsbury."

While Jake and his escorts were on the way to the Thornsbury ranch, Sinclair Thornsbury, red-faced and angry, stood at the head of a large oak table that occupied most of his study. His fists were clenched, and he leaned on his knuckles as he talked, lifting his right arm occasionally and shaking a chubby forefinger to make a point. "It is my intention to see every horse thief, every cattle rustler, and their dogs strung up from the nearest tree strong enough to hold them!" he roared.

The other men seated around the table had never seen their leader quite so animated. Thornsbury paused for effect then continued, "I came to this country and built one of the finest cattle operations west of the Mississippi, and I will be damned if I am going to lose another head of cattle or another horse to those bastards. Are you with me?"

Thornsbury was a short, overweight, middle-aged Englishman and the undisputed head of the White Sands Land and Cattle Association. Of the seven men in the room, he had the second largest spread. Patrick Dunnigan owned the largest ranch in terms of area, but it was Sinclair Thornsbury who ran things in the region. He had come from England in the early 1870's and settled in the area when no one else dared venture into Apache country. He ran cattle on the open range and sold them at a huge profit to the army at Fort Craig, Fort McRae, and Fort Selden.

"I've always sided with you on most matters," said Patrick Dunnigan, "but don't you think you're flying off the handle on this one? I mean, we've always had rustlers and horse thieves. It's part of the business." Dunnigan had arrived in the area a couple of years after Thornsbury and set up operations at the opposite end of the valley. The two men respected each other and often ran their cattle together, separating them after the fall roundup.

Over the next ten years, about a dozen or so settlers had taken up residence and established smaller operations scattered throughout the basin. Sinclair Thornsbury had a shrewd business mind, and he saw the advantages in a cooperative where the members could combine their resources and get top dollar for their cattle. At the same time, by buying their supplies in bulk they could cut their operating expenses. Thus, the White Sands Land and Cattle Association was born.

Thornsbury took the floor and said, "Patrick, I understand your thinking. I used to think the same way, too. What's a few head of cattle or a horse or two? Well, the old adage applies — give them an inch and they will take a mile. By letting it slide, we have delivered a message that announces: '*Come help yourselves. We won't do anything about it.*' We have to delivery a new message that states emphatically: '*No more! Steal from the Association and you will face the consequences.*' We must take a stand."

Michael Conklin spoke up, "Mr. Thornsbury, I have a question." He looked about the table at the other members as is for support and then continued, "What are you going to do to stop the rustlers and horse thieves?"

"You needn't concern yourself with the details, Mr. Conklin. All you have to do is pay your share of the expenses," replied Thornsbury.

Conklin owned one of the smaller spreads near Dunnigan's end of the valley. He was a hard worker who minded his own business and expected others to do the same.

Sinclair Thornsbury did not like Michael Conklin. To Thornsbury, Conklin was a stubborn pain in the ass. It was like pulling hen's teeth to get him to do anything without a lengthy explanation or an argument.

"Just what is it I'm paying for?" asked Conklin.

Thornsbury could see that all eyes in the room were focused on him, and they all wanted an answer to Conklin's question. After a momentary pause, he said, "I have taken the liberty of hiring three gentlemen who are experienced in this sort of business."

Conrad Mueller was a German immigrant who had settled in the area not long after Thornsbury and Dunnigan. He and his two grown sons had built a respectable horse trading business. They rounded up wild stock and saddle broke them before selling them to the army and the ranchers in the area. Conrad said, "You mean gunmen? I will have no part of this!"

Thornsbury had not anticipated any opposition to his plan. He replied with an angry undertone, "If you want to remain a member of this association you will go along with whatever this group decides. That's the way it works in this country, Mr. Mueller; we vote and the majority rules."

Joseph DeLarosa and John Ballard, two small time ranchers, looked at each other and nodded. It was as if they knew what the other was thinking. They folded their arms across their chests and sat silent with scowls on their faces.

The last man at the table was a southerner, Colonel Ben Hollister, who still considered himself an officer and a gentleman. After the Civil War, having lost everything he owned to carpetbaggers, he left North Carolina to wander about Texas and Mexico. After a dozen years of the saddle tramp lifestyle, he had settled in the basin. He was an easy going man with little ambition or motivation who still hated the Yankees for having taken away his life of rank and privilege. He did just enough work to keep his small ranch from foreclosure. He didn't really care about the matter currently before the members, but he was driven by his need for acknowledgement of his self-perceived importance when he asked, "Mr. Thornsbury, just exactly who are these men that you have hired in our good name?"

Thornsbury got up and walked to the study entrance, opened the door, and said to someone in the hallway, "Won't you please come in?"

Three men entered the room and stood at the head of the table. Thornsbury said, "Gentlemen, permit me to introduce Deacon Samuel Fletcher, his son Nathaniel, and Mr. Gus Haines."

Samuel Fletcher was a short man; maybe five foot six or seven, at best. He was a self-proclaimed minister, and though not ordained by any church, he believed it was his mission to punish those that he deemed wicked. He was dressed all in black, which included a long black coat with tails and tall Spanish riding boots. He sported a priest's white collar and an old, weather-beaten, black, Stetson hat. The entire ensemble was set off by a metallic cross on a silver chain, hanging from his neck. The only weapon he carried was a short-barreled Winchester .44 carbine.

Nathaniel Fletcher, much taller than his father, was dressed in similar fashion to the older Fletcher, including the black coat with tails and high boots, but he wore no collar or cross. His weapon of choice was the somewhat longer

Winchester .44 rifle. Nathaniel always had a smirk on his face like he knew something you didn't and was taunting you with it.

Gus Haines wore grey dungarees, held up by canvas suspenders overtop his red long underwear. He wore no shirt, but sported a brown leather vest from which dangled a gold chain attached to a pocket watch that Gus took out of his right vest pocket and checked every few minutes as if he were waiting for a late train. His dirty, brown hat hung on his back, secured by a leather string around his neck. Gus was armed with a holstered Starr double-action .44 army pistol. On his horse, in a scabbard, was a Sharp's .50 caliber rifle with a telescopic sight, in case they needed to do some long distant shooting.

Colonel Hollister interrupted the proceedings when he said, "I have heard of this Sam Fletcher and the two poor excuses for human beings riding with him. They are wanton killers for hire, and there is nothing reverent about them."

Thornsbury was about to say something when the elder Fletcher cut him off, "I do the Lord's work, Sir! I am the mighty sword that cuts down the wicked and the evil ones who prey upon the good Christian people of this land." As he spoke, his eyes grew wide and he turned his head to one side. He paused and held his head in a sideways position, rotating his eyes, so that he made visual contact with everyone in the room. There wasn't a single man who didn't feel uncomfortable. Nathaniel Fletcher chuckled and grinned.

There was, what seemed, a very long pause before Thornsbury cleared his throat and spoke, "Uhh, yes. Seems like the Deacon is passionate about his work. That's a good thing, I'm sure."

Thornsbury wasn't wrong with his assessment. The Deacon, his son, and the Deacon's nephew, Gus Haines, had a reputation across the South from East Texas to New Mexico. They were unaffectionately called "The Father, The Son, and The Holy Ghost." They were, essentially, guns for hire, and many a rustler, petty criminal, or horse thief would leave the territory as quickly as possible when he heard the trinity was on their trail.

CHAPTER TWO

"Who the hell is this?" demanded an irate Thornsbury. He was doubly upset; Pat Wilkens and his two cronies were two hours past due, plus they had just made a mess of his polished hardwood floor with their mud-caked boots.

Pat Wilkens replied with a tone of indifference, "This here's Jake Romero, the fella you sent us after."

"I asked for one of the best trackers in the country, and you bring me this derelict!" retorted Thornsbury, nearly shouting.

Jake turned to leave. "Where in blazes do you think you are going?" asked Thornsbury.

"I have decided I do not want to work for you," replied Jake.

Thornsbury was taken aback, "What — what do you mean? Nobody talks to me like that!"

Wilkens interrupted, "I know he don' look like much, Mr. Thornsbury, but without a word of a lie, this here's Jake Romero."

Thornsbury looked shocked. "I apologize, Mr. Romero. I was expecting a white man suitably dressed in civilized apparel, not someone who — who looks like — well, you know what I mean," he stammered.

Jake turned back to face Thornsbury and asked, "How much does the job pay?"

"Don't you want to know what the job is before how much it pays?" asked a surprised Thornsbury.

Jake didn't reply. He had asked a question, and he was still waiting for an answer. Thornsbury understood what was happening, and clearing his throat, he replied in a very business like manner, "The job pays a dollar a day and provisions."

Jake responded without hesitation, "Two dollars."

Thornsbury was flabbergasted, "Why—why this is an outrage! The rate is a dollar a day!"

Again, Jake turned and started toward the exit. Thornsbury let him get to the door before he spoke, "Alright, alright. I'll pay you two dollars a day. You are damn lucky there isn't another scout in the area." Turning to Wilkens, he added, "Take Mr. Romero and put him with the other troglodytes."

Wilkens didn't have the slightest idea what a troglodyte was, but he assumed Thornsbury meant the three men that he had noticed entering one of the bunkhouses earlier. Wilkens, Jim Clemfeld, and the man they called Mex escorted Jake out of the ranch house and across a large yard to the first of three identical buildings; the bunkhouses for the men working on the ranch. The cowboys had been moved to the other two bunkhouses to accommodate Deacon Fletcher, his two cohorts, Pat Wilkens, his two partners, and Jake Romero.

When Wilkens and company came through the bunkhouse door, Gus Haines stood quickly, drew his pistol, and cocked the hammer. Pat Wilkens said, "Whoa, whoa—hold on there, cowboy. Put the gun away. You're amongst friends here."

Samuel Fletcher rose from where he was sitting on the bunk and said, "I apologize for Brother Haines. He is a little over protective of me sometimes." He paused briefly and then turned his head sideways. His eyes went wide when he asked, "And who might you gentlemen be?"

Pat made introductions, and when he was done, Deacon Fletcher looked Jake up and down several times. Noticing what he thought was a dog standing beside Jake, Fletcher actually snarled at Azul, who merely turned his head and looked quizzically at him. Fletcher turned to face Pat and asked, "Is this heathen and his mongrel going to live under the same roof as the rest of us God-fearing men?"

An uncomfortable Pat Wilkens made eye contact with both men; first Jake, then Fletcher, and back to Jake again before he spoke. "Why, this man ain't no 'Pache. He's as white as you or me. Just look at them baby blue eyes."

Fletcher asked Jake, "Well, Mr. Blue Eyes, then why do you dress like a savage?"

Jake didn't answer. Instead, he walked towards the nearest bunk and lay down on the bottom half which prompted Fletcher to mutter something about Jake having the manners of a heathen. Gus Haines covered the distance between himself and the bunk Jake was occupying in three long strides. "That's my bunk," he stated firmly.

Jake rose and walked the few feet to the next set of bunks and lay down on the bottom one. Again, Haines followed him and told him the bunk belonged to Nathaniel Fletcher. Jake repeated the process a third time, and for a third time Haines said the bunk belonged to the Deacon Fletcher. Jake's patience had reached its limit. He sat up and asked, "Which bed is not taken?"

There were four sets of double bunk beds in the room, enough for eight men. Haines replied, "They are all taken!"

Jake rose quickly and headed for the door. Wilkens asked, "Where ya goin', Jake?"

Jake replied, "The air is foul in this place. I will sleep outside where there is no stench of hypocritical righteousness."

Wilkens was taken aback by the big words coming from Jake. Deacon Fletcher cocked his head to one side and smiled. He said, "One moment, if you please, Mr. Romero. It seems we have misjudged you. You sound like a very educated man. Pray tell, where did you learn to speak the Queen's English so eloquently?"

Jake had paused to hear Fletcher out and then turned and started towards the door with Azul close behind. Gus Haines followed him with the intention of spinning Jake around and giving him a solid backhand for his insolence. The moment Gus's hand touched his shoulder, Jake dropped into a squat, and balancing himself with his left hand on the floor, he swung his right leg in a wide arc, knocking the surprised Haines off his feet. Before Haines hit the floor, Jake had maneuvered behind him and put Haines in a choke hold with his right arm. His left hand held an eight inch knife, the point of the blade under Haines's right eye.

Deacon Fletcher picked up his Winchester from one of the top bunks and levered a shell into the firing chamber. Nathaniel, following his father's lead, did the same. "I suggest that you let go of Mr. Haines," said the older Fletcher. "He's family, and we wouldn't want to see any harm come to him, now would we?"

Azul, sensing danger, spread his legs for balance, barred his teeth, and emitted a deep guttural growl. Jake never moved a muscle. He continued to stare at the preacher and his son, like a bird of prey watching and waiting for his quarry to make the next move. After what seemed an eternity, Pat Wilkens broke the tension by clearing his throat and saying, "Shithouse mouse, but that boy is quick. Ain't he? I seen 'im catchin' rattlesnakes with his bare hands." He took a few steps and positioned himself between the combatants. With his back to Jake and facing the Fletchers, he continued, "You don' want to kill him, Deacon. We need him. He's the best damn tracker in seven counties. Not to mention the fact that Mr. Thornsbury might be a tad upset."

Samuel Fletcher turned his head to one side, and a wide, maniacal grin appeared on his face. He stated, "Brother Haines can track just fine. We don't need two trackers, do we, Mr. Wilkens?" Fletcher didn't expect an answer, so he continued, "Seems like we should get rid of one." He cocked the hammer on his rifle, and as he did so, he could hear the distinct clicks of a pistol and a shotgun being cocked, off to his right.

Jim Clemfeld and Mex had drawn and readied their weapons. Deacon Fletcher turned his gaze to the two men and then looked back at Pat. He spoke slowly and deliberately, "Wherefore, let him that thinketh he standeth take heed lest he fall."

Wilkens slowly shook his head from side to side and said, "I'm not exactly sure what you just said, but I ain't fallin' anywheres. Best thing we all can do is calm down and learn to get along. We got a lot of hard ridin' ahead of us." He glanced at Jake, who was still holding Haines in the choke hold with the knife to his face. Wilkens continued, "Let him up, Jake." Looking at Fletcher, he added, "There ain't gonna be any more trouble. Ain't that right, Deacon?"

Fletcher tilted his head to one side and glanced at Clemfeld and Mex still holding their weapons at the ready. He quoted the Bible again, "Patience is the companion of wisdom." After a short pause, he completely changed the subject when he said to Jake, "You and your four legged companion are welcome to share this humble abode with us."

Jake released his hold on Haines but not before giving him a little nick on his cheek with the point of the knife. Jake rose quickly as did Haines, and it appeared that trouble would start again, but Fletcher intervened when he said, "That will be all, Brother Haines."

"But he cut me!" whined Haines.

Wilkens interrupted, "He had to. 'Pache tradition. He pulls his knife in anger, he has to use it, if not on someone else then on hisself."

Haines wiped the tiny trickle of blood from his cheek and glared at Fletcher as if he was asking permission to continue the fight with Jake. The

Deacon simply smiled and said, "Not to worry, Brother Haines. I am sure an opportunity for retribution will present itself."

Wilkens took everyone's attention in another direction when he asked, "Anybody for some cards?" Jim Clemfeld and Mex joined Wilkens at one end of the long table that filled the center of the room. As he picked up a dog-eared deck of cards from the table and shuffled them, Wilkens looked at the Fletchers and Haines once more as if he was offering the invitation to play one last time.

"Gambling is a sinful practice, and those who indulge in it shall be punished, sayeth the Lord," uttered Fletcher.

"Oh horseshit! I never heard nothin' of the sort. I think the good Lord didn't *sayeth* no such thing," retorted Wilkens.

"Are you calling me a liar, Sir?" As he asked the question, Fletcher's head turned sideways, his eyes opened wide, and the maniacal smile they had seen before, appeared on his face, making Wilkens feel very uncomfortable.

Wilkens stammered, "No — no — it's just that I never heard of no quote like that from the Bible. Uh - that don't mean there ain't one. Like I said, I ain't never heard of one, is all. Besides, we don't play for any serious money. Match sticks most often."

Fletcher straightened his head, relaxed his eyes, and said, "And withal they learn to be idle, wandering from house to house; and not only idle, but tattlers also and busybodies, speaking things they ought not."

Wilkens, losing his sense of humor, had reached his toleration point. He threw the tattered deck of cards on the plank table, stood up abruptly, and remarked. "It's gettin' a little thick in here from all the horseshit. Think I'll go out for some air." With that in mind, he quickly covered the few paces to the door, opened it, and started out, only to be confronted by Sinclair Thornsbury, Patrick Dunnigan, and Ben Hollister.

"Ah, just the man I want to see," said Thornsbury. He forced his way past Wilkens and into the middle of the room, with Dunnigan and Hollister close behind. He scanned the room slowly, taking note of everyone inside. "Gentlemen, I am glad that we have you all together. I know it is getting late, and you all need your beauty sleep, so I won't keep you long. Tomorrow morning, bright and early, the seven of you, accompanied by Colonel Hollister, will be going on a lengthy hunting expedition."

He paused momentarily, and then his voice went up several octaves and filled with emotion when he said, "Your prey — every cursed horse thief, every saddle bum, every Mexican bandit, every heathen renegade who think they can come into this basin and steal from The White Sands Land and Cattle

Association! I want them brought to justice, and if they resist, shoot them where they stand, or hang them from the nearest tree big enough to hold their miserable corpses!"

He took several deep breaths which seemed to calm him somewhat. "Gentlemen, you have all the tools you need to carry out the task. We have, supposedly, one of the best trackers that good money can buy. Deacon Fletcher and friends, hopefully, will live up to their reputation, and Mr. Wilkens, it's about time you and your two cronies earn what I pay you. That's all, Gentlemen. Any questions?"

Jake asked, "Do I get paid for today?"

Thornsbury completely ignored him. Deacon Fletcher stepped forward and asked, "Where shall we begin this mission?"

"Mr. Wilkens knows the territory well, and he is familiar with the locales of the thievery and the routes these scoundrels take to escape with their booty. You will all take your orders from Colonel Hollister, who in turn will rely on the knowledge and experience you all have to offer in order to make his decisions," Thornsbury replied.

Thornsbury, impatient to leave, paused long enough to see if there were any more questions, and as he turned to go, Jake stood up and said with a hint of sarcasm, "I have no weapon. To hunt such bad men, I must have a weapon."

Thornsbury looked at Pat and gave an order, "See to it that he has a rifle and some ammunition." Then he added with the same amount of sarcasm Jake had used, "God knows, we wouldn't want Mr. Romero unequipped for the job." He added, "Goodnight Gentlemen," and he and Dunnigan left the bunkhouse, while Colonel Hollister remained.

Hollister sat down at the head of the long table and invited everyone to take a seat. There was a natural, subconscious gravitation to separate sides of the table, with the Fletcher clan sitting to Hollister's left and Wilkens and his crew occupying chairs to Hollister's right. Jake Romero sat at the other end of the table, leaving quite a distance between himself and the rest of the group which caused Hollister to say, "Why don't you come closer, so you can hear what I have to say?"

Jake rose and sat in the chair at the end of the Wilkens line, next to Mex. As he got comfortable, he looked up and saw Gus Haines staring at him with pure hatred in his eyes. Jake returned the stare for a few seconds, smiled slightly, and pursed his lips, imitating a kissing motion. Haines, his blood boiling, was incensed. As he rose, he kicked his chair backwards and lunged across the table at Jake, both hands reaching for Jake's throat. As quick as Haines was, Jake was a lot faster, and he was up on his feet, standing several feet back of the table with his knife drawn, leaving an embarrassed Gus Haines sprawled across the table.

Hollister defused what could have been a volatile situation when he rose from his chair and shouted, "That will be enough, Gentlemen! I don't know what your differences are, but they stop here! You want to kill each other? I personally don't give a damn, but you will set your differences aside for the purposes of this mission! Do I make myself clear?"

Haines crawled back off the table to a standing position, Jake put away his knife after cutting his finger slightly, and they simultaneously sat back down in their chairs. Deacon Fletcher turned his head sideways to face Haines and said, "As I said before, Brother Haines, the Lord shall provide an opportunity to punish this heathen when the time is right."

Pat Wilkens laughed out loud and said, "Lord or no Lord, when the time comes, my money is all on ole Jake, here. Yes, Sir."

Hollister, who was still standing, was growing impatient. "Deacon, perhaps you and your party should pack up your things and get out. I'm sure the Association can find adequate replacements in short order."

Fletcher backed down. "You have my word. You will have no more trouble from us until the job is done," he said. He paused and then added, "But when the mission is completed to the Association's satisfaction, there will be a reckoning. On that, you also have my word." He paused briefly for effect, and then looking at Colonel Hollister, he quoted the Bible again, "Give to everyone what you owe them. Pay your taxes and government fees to those who collect them, and give respect to those in authority."

Hollister wasn't really sure what Fletcher had just said, so he cleared his throat and said, "If you children are done squabbling, let us get busy and figure out how to catch some rustlers."

CHAPTER THREE

THE DULL GREY of the early morning light, mixing with a rising ground mist, left Hollister and his eclectic posse with an eerie, mystical feeling. The mood was sullen as each man, alone with his thoughts, finished the task of saddling up and tending to his personal gear. Two of Thornsbury's ranch hands had packed enough provisions for at least three weeks on three pack horses along with some cooking gear, a couple of axes, and a small buck saw for cutting firewood.

Colonel Hollister mounted and turned his horse back in the direction of the ranch house, slowly heading toward it. The rest of the men followed suit. Sinclair Thornsbury came out onto the veranda and walked to the top of the stairs just as Hollister and company arrived. It was as if he had been waiting behind the door until the timing was right to step out and make a grand entrance. He said, "Gentlemen, I just want to say a few words before you head out on your mission. You all know the task at hand. You are to rid the territory of every horse thief, cattle rustler, and renegade who dares set foot on Association property. Hopefully, in a short time, word will spread, and these human vermin will think twice about coming into this valley to do their business. You have the blessing of local law enforcement. Deputy Sheriff Gunderson gets paid by the Association and is fully supportive of this initiative. Colonel Hollister represents the Association, and he will be judge and jury when it comes to the dispensation of justice. Good Hunting!"

As Thornsbury turned and went back inside the ranch house, Hollister reined his horse around, shouted some orders, and headed out of the yard and down the road. The Fletchers and Gus Haines took their place behind the Colonel as ordered, while Pat, Jim, and Mex followed with Jim Clemfeld leading the pack horses. Jake was the last to leave the yard, and remembering the Colonel had told him to ride up front, he spurred his horse gently and caught up to Hollister.

Noticing Jake beside him, Hollister remarked, "Hope you are as good as Pat seems to think you are."

"I am a tracker. That is what I do best," replied Jake, and then he asked, "Where do we start?"

Hollister explained, "One of the line riders noticed three or four men herding a dozen cattle or so along the western edge of the ranch just north of canyon country. Once they get into those canyons it will be very difficult to track them over the table rock. That's where you come in. In a few hours you can start earning that two dollars a day."

Hollister was a stickler for detail, and when something was out of place he noticed it right away. Not seeing Jake's dog, or wolf, or whatever it was, he asked the inevitable question, "Where's your dog?"

Jake looked all around and then answered, "I do not know. He comes and goes as he pleases. I am sure he is close by."

Hollister scanned the area to his left, to his right, and lastly, straight ahead. Unable to see Azul anywhere, he yielded to the temptation to look behind. As he turned his head back to the front, he made eye contact with Jake. It annoyed him slightly to see Jake smiling because he thought the man was toying with him.

The group rode along the well traveled road for about three miles and then took a sharp turn towards the outline of the mountains on their right. Each man in the troop rode in relative silence, broken only by the intermittent rants of Deacon Fletcher. Sometimes he quoted the Bible; while other times his outburst was something he made up to get his thoughts out. Fletcher truly believed he was doing God's work, and that his ideas of doling out punishment and retribution to those whom he perceived to be the wicked, came from God. With every outburst, Colonel Hollister would turn in the saddle, stare at Fletcher, and then face forward again, muttering something about a crazy old fool under his breath.

Pat Wilkens, the joker in the deck, smiled every time Fletcher hollered. Soon after the Deacon started his exaltations, Pat would shout a loud *'Amen'* and turn and smile back at Jim and Mex. After the third *'Amen'*, Fletcher stopped, turned his horse in Pat's direction, and asked, "Are you mocking me, Mr. Wilkens?"

Pat looked very serious when he replied, "No Sir! I'm just agreein' with what you're sayin', Deacon." He spat a large gob of brown juice onto the ground, wiped his big moustache with his shirt sleeve, and smiled.

Fletcher stared hard at Pat for what seemed an eternity and then quoted the Bible, "All manner of sin and blasphemy shall be forgiven unto men, but the blasphemy against the Lord shall not be forgiven unto men."

Pat reciprocated with a resounding, "Amen, Brother!" which prompted another hateful look from Fletcher.

What could have escalated into a clash, was defused by Hollister who had ridden back to see why they had stopped. "Is there a problem, men?" he asked.

Pat had a smirk on his face when he replied, "We was just listenin' to a short sermon from the good Preacher, here."

"Let us focus our energies on the business at hand, shall we?" said Hollister rather sternly.

"Blessed are the peacemakers for they shall be known as the children of God," said Fletcher as he turned his horse forward and nudged it gently in the ribs. Hollister simply shook his head and spurred his horse to take his spot at the front of the column.

After another three hours in the saddle, they stopped to rest the horses and to have a bite to eat since none of them had eaten any breakfast. While they were gnawing on some very salty beef jerky and some dry, rock-hard biscuits, a lone rider approached them on their back trail, pushing his horse pretty hard. As the man came into range, Hollister recognized him as the line rider who had reported the rustling. The cowboy dismounted, tipped his hat, and said, "Colonel Hollister?" He waited for a return acknowledgement from Hollister and then continued, "Mr. Thornsbury sent me out to show you where I saw them rustlers. I didn't know you were leaving so early, or I would have come with you. Nobody told me you were leaving —"

An understanding Hollister cut him off, "That's fine, Taylor. Don't worry about it. I'm sure we would have picked up their trail, but you can show us where it is. That will make things a lot easier."

"It ain't far. You're just about there. Another half hour or so. Right below Burnt Timber Ridge," said Taylor.

Burnt Timber Ridge got its name from the stand of ancient fire-blackened pines that extended for the better part of two miles under some sandstone cliffs which sat atop a low row of foothills that ran parallel to the mountains behind them. A half hour of easy riding brought the group to a well used area, just as Taylor had described. There were hoof prints everywhere in the sandy soil, belonging to both cattle and horses. A large fire circle with partially burnt logs appeared to have been the center of activity.

Without being asked, Gus Haines dismounted quickly and began walking back and forth across the area, stopping and kneeling every few feet to examine anything that caught his attention. After some close scrutiny, he would rise and gently push the dust around with his right foot and then try another spot. After several minutes he stopped and addressed Deacon Fletcher, "Looks like three or four horses and maybe a dozen cattle, Reverend."

All eyes were on Hollister who wasn't sure what to do. The Association was paying good money to an expert tracker, and yet one of Fletcher's men had assumed the role. He cleared his throat and said very diplomatically, "Thank you, Mr. Haines. I am sure you are a fine tracker, but I would like Mr. Romero to verify your findings, if you wouldn't mind?"

At the mention of his name, Jake dismounted and starting at the fire pit, he walked in expanding circles around it. Forty feet from the fire pit, he walked in a straight line in a southerly direction for a hundred feet. He crouched down on his haunches and picked up some horse dung, crumbling it in his hands. Returning to the group, he related his conclusions to Hollister, "Two days ago, there were four riders. They changed the brand on seven steers."

Gus Haines laughed out loud and then remarked, "Horseshit! How in God's green earth can he possibly tell if any cattle were branded here, let alone the exact number?"

Hollister, wanting to know as well, looked at Jake and said, "Explain it to him, Mr. Romero."

Jake sighed heavily with impatience and explained his findings, "I also see tracks of four horses. The dung is almost dry. The day before yesterday it was still in the horse. The big fire pit is where the branding was done." As far as Jake was concerned, there was no more to explain, but he sensed Hollister and company were looking for more detail, so he walked the few paces to the fire pit and picking up a small unburned log, he held it up for all to see and continued, "When changing a brand you do not put a red hot iron to the animal. If you do, it is very easy to tell the brand has been changed because the new burn is much darker than the old. A cooler iron does not burn so deep which makes it difficult to see that the brand has been changed. To cool the iron, you can press it on some wood. This log shows it was done seven times." Jake could have told them much more; that one of the horses had a crooked shoe, that the riders treated their mounts well, judging by the undigested oats in the road apples, or that one or more of the riders smoked a lot, considering the numerous cigarette butts scattered about.

Hollister seemed satisfied with Jake's analysis and had no desire to continue the discussion with Gus Haines or Deacon Fletcher. "Let's move out and catch us some rustlers," he commanded.

For the rest of the day they made good time. The trail was plain and easy to follow. In the western foothills the lush pastureland of the basin, where several thousand of the Association's cattle grazed, gave way to desert scrub and creosote bush. Late evening brought a new set of problems for Hollister. On most cattle related ventures, such as roundups or spring branding camps, there is always someone responsible for all the tasks centered on the preparation of meals for the rest of the crew, usually consisting of a cook and a helper or two. In this group there was no one willingly to be the chief cook and bottle washer, so Hollister gave orders that everyone would pitch in and get a meal going, which included gathering firewood, building a fire pit, and retrieving all the hardware needed for cooking the sowbelly, beans, biscuits, and the coffee to wash it all down. He also stated they would all take turns actually cooking the meals.

Everyone grumbled slightly, but they all did their share, and in a few minutes there was a hot fire blazing. Pat Wilkens asked Mex to do the cooking who vehemently objected, but Pat convinced him it was a good thing to get your turn out of the way first. The sun was just setting when Mex picked up a tin plate, doled out a generous helping of the sowbelly and beans out of the big pot, and grabbed a couple of hardtack biscuits before he yelled, "Come and get it."

Not many people knew Mex's real name; Antonio Carlos Miguel Hernandez. He was always introduced as 'Mex' and he never did nor said anything to correct the faux pas. All of the men who knew him would have been very surprised to learn he was as American as they were. He was born on the American side of the border in the Rio Grande Valley. His father was one of fifty or so farmers who had moved to a better future near Fort Comfort.

Mex was the third of eleven children; eight girls and three boys. As the eldest male, Mex was expected to work the farm and the fields alongside his father at a very young age. Unfortunately for him, his younger brothers were the last two children born and were too young to ease his burden.

When he was fifteen years old, his two older sisters, Maria and Carmen, who were eighteen and seventeen years of age, respectively, were brutally raped by three drifters while the girls were in the village getting some supplies. Their father had gone to confront the men and had received a horrendous beating for his trouble. Two days later, the three culprits were found with fatal shotgun wounds. In each case, their arms were folded reverently across their chest. Each man's genitals had been cut from his body and placed neatly in their hands as if they were holding a bouquet of flowers.

Deputy Sheriff Albert McKinley had ridden out from Las Cruces to investigate, and after a week of interviewing just about everyone in the village, he learned nothing. Two witnesses claimed they had heard three or four loud gun shots about three in the morning. "Could have been a shotgun, I guess?" one of them remarked.

Based on a rumor that two young girls from a family by the name of Hernandez had been molested, McKinley made a trip to their farm and asked to speak to the head of the household. Antonio emerged from the adobe house and asked the Deputy what he wanted. McKinley indicated he wished to talk to the boy's father. Antonio assured him his father was quite ill. According to the boy, the father had been kicked and stomped by one of their mules and was too sick to be disturbed. The boy said he could answer any questions the Deputy might have. McKinley grilled the boy extensively, asking about their whereabouts on the night of the killings. The boy didn't flinch, nor did he seem the least bit nervous as McKinley asked his questions.

Satisfied he wasn't going to get any information, McKinley called it a day. Not that he believed the boy, but there was no evidence to indicate anyone had left the farm on the night of the murders. Had he looked behind the woodpile, where Antonio had hidden the shotgun, he might have done things differently. But he didn't, and people soon forgot the incident.

From that day forth, Mex said very little and smiled even less. He had a sadness in his eyes, and his youthful spirit and a young boy's zest for life had died along with the three strangers. Now, ten years later, he still carried the 12-gauge, but he had cut the barrels down and carved the bulky stock into a handle, not unlike a pistol grip, which made the weapon a lot easier to handle. Those who knew Mex would tell you he was never seen without the sawed-off shotgun. They would also tell you that in the event of trouble, his standard operating procedure was to cock one barrel of the shotgun, and if it appeared the trouble might escalate into gunplay, he would cock the other hammer, ready for the fight.

Gus Haines came running when he heard Mex call supper. Noticing Mex had already helped himself to the food, Haines, bully that he was, saw a opportunity and said loud enough for everyone to hear, "Since when does the kitchen help eat before the real men?"

Mex, ignoring him, concentrated on his food. Haines, somewhat annoyed, tried again, "I'm talking to you," he snarled.

Again, Mex completely ignored him. Haines was incensed. He rapidly covered the short distance between himself and Mex and with a well placed boot, kicked the plate out of Mex's hand. Mex slowly looked up at Haines, reached for the shotgun by his side, and all in one motion stood up while cocking one of the hammers of the double-barrel 12-gauge.

With his hand on his big pistol, Haines laughed nervously when he said, "What are you going to do, Greaser? Shoot me?"

"Only if he pulls that second hammer back," interjected Pat Wilkens. "Trust me, Mister. You ain't fast enough to get that .44 out 'fore he cuts you in half. Now, I don' know about you, but the sight of that would just set me off my supper. I think you should apologize to Mex, and then we can all get something to eat."

Haines, angry and embarrassed, didn't apologize. In fact, he didn't say a word. He glared at Pat and Mex then turned and walked off into the fading light, away from camp. Mex cocked the second hammer of the shotgun and stood waiting, staring into the direction Haines had gone. Pat figured out what Mex was thinking and said, "I don' think he's stupid enough to come runnin' back into the light to shoot you, but I'd sleep with one eye open tonight." With that, he picked up a plate and doled out a big helping of the sowbelly and beans.

The rest of the group followed suit, with Hollister and Jake being the last to dine. Hollister took a couple of spoons full of the mixture and handed the ladle to Jake who helped himself to the food. He took his plate and a cup of coffee and walked toward the edge of the camp where he sat cross-legged on the ground with his back to a huge boulder. Hollister watched Jake until he was seated, approached him, and asked, "Mind if I join you?"

Jake replied, "Suit yourself. You are the boss."

Hollister sat down on a rock directly across from Jake. He quickly shoveled down his food before he spoke. Most people would talk between mouthfuls, but Colonel Hollister thought the food was an inconvenience and should be dispensed with quickly before conversation began. He set his empty plate on the ground and asked, "Jake, is it?" When Jake didn't answer, Hollister assumed he was correct and continued, "Jake, I like to get to know all the men

I ride with. I know Pat, Jim, and Mex. I understand men like Samuel Fletcher and his entourage. But you — you, I'm having a little difficulty figuring out. I have been watching you, and you seem to have an air of distain for the rest of us. Why is that?"

Jake thought for a moment before answering. "You are mistaken. You take my indifference for distain. I neither like nor dislike any of you."

Seeing an opportunity to challenge Jake, Hollister replied, "Are you telling me you have no dislike for Gus Haines after his treatment of you in the bunkhouse?"

Jake smiled before speaking, "This man Gus is like a mongrel dog that is always trying to prove to its master how brave it is. I believe when the master is not around, this dog does not growl so loud."

Hollister chuckled and said, "Jake, you certainly have an interesting perspective on things. Yes, you certainly do."

CHAPTER FOUR

THERE WAS A small but hot fire burning, and the morning coffee was brewing before any other members of the group opened their sleepy eyes to greet the new day. Jake's gesture was much appreciated by everyone, although the only one who acknowledged it was Pat who poured himself a cup, took a big bite out of his Drummond Chewing Tobacco, and after working the wad for a few minutes, spat a big brown gob on the ground. After wiping his big handle-bar moustache on his sleeve, he took a long sip of the black coffee and said, "Yes sir, 'nother fine day to be 'bove ground. Thanks Jake. Damn good coffee!"

Jim Clemfeld, grumbling under his breath, took his turn at rustling up some grub; burnt pancakes and crisp bacon were the order of the morning. Pat, a twinkle in his eye and a mischievous smile on his face, remarked as he filled his plate, "Guess a fella will eat just 'bout anythin' if he's hungry 'nough."

Colonel Hollister was anxious to get going, so anyone who wanted to eat wolfed down some breakfast and washed it down with Jake's coffee. For three days they had been following the rustlers' trail, and Hollister was getting inpatient. He thought they should have caught up to the thieves by now.

Everyone saddled and packed up, and they were aboard within the half hour, waiting for orders. "We are going to do some hard riding, and maybe, just maybe, we can catch those rustlers today," was the only thing Hollister said before he turned and spurred his horse.

For the rest of the morning, they pushed their mounts hard, stopping briefly every hour to stretch their legs and let the horses get their wind. Midday found them on a small rise overlooking a narrow valley that was split in two by a shallow, winding creek. From their lofty position, they could see the smoke of a campfire. Hollister reached into a saddlebag and brought out a long brass spy glass, which he used to survey the camp area. After several sweeps with the glass back and forth across the encampment, he reported that he'd seen three covered wagons, several semi-permanent shelters, and from what he could tell, there were at least half a dozen people wandering about.

After putting away the glass, Hollister turned to face the men and said, "We will ride in nice and slow with firearms cocked and ready, but no one, and I mean no one, fires a shot unless fired at first, or I give the command to shoot. Is that clear?" He looked for signs of dissension. He didn't see any which made him feel he was in complete command and the men would follow his orders.

They rode down the slope, crossed the creek, and made their way the hundred yards or so into the encampment with Hollister and Jake in the lead, followed by the rest of the men in their assigned positions. As he got closer to the center of the camp, Hollister could see he had miscalculated the number of people; it appeared there were closer to a dozen. He looked at Jake and asked in a low tone, "What do you think?"

Jake looked back at him as if he didn't know what Hollister was talking about.

Hollister, somewhat annoyed, tried again, "Assess the situation for me. Tell me what you see!"

Jake knew all along what Hollister wanted, but he liked to feign stupidity. It kept other people unsure about him, and he enjoyed seeing the exasperation in their faces. After a short pause and a look around the area, he said, "I see three men, four women, four or five children, and I hear a baby crying. There are three families traveling together. They have been here two days. These people are not the rustlers, but you should ask them about the meat cooking over the fire.

Hollister was amazed at Jake's power of observation. He didn't have time to dwell on it, however, as the people had gathered all around, and three men stepped forward. Two of them were unarmed while the third one, who looked like he was in charge, cradled a weather beaten Spencer rifle in his arms that looked like it had seen better days.

Hollister stopped his mount a few feet from the men, leaned forward in the saddle, tipped his hat, and cordially said, "Afternoon."

The man with the Spencer took a step forward and dropped the rifle from a cradled position to one where he held the rifle in both hands. He didn't return Hollister's greeting. Instead, he asked rather impolitely, "What do you want?"

If the man hadn't taken a defensive position with the rifle, and if Deacon Fletcher hadn't intervened when there was no call to, trouble could have been avoided. As soon as the man with the rifle asked his question, Fletcher moved his horse between Hollister and the man and said, "Sinner, what we want are the thieves who have been stealing the Association's livestock. When thou sawest a thief, then thou consentedst with him and hast been partaker with adulterers."

Somewhat unsure of Fletcher had said, the man with the Spencer spoke, "What in God's name are you goin' on about?"

Fletcher opened his eyes even wider, and he turned his head sideways before he answered, "Blasphemer, you know of what I speak. We seek cattle thieves and there lies the proof!" He pointed to the large chunk of meat, roasting over the fire, which Jake had referred to earlier.

Whether it was intentional or not, the man raised the point of the rifle as he turned back to look at the fire. Nathaniel Fletcher quickly aimed his Winchester and shot the man square in the kneecap. At the sound of the shot, Samuel Fletcher levered a shell into the chamber of his Winchester, and Gus Haines drew and cocked his pistol. Before any further damage could be done, Hollister shouted at the top of his lungs, "Cease fire! No more shooting!"

Reluctantly following Hollister's orders, the Fletchers and Gus Haines uncocked and lowered their firearms. Hollister moved his horse closer to Nathaniel Fletcher and asked in a much calmer, quieter tone, "Why in hell did you shoot this man?"

"He raised his hand against my father! You saw it yourself," retorted Nathaniel.

Hollister was convinced the squatter had no intention of using the Spencer; it was all just for show. In fact, he believed the rifle rose up as a reaction to the man turning to look back. He was also convinced Nathaniel knew this as well, but he had used it as an excuse to shoot the man. Before either Nathaniel or Hollister could say anything more, Samuel Fletcher spoke up. "If you have something to say, you say it to me, Sir!" he shouted at Hollister.

Hollister glared directly at Samuel for a long moment before he spoke to the Fletcher bunch as if he were a school headmaster admonishing unruly boys. "Let's get one thing perfectly clear, Reverend. I don't like your kind, and I especially don't like you. I didn't go along with the decision to hire you, but as sure as I'm sitting here, I can see to it that the Association fires you, and I will, believe me, the next time any of you makes a move without orders from me! Now, scour the camp and see if you can find anything that would indicate these people might be rustlers and for God's sake don't shoot anybody else!"

By this time, a middle aged women had rushed out from the crowd of onlookers and knelt down beside the wounded man, cupped his right hand in hers, and began to sob, rocking her body back and forth as she wailed. The Fletchers and Gus Haines turned their horses and rode off in three different directions to scout out the camp as ordered. Pat Wilkens turned in his saddle and instructed Jim and Mex to have a look around as well. Jake didn't know if he was expected to check things out, but he decided he would have a look to satisfy his own curiosity.

Pat spurred his mount gently, moving it next to Hollister's, and asked, "Colonel, maybe it ain't my place to ask, but why are we ridin' with the likes of them three?"

"Pat, if it were up to me, we wouldn't be," replied Hollister. "I am only one voice of many. Thornsbury usually gets what he wants, and he thinks he can stop all the rustling and horse thieving by putting the fear of God into the culprits. He believes the good Reverend's gang are the ones to do just that. I tell you, Pat, I've had just about enough of them. Next time they step out of line I will send them packing, and I will deal with Thornsbury when the time comes."

While they waited for the men to return and report their findings, Hollister rolled a cigarette, and Pat took a big bite of his tobacco as he lifted his left leg out of the stirrup, turned his body sideways, and hooked his free leg around the saddle horn. The two men, who had been standing beside their wounded leader, hadn't moved and were glaring intensely at Hollister and Wilkens. Hollister noticed the hateful stares and asked the closest man, "What's on your mind, friend?"

"You had no call to shoot James. We have done nothing wrong!" the man replied.

"That is yet to be determined," answered Hollister.

By this time, three women and five children, ranging in age from four to eight years old or so, had gathered in a group near the two men. One young woman was holding a crying baby while another older one knelt down beside the wounded man and his wife to see if she could be of some comfort. Pat leaned over and spit out a big brown gob of chewing tobacco juice which brought a look of disgust from the two standing women. Pat wiped his handle bar mustache with the back of his hand, smiled, and said, "Beg pardon, Ma'am."

"What are you planning to do next?" asked the man who had spoken before. Before Hollister could reply, the Fletcher party had returned and gathered in a semicircle in front of him. Hollister directed his question to Samuel Fletcher, "Well, did you find anything?"

"Just this," replied Gus Haines as he threw an untanned cowhide into the dirt in front of the two men.

Samuel Fletcher added, "The carcass is hanging in one of the wagons."

Hollister glared at the man who had been doing all the talking, and after a long pause, he asked, "Where did you get this steer?"

The spokesman, nervous and unsure, changed his demeanour as he realized there could be more trouble coming. "As God is my witness, Mister, we bought that steer from four fellas who come through our camp last night. They was pushing a small herd, maybe six or seven. They asked for water for the cattle and for themselves. When we told them we couldn't invite them in to share a meal because we had no food to spare, one of the fellas offered us one of the steers for five dollars. I asked him why he was selling so cheap. He says he don't like to see children go hungry. We weren't going to argue, so we bought the steer and dressed it out, and we're roasting some of it up now, as you can see."

Pat stepped down, picked up the cowhide, and manoeuvred it so he could see the brand which read *8J*. Pat brought the hide closer to Hollister so he could examine it as well. Hollister dismounted, took the hide from Pat, rubbed his fingers over the brand, and turned the hide over to look at the underside. Most working cowhands knew that when you are using a branding iron on an animal the burn goes much deeper than if you use a running iron to create or change a brand. Consequently, with a branding iron, there is usually a faint impression left on the underside of the hide after the wound heals; not so with a running iron. The back side of the hide in question clearly showed an *ST*. The brand on the front of the hide looked old, but part of it seemed new. It was obvious that someone had recently used a running iron to change the *ST* to an *8J*; not hard to do.

Hollister, with hide in hand, took three strides, bringing him face to face with the two men. He showed them the difference in the brands and then said in a commanding tone, "Explain this to me!"

The man who had previously done all the talking answered, "Like I said before, Mister, we didn't steal no steer. We bought it from the fellas who come through last night. I swear, we don't know nothing about any rustling."

Hollister thought for a moment before speaking, "Alright, let's say I believe you. What do these fellas look like?"

Sensing an ease in tension, the spokesman replied civilly, "One of them was a very tall, but very thin man. Ordinary looking. Had a week's worth of whiskers on his face. Other fellas called him '*Stick*'. Two of them were just youngsters, fifteen—sixteen, maybe. One of the kids was white, and the other was an Apache—mixed blood, I think. White kid was really nervous. Kept looking around all the time. The fourth one was a full blood Apache. He looked like a reservation Indian."

"Anything else?" asked Hollister.

"The tall one, he seemed to be the leader. He was doing all the talking and giving all the orders," was the reply.

When it looked like the man had said all he was going to say, Hollister asked, "What were they dressed liked? What kind of horses were they riding?"

The other man said, "The boss man was wearing a pretty beat up black leather coat and grey dungarees and a brown hat. Stetson, I think. The white kid was wearing a white cotton shirt with black suspenders holding his britches up. He had a big red bandana with white flowers all over it around his neck and a fancy pistol stuck in his pants. I noticed a white pearl handle. The Apache kid had on a blue army jacket. I think the others called him '*Breed*'. The older Apache had on a calico shirt and a leather vest. He wore them knee-high moccasins. Neither one wore a hat, I don't think. As far as their horses, I don't know horses from mules. They were horses!"

Hollister looked annoyed. The first man, sensing that Hollister wanted more, added, "I know something about horse flesh, and they were all riding good stock. The leader was riding a big grey, and the others were all roan coloured. I think they might have been army horses 'cause I saw a big '*U.S.*' brand on a couple of them."

Hollister sensed he wasn't going to get any more out of the two men. He looked around the camp once more, glanced at his men, and then said to the squatters, "You are trespassing on White Sands Land and Cattle Association territory. We will be back this way in a few days, and we better not see you here, or we will burn you out. Is that clear?"

The squatter spokesman started to protest, "We need another week to rest up. James can't travel with that shot up knee. He needs time to —"

Hollister cut him off, "I don't care about your problems. Be gone when we get back!" With that, Hollister remounted and shouted, "Let's move out!"

The men rode past Hollister and south through the camp. Gus Haines pulled up in front of the squatters. With a maniacal sneer on his face and a threatening tone in his voice, he said, "Personally, I hope you are still here in a few days. I would really enjoy stomping you." As he turned his mount and rode past Hollister, he gave the Colonel a hateful stare.

Pat was the last to leave the camp and as he approached Hollister, he stopped, spat, and said, "Somebody needs to teach that boy some manners."

A couple of hours later the group stopped and dismounted to rest the horses. Jake had dug into the oat supply and was feeding his pony a handful. Deacon Fletcher, his son Nathaniel, and Gus Haines were involved in small talk as were Hollister and Jim Clemfeld. Mex, who seldom participated in lengthy conversations, was listening to Hollister and Jim. Pat Wilkens broke away from the Hollister group and made his way to the Fletcher party. When he was within a few feet of them, he stopped and said, "Mr. Haines, could I have a word with you?"

Haines, who had been talking, said to Samuel and Nathaniel Fletcher, "Excuse me. I'll just go and see what he wants." He crossed the short distance to Pat and planted himself firmly with not more than two feet distance between them. He moved his head in closer to Pat's until their noses were no more than six inches apart and said, "What can you possibly say to me that I would want to hear, you squinty-eyed piece of horseshit?"

Pat didn't react immediately. He moved away slightly by pulling his head and shoulders back. He turned his head sideways and spat out some tobacco juice right on top of Gus's left boot. Gus looked down, and he was immediately filled with rage. His thoughts centered on beating the living daylights out of Pat, but he never got the chance. As Gus raised his head, Pat drove his forehead into Gus's face, catching him right between the eyes on the bridge of his nose. Gus went down like he'd been shot. As soon as he hit the ground, he tried to sit up, but he was too stunned to make it all the way up. He fell back to the ground and flopped onto his back, where he stayed, holding his dislocated nose and yelping in pain.

Assured that Gus was no longer a threat, Pat looked up at Samuel Fletcher and his son for a reaction. Although they both held their rifles in their hands, it didn't appear either one of them was going to interfere. Pat turned his gaze to Colonel Hollister who had a stern look on his face. Inwardly, he was elated that Pat had taken charge and put the bully in his place, but outwardly he had to appear all business if he was to maintain order in the group. He said, "That's enough, Pat. I think he gets the point."

Pat backed up several paces while Gus got to his feet. Gus stood bent over with his hands on his knees, trying to catch his breath. After a moment, he straightened up and glared at Pat. With dripping hatred in his voice, he said, "Before this is over, I am going to kill you!"

Pat paused for a few seconds before he responded with, "Anytime you can work up the nerve, you know where to find me."

CHAPTER FIVE

NEAR MID MORNING of the following day, Jake was riding point about a half mile ahead of the rest of the group when he spotted the rustlers. Accompanied by Azul, he went part way up a small rise and dismounted before reaching the top. In a crouched position, he made his way to the crest of the hill, where he lay flat amongst the dry, brittle prairie grasses, and using the field glass Colonel Hollister had given him, he surveyed the area below. He saw six mangy range steers gathered around a brackish, algae covered pond, where they were munching on marsh grasses, stopping occasionally to take a drink from the stagnant water. Jake saw four men, three of whom were sitting on a large rotting cottonwood log while the fourth one stood facing them. Jake recalled the sodbuster's description of the rustlers and concluded they were right on the money. The two youngsters (one a white and the other of mixed blood) and an Apache were the ones seated while the thin, tall man was the one standing. It appeared they were having a bite to eat while they let the stock rest and water. Their horses were fifty feet away on the far side of the spring-fed pond, tied to a huge old cottonwood tree.

Jake continued to watch the rustlers until he heard the sound of Hollister and the others approaching. Seeing Jake's unoccupied horse, Hollister hand-signaled for the rest to dismount and be quiet, and then he made his way up the rise on foot. He was still wary of Azul, and he cautiously shooed him away before he lay down next to Jake. "What have we got, Jake?" he asked.

"Those men are the ones the wagon people described," replied Jake as he handed Hollister the field glass.

Hollister took his time surveying the rustlers, the cattle, and the terrain around them. After several passes, he returned the field glass to Jake and said, "We need to figure out a way to approach them without spooking them."

Hollister backed down the hill a short distance, keeping a low profile before rising to his feet. He indicated to Jake to come as well, and the two of them made their way to where the rest of the group was gathered, all of whom were anxiously waiting to learn what Jake had found. Hollister took the initiative and explained what lay over the hill. "Looks like we found the rustlers, boys. There are four of them just like the sodbuster described. Getting close without scattering them is going to be difficult."

A fiery, boisterous Deacon Fletcher shouted, "For, behold the Lord will come with fire, and with his chariots like a whirlwind to render his anger with fury and his rebuke with flames of fire."

Hollister, somewhat amused at Fletcher's pontification, shook his head and said, "No, Mr. Fletcher, we can not go charging down that hill like the U.S. Cavalry. They will bolt in four different directions, and we'll be lucky to catch any of them."

Fletcher, stubborn and determined to be in control, was not to be deterred, "Fine, then we can put Brother Gus up on the hill with his long rifle. He can get a couple of them, and then we can catch the ones that are left."

Hollister paused to think, which gave Jake an opportunity to speak. "I can take their horses away," he suggested.

Hollister was expectantly waiting for more detail, and when he deduced there was no more information forthcoming, he asked, "What do you mean, Jake?

Jake wasn't sure why Hollister couldn't figure it out, but he explained anyway. "I will make my way to their horses and take them away. When you see the horses are gone, the rest of you can ride down the hill."

Hollister didn't hesitate this time. "Sounds like a good plan, Jake. I'll be watching from the top of the rise."

Jake took off running in a direction that would take him around the left side of the hill. Azul was right behind him, keeping pace. Hollister climbed the short distance back to the top of the rise and watched as Jake executed his plan to outflank the rustlers, quickly gather their horses, and quietly walk away with them. Although he had plenty of cover, there was still a large open space between one clump of Juniper bushes and the clump directly in front of the cottonwood tree to which the horses were tied. Hollister thought if the rustlers spotted him, it would be there.

The plan went off without a hitch, but Hollister thought there was something odd about the venture. He had expected to see Jake dash across the open space, but he never did. Hollister concluded Jake must have found a different route, one he couldn't see from the hill, but what stuck in his mind was even though Jake hadn't crossed the open space, about the time Jake should have been doing so, he thought he saw a coyote run between the two clumps of juniper bushes.

Jake commanded Azul to stay put, so he would not frighten the horses. He made his way quickly to the rustlers' mounts, untied them, gathered them all together, and gave Hollister a wave; the signal to advance. A few minutes later, the Hollister posse made their way down the hill at a leisurely walking pace. The rustlers looked in the direction of the sound of the oncoming riders, but they didn't panic, or scatter as both Hollister and Fletcher had anticipated. The three seated individuals stood up, and the tall, thin man turned in the direction of the approaching ensemble.

The tall, thin man, whom the homesteader had referred to as 'Stick', was armed with a holstered six-shooter. The white kid sported a white handled pistol tucked in his belt, while the two Apaches carried Winchesters, just as the squatter had described. As Hollister and his group approached, all of the rustlers readied for a fight. The two white men put their hands on their pistols while the two Apaches brought their rifles forward into a firing position.

Hollister's group rode slowly towards the rustlers to within a few feet of the gang, where they stopped in formation with Hollister out front and the rest in a parallel straight line a short distance behind him. Hollister leaned forward in the saddle with his arms crossed on the saddle horn. He spoke in a friendly, cordial tone as if he were visiting a neighbor, "Good afternoon, Gentlemen." He paused and looked at each of the rustlers and then stared into Stick's eyes as he said, "State your business, Mister."

"Our business ain't no concern of yours!" spat a defiant Stick.

Hollister, irritated and impatient, was just as adamant when he replied, "Maybe so. Maybe not. You explain to me where you got them cattle, and if I believe you, we won't have a problem." Hollister uncrossed his arms and settled his right hand on his pistol, a short-barreled Peacemaker that he wore in a shoulder holster under his coat.

Stick saw the suggestive movement, and he made a quick decision that prevented any gun play and probably saved his life for the moment. He raised his arms in the air and said, "Easy there, Mister. We work for the boy's father." He nodded in the direction of the young white boy. "Owns a small spread near the border called the Eight Junipers. We bought them cows from a bunch of sodbusters a ways back. Check the cattle. You'll see our *8J* brand."

Hollister shifted his gaze to the young white man and asked "What's your name, son?"

The youngster stared back with a hateful glare and replied, "I ain't your son! We're minding our own business. Why don't you do likewise?"

Ignoring the kid for the time being, Hollister looked back at Stick and said, "You see, Mister, I have a problem here. You say you bought the cattle from the sodbusters, but the dirt pushers say you sold *them* a steer. I don't know who to believe, but I am not as dumb as you think I am. If you bought those cows from the sodbusters, they should not have a brand on them?" As an afterthought, he added, "And don't tell me you took the time to brand them all between yesterday and today. We have been trailing you for three days, and we only saw one branding fire. Now, here's the odd thing; we saw *that* fire long before we ran into the sodbusters. In fact, if we checked your pack horse, I am sure we would find a running iron or two."

Stick maintained his pseudo-innocent, defiant demeanour. Hollister took a glance at the other three rustlers. The two youngsters were very nervous, furtively looking around and at one another, while the older Apache seemed unconcerned. Hollister assumed he knew little English and therefore, had no idea what was being said. Stick looked down at his boots and then lifted his head slowly to meet Hollister's gaze. As his head came up, so did his right hand as he casually reached for his holstered pistol. Hollister had anticipated the move and had his pistol out and cocked by the time Stick's eyes met his.

"I've had just about enough of your bullshit," snarled Hollister. "Before any of you bastards lie to me again, let me give you a little information. We are regulators for the White Sands Land and Cattle Association, and you are cattle thieves who have clearly helped themselves to the Association's property. The only question remaining is what are we going to do about it?"

He paused long enough for what he had just said to sink in, and then he continued. Centering his gaze on the white youth, he asked again, "I asked you your name, boy, and if you give me a straight answer, it might save you from a rope."

The kid wasn't quite as insolent. In fact, he was visibly shaken. "I—uh—my name—my name is Tommy Kulbane. Like Stick says, my father has a small ranch south of the border, and we are just rounding up strays and unbranded stock to build up the herd." He stopped talking and glared at Hollister, watching for a reaction.

Hollister turned to Jake and asked, "Jake, you speak Apache?"

Jake simply nodded; his response to an obviously rhetorical question.

"Take the Apache kid aside and ask him the name of the rancher they work for and where exactly this ranch is," ordered Hollister.

Jake moved the young Apache away from the group and grilled the kid. He knew the youngster spoke English and was pretending not to understand. He tried several dialects before the young man answered. Jake listened, escorted the youth back to the group, and was about to translate when Hollister stopped him, stepped down from his mount, and approached Tommy. He put his arm around the boy's shoulder and walked him out of earshot. In a low tone, which no one else could hear, he asked, "Tommy, what is your father's first name and where exactly is his ranch?"

Tommy tentatively answered the questions, and then Hollister walked him back to the rest of the men. Hollister glared at Stick and said to him very deliberately and slowly, "I am only going to ask you this once and you best answer quickly and correctly, "The kid's father, what is his first name?"

Stick looked in Tommy's direction, back at Hollister, and said, "George! His name is George!"

Hollister turned quickly, walked to where Jake was holding the Apache lad, moved his head in close to Jake's and whispered, "Just play along." He turned back to face Stick and said, "That's not what this kid says."

Jake realized what Hollister was up to, and he answered accordingly, "It was not George."

Tommy jumped in and screamed, "You're a liar!" But it was too late, for just as Hollister had planned, Stick had made his play, drawing his gun. Hollister, fully expecting the move, covered the short distance between them in three long strides and hit Stick on the side of the head with the pistol butt before he could clear leather, and the rustler went down in a heap at Hollister's feet. Any thoughts of fighting their way out of their predicament were quickly dissipated when the rest of the rustlers saw seven weapons cocked and aimed at them.

Stick sat up, rubbing the side of his head, and began to speak, desperation in his voice, "I tell you, we didn't steal those cows! They are free range stock with no brand and are there for the taking."

"Well that's a matter of conjecture," retorted Hollister, eluding to the fact that many small ranchers believed any unbranded cattle found on unclaimed land were free for the taking while the larger ranchers and various cattle associations strongly opposed this view. They felt these cattle were offspring of stock they owned. It was inconsequential where they were found; the cattle belonged to them.

Stick wasn't sure what Hollister was alluding to, and his silence allowed Hollister to continue, "Besides, these cows are not free runs. I believe you boys did some doctoring with running irons. Pat, check the pack horse."

"Okay! Okay!" stammered Stick. "We stole a few head. So what? A fella has got to eat, don't he? We was generous enough to sell one to the sodbusters for a pretty cheap price. Don't that count for something?"

"Sure," answered Hollister, "if you were planning on sending the money you got for the steer to the Association. I don't think you were going to do that, were you?"

Stick sensed the sarcasm in Hollister's tone, and he changed tactics. "You fellas have thousands of cattle. You ain't gonna miss a few head."

"You can still save your neck from a rope, if you tell me who buys the cattle you steal?" said Hollister.

"We don't sell them! Mister, I told you we take them to the Eight Junipers ranch to build the herd."

Hollister removed his hat and ran one hand through his hair. He shook his head from side to side and then gave an order. "Men, take this rustler to that cottonwood yonder and string him up!"

On Hollister's command the regulators jumped into action and pandemonium broke loose. Everything happened at once. Stick turned to run, but before he got two steps Hollister shot him in the leg. At the same time, the older Apache turned and started to sprint in the opposite direction. He didn't get far as a shot from Samuel Fletcher's rifle caught him dead centre between the shoulders. He would live long enough to say a short death prayer as he crossed into the afterlife. Tommy raised his arms over his head as far as they would stretch while the young Apache lad threw his rifle into the dirt, dropping to his knees in a submissive position with his head bowed and his arms extended forward.

Pat, Mex, and Jim Clemfeld dismounted quickly. With weapons cocked and ready, they surrounded the three rustlers while Samuel Fletcher, his son Nathaniel, and Gus Haines remained mounted with their guns ready. Hollister holstered his pistol, and reaching down, he pulled Stick to his feet with a fistful of the man's shirt. Stick howled in pain as he inadvertently put his weight on his shot-up leg. Hollister said to Stick, "Tell me where you take the stolen cattle, and you might live to see another day."

Stick looked up, tears in his eyes from the excruciating pain in his leg and spat in Hollister's face. Hollister had been patient with the rustlers, but Stick's personal act of defiance caused him to lose his temper. "Hang the son-of-a-bitch!" he barked.

Pat Wilkens looked first at Jim and then at Mex. All of them seemed reluctant to follow Hollister's orders. It was as if they thought it was all a bluff, and Hollister wasn't really going to go through with the hangings. Samuel Fletcher, seeing an opportunity, dismounted quickly and shouted, "Gus, bring your rope."

Gus Haines leaped down from his saddle, and with rope in hand, he hit the dirt running over to Stick who was back down on the ground. Haines roughly lifted the wounded man back to his feet, not caring what pain he may be inflicting. At the same time, Samuel and Nathaniel Fletcher took the young Apache lad, one by each arm, and lifted him to his feet. The youngster realized what was happening and began to struggle violently to break free. Nathaniel Fletcher let loose his hold on the boy, and bringing up his rifle, he butted the boy in the head, knocking him unconscious. Then he and Samuel dragged the inert body to the cottonwood tree on the far side of the pool. They dropped the boy face down in the dirt and came back to assist Gus in tying Stick's hands behind his back. Stick was putting up a valiant fight, but after several kicks to his injured leg from Gus's well placed boot, the pain was too much for him to bear, and he gave in. Samuel and Nathaniel dragged him to the cottonwood and held him in place while Gus fashioned a crude noose, threw the loose end of the rope over a thick branch about a dozen feet off the ground, and draped the looped end around Stick's neck. Grinning from ear to ear, Gus waited momentarily and when Samuel nodded his headed slightly, he pulled the loose end of the rope with all his might. As soon as Stick was airborne, Nathaniel ran to help Gus pull the rope. Rather than tie the loose end of the rope to a lower branch or the tree trunk, the two hangmen held onto it while Stick gasped, coughed, and kicked violently. It seemed to take forever, but eventually Stick stopped kicking and twitching. For the longest time, the only movement was Stick's body swaying back and forth, and the only sound that could be heard was a creaking noise as the taut rope rubbed against the dry cottonwood branch. Assuming that Stick had moved on to meet his maker, Gus and Nathaniel interrupted the eerie silence by letting go of the rope, and Stick's body hit the ground with a dull thud.

"Alright, the next one!" shouted Samuel.

Gus removed the rope from Stick's body, and he and Nathaniel turned the young, unconscious Apache on his back. Nathaniel put the loop around the young man's throat while Gus threw the other end over the same branch they had used to hang Stick. They were about to pull the body up when they were interrupted by Jake, who had a strong hold on the rope a few feet from the kid's neck. Jake stared at Hollister and said, "He is a boy. Fourteen summers, maybe. Are you going to hang a child?"

Hollister looked like he was about to change his mind, but he never got the chance. While his attention was diverted, Jake failed to notice Samuel Fletcher sneaking up on him from behind. Jake's senses told him someone was there, but he turned too late. A well aimed rifle butt caught him above his left ear and knocked him to the ground. Samuel levered a shell into the chamber of the Winchester, knelt down beside Jake, and shoved the barrel into his throat. Azul came within a few feet and barred his teeth, snarling at Samuel, who ignored the animal, turned to Gus and Nathaniel, and commanded, "Finish it!"

The echo of Samuel's order had barely died out when Gus and Nathaniel yanked on the free end of the rope, and the young Apache lad was swinging. They hadn't bothered to tie his hands behind his back, so in frantic desperation the lad was grabbing at his throat to free the rope while his eyes bulged and his face turned a plum purple color. Not having any success, he reached behind his neck, grabbed the rope with both hands, and pulled himself up, taking the pressure off his neck. Samuel saw what was happening, left Jake's side, and rifle butted the kid in the middle of the back. The blow knocked the wind out of him, and he immediately stopped struggling as the rope around his neck did what it was supposed to do. Gus and Nathaniel let the body drop, and Samuel, with the wide-eyed expression on his face, shouted, "And the wicked shall be punished, sayeth the Lord." He turned to Gus and Nathaniel and commanded, "Now, the last one!"

As Gus and Nathaniel moved in Tommy's direction, Hollister drew his pistol and fired a shot in the air, stopping the two henchmen in their tracks. "Everybody take a breath and relax!" Hollister turned his attention to Tommy and said, "I want you to understand something." He was talking to Tommy, but he was also explaining himself to the rest of the men. Hollister paused long enough to glance around at everyone before he continued, "By hanging these men, we have delivered the message that rustlers will be dealt with harshly. Hanging you won't do much more to add to that. What I need to know is who buys your stolen cattle. We will deal with them, and I believe if there is no market for stolen stock, there will be less rustling. Do you see my point?" Again, he was directly asking Tommy the question, but indirectly he was talking to the Fletcher bunch.

Tommy's defiant look returned as he sneered, "You hang me and my father will hunt you down, and your death will be a slow one."

Hollister changed tactics and said, "We're done here. Hang him!"

Tommy's bluff had been called. As Gus and Nathaniel grabbed his arms and began to tie his hands behind his back, Tommy began to shout, "Alright! Alright! What do you want to know?"

With all the attention centered on Tommy and Hollister, no one noticed that Jake had regained consciousness. He sat up, rubbed the back of his head, and looking around, he picked up the Winchester from the dirt beside him and rose on wobbly legs. He walked up behind Samuel Fletcher, drew his knife, slashed the preacher's cheek, and smashed the knife handle across his temple. He cocked his rifle as he knelt down beside the dazed preacher and shoved the rifle barrel into his right ear.

Pat caught the tail end of the action and interrupted Hollister, "Boss! Boss! Jake's gonna kill the Preacher!"

Hollister fired another shot into the air and shouted, "Jake, you kill him, you'll force me to hang you. I don't want to do that."

Jake moved the rifle barrel a quarter inch away from the preacher's ear and pulled the trigger. The shot only grazed Samuel's ear lobe, but the report deafened him. He jumped up hollering, "He shot me! He shot me!"

Before anyone overreacted, Jake pointed his rifle to the ground and said, "I did not shoot him. He will have a ringing in his ear for a few days. That is all."

"Gus, shoot that white Apache. That's an order!" bellowed Samuel.

Gus would have obeyed his boss's command if it weren't for the four weapons aimed in his direction and Hollister's quick action when he stated, "Anyone shoots Jake, and I shoot him!"

Samuel Fletcher, blood dripping from his earlobe, stared into Jakes eyes, and through clenched teeth, he stated. "Sleep with one eye open, you heathen. You will pay for this."

Jake responded with the same intensity, "If you ever lay your hand on me again, I *will* kill you." He turned his gaze to Hollister and when their eyes met, Jake stated, "You did not need to kill the boy!"

To divert the focus of attention, Hollister said, "Gentlemen, gentlemen, let us get back to the matter at hand. We are not going to hang young Tommy, just yet. In return, he is going to tell us who buys the stolen cattle. In fact, he is going to lead us there. Isn't that right, Mr. Kulbane?" Tommy paused, so Hollister added in a much sterner tone, "Or perhaps, Gus and Nathaniel can finish what they started."

"No! No, I'll take you to the place," replied Tommy.

Hollister looked at Jake and asked, referring to the rustlers' mounts, "Were there any ropes on their horses?"

Jake replied, "There were two."

Hollister looked at Pat and commanded, "Get the other ropes and hang all three of those bodies back up in the tree. I want to leave a gentle reminder about what happens to rustlers in this neighborhood."

CHAPTER SIX

VARYING SHADES OF purple, pink, and crimson were beginning to appear in the western sky by the time Pat Wilkens, Mex, and Jim Clemfeld hung the three bodies in the old cottonwood tree. Pat didn't like what he was ordered to do, so he made light of it by remarking, "Cattle rustlin' is a serious offence in these parts." He took the time to spit out a huge brown gob and then added, "They hang ya twice for it."

Seeing Samuel Fletcher and his son Nathaniel with bowed heads in reverent prayer, Hollister couldn't help but think what hypocrites they were. It was late enough in the day to camp for the night, but Hollister wanted to put a little distance between themselves and the waterhole. He didn't like the idea of trying to sleep while listening to the creaking sounds the ropes attached to the swaying bodies made as they moved ever so slightly back and forth across the dry branches.

Another half an hour's ride found them in a small grove of Ponderosa Pine where Hollister called a halt for the night. The entire troop went about the required ritual of caring for their horses and getting themselves something to eat. Jim Clemfeld looked after the extra mounts they had picked up when they had hung the three rustlers. He thought they should have taken the gear off the horses and turned them loose, but Hollister argued it might be beneficial to bring the extra mounts to spell off their own horses. Jake gathered firewood while Pat and Mex got a fire going and cooked up some beans and pork belly.

After Tommy Kulbane had eaten, Hollister approached him and said, "Time for some conversation." He paused long enough to see if Tommy was paying attention and satisfied that the boy was, he continued, "I want to know where you people sell the cattle you steal. I don't want any backtalk or lies. If I don't like what I am hearing, I can still hang you."

Tommy took a sip of his after-meal coffee and said, "I ain't stupid. I know when I'm done. We take the cattle to a place called Dry Haven Creek. It's about ten miles or so south of the border, about three days from here. Fella that runs the place will pay a good price, no questions asked."

Hollister changed the direction of the conversation when he asked, "How in hell did you get mixed up in this stealing for a living? It always leads to a bad end. How old are you anyway?"

Tommy was willing to talk about the rustling, but he clamed right up when Hollister started asking personal questions. After a few moments of awkward silence, Hollister rose with cup in hand and said, "Well, when you do feel like talking I'll be here, ready to listen."

He refilled his coffee and tried to make conversation with Pat and Jim, but they didn't want to talk much, either. He walked to where Samuel Fletcher and his two cohorts were sitting with intentions of starting up a conversation, but as he approached them, he got a feeling he might not be welcome, so he merely tipped his hat in acknowledgement and continued walking past them on the pretense of checking the horses.

On the trail the next day things hadn't improved, for everyone rode in silence. Tommy stared off at some distant point on the horizon and there was not the usual banter between Pat, Jim, and Mex, and no thunderous biblical quotes from Samuel Fletcher broke the stillness.

After the evening meal, the chatter around the campfire centered around who could come up with the biggest whopper about some exploit of theirs with regard to cowboying, shooting, drinking, or in the area of romance. Pat won the prize when he told a tall tale of how he had fought a grizzly bear blindfolded. He described in great detail the battle, even lifting his shirt to show a long scar he claimed came from one of the bear's claws. Just when he had his audience all agitated and ready to call him a liar, Pat finished the story with, "I don't know who blindfolded that bear, but I'm sure glad he did!"

For the next two days the atmosphere was lighter. Pat told his tall tales between spits of tobacco juice, Samuel Fletcher shouted biblical quotes intermittently, and Hollister carried on a mostly one sided conversation with Tommy, trying to learn more about the boy's background.

About mid-morning on the third day after the hanging, Colonel Hollister calculated they had crossed the Mexican border into Chihuahua. Mex knew the country well, and when questioned by Hollister, he relayed all that he knew. They had crossed the Southern Pacific Railway tracks yesterday afternoon, and Hollister concluded they were somewhere between Lordsburg to the west and the Rio Grande river to the east. Mex confirmed Hollister's assumptions, and added that if they ventured much further, they could run into bandits who crossed the border back and forth plying their trade.

Hearing this news, Samuel Fletcher crowded his horse next to Hollister's and stated, "We didn't sign up to fight no greaser bandits."

Hollister smiled and replied, "What? You figure they won't be so easy to hang?"

The insinuation that he might be a coward spurred a rant from Fletcher. He turned his head sideways, and his eyes bulged out in the fashion Hollister had witnessed several times since their journey began. He shouted loud enough for everyone to hear, "I am not afraid of any man that God has chosen to set upon this earth! You would do well to remember that fact, Colonel." He stared at Hollister, expecting an answer or an apology, but none was forth coming. Hollister merely smiled and spurred his horse away, trotting the short distance to join Pat, Mex, and Jim Clemfeld.

Hollister stopped his mount close to Pat's and asked, "What do you think, Pat?"

Pat spat out a big brown gob, wiped his lips on his sleeve, and fingered his moustache before he answered, "I ain't no coward, Colonel, but I kinda agree with the good Deacon. I sure don' want to run into no bandits. The kid says we got another ten miles to go. I'm thinkin' it might be good to go that far and put some fear into these fellas 'bout buyin' White Sands cattle, and then we head back across the border and go huntin' for more rustlers."

Tommy was within earshot, so Hollister got his attention. "Hey kid, how far to this Dry Haven place?"

Tommy answered immediately, "Two hours ride, at most."

An hour and a half later, Hollister and company could see some buildings in the distance. Through the shimmering heat, they could make out the silhouettes of two large structures and several smaller ones. Tommy indicated that the nearby dry creek bed, which they had been following for a couple of miles, led to the ranch. As they got closer, the buildings became clearly defined; a ranch house, a large barn, and several smaller shed-like structures.

The regulators rode slowly up the weed infested, wheel rutted wagon road, and as they neared their destination, Hollister looked around several times and took in all there was to see. The 'ranch house' was an old adobe building that had seen better days. The roof had once been covered with clay shingles laid out in uniform rows, but as time took its toll on them and leaks appeared, they were replaced by wooden shingles held down with misshapen, haphazardly placed pieces of tin. A large veranda, which looked like a recent addition, ran along the entire front of the building. It was held up by four evenly spaced posts, and a set of five steps invited one to come up and sit in several pieces of crudely fashioned furniture that passed for chairs scattered along the length of the veranda. The barn had been hastily constructed with little concern for keeping out what little rain did fall in this part of the country. The clap boards used for the roof and the sides of the building were uneven with gaps everywhere, but it kept the livestock and their feed relatively dry.

Hollister concluded that the three other smaller buildings were perhaps once used as storage for tools, gear, harnesses, and tac, or vegetables, corn, and grain. Between the buildings was a myriad of corrals with perhaps a dozen horses in one large enclosure, several steers in a smaller corral, and a burro had one small pen all to himself. In the middle of the front yard was a sizeable pile of split firewood next to a large stump with an axe buried in it.

Several hundred yards downstream from the ranch house, Hollister could make out a collection of adobe brick buildings, one of which he assumed was a church because of the prominent steeple. He thought that at one time the village was full of people when the ranch might have been a thriving operation, providing work and commerce for the occupants. Now, its few residents probably scratched a meager existence from the dry earth and whatever work they could get from the present residents of the ranch.

As they came closer, Hollister and his entourage could see three men; one seated and two others leaning against a couple of the central posts. The seated man was Charlie Goodnall, an ordinary looking gent dressed in dungarees and a denim shirt. Charlie was an observer rather than a participant in life. He would follow a conversation by intently moving his gaze from one speaker to the other. He had a lazy left eye, and at times, if Charlie spoke, it was difficult to tell if he was talking to you or not because he wasn't looking directly at you. Charlie would never initiate any action, although he was quick to jump into a situation when ordered to do so, similar to an expectant dog waiting at his master's side for a command.

The two men leaning on the posts were a man of Spanish decent by the name of Carlos Ruiz Ortega and a full blooded Mescalero Apache called Too-ah-yay-say which translated to '*Strong Swimmer*'. It was rumored he once stole two hundred horses from the Mexican Army and dared to swim across a flood swollen Rio Grande, drowning half the horses and almost killing himself.

Too-ah-yay-say was very tall for an Apache, several inches over six feet in height. He was a very handsome man with chiseled features. He was very proud and considered himself an equal to the white men with whom he kept company. He was dressed in traditional garb consisting of an off-white cotton shirt and pants, knee high moccasins, and a red headband held his jet black, shoulder length hair in place. Tucked in a sash around his waist were a big Bowie knife and an old navy colt. He was an opportunist of the highest order, and his comrades had learned not to leave anything of value lying around if they ever wanted to see it again.

Carlos Ruiz Ortega told anyone who would listen that he was a Spaniard, descended from royal blood. He was attired in a black sequined vest that complimented his frilly white shirt and skin tight, black pants tucked into tight fitting riding boots. A wide sombrero was his hat of choice. He walked with a swagger and was always correcting people in an angry tone whenever someone referred to him as a Mexican. In fact, he often treated others with distain because in his mind he felt he was their superior.

When Hollister and company reined up in front of the veranda, Charlie lifted the brim of his hat, looked out at them, rose from the chair, walked to the door of the house, opened it, and shouted to whomever was inside. Hollister didn't hear what he said, but it sure got a response. Five other armed men rushed through the door and took up various positions across the length of the veranda.

The man in the middle was a big man named Curly MacTavish. He stood six foot, five inches tall and weighed two hundred and thirty pounds. He always sported a three day growth of whiskers, and under his weathered Stetson, he was nearly bald. The sparse red hair growing on the lower half of his head was very curly, hence his nickname. He was seldom seen without a half-smoked, chewed up cigar dangling out of the corner of his mouth.

The only weapon he carried was a Bowie knife with a fancy handle carved from a deer antler that he kept in a buckskin sheath tucked in his belt. He was extremely fast and accurate when throwing the knife and knew how to use it in close quarters. Many men who were good with a gun were afraid to go up against Curly and his knife. He was the undisputed boss of the outfit. What he said went—no argument. Curly was bad tempered, and he dealt with people with force and power.

On Curly's left stood two brothers, Dirty and Foolish Johnston who hailed from the back country in Tennessee. They had little or no formal education, and neither one could be called the sharpest knife in the drawer. Dirty, the older brother, was mean spirited, never happy, never smiled, and he found no joy in life. Foolish was even dumber than Dirty, and he depended totally on his older brother to get him through life. He was devoted to Dirty and would do anything for him, when asked.

Their names were a cruel gift from a father with a moonshine soaked brain. Papa Johnston observed his dogs for a few weeks when they were pups, and he named them according to some behavior he'd noticed the dog exhibit, such as '*Scratch*' or '*Howler*'. The boys had been given Christian names by their mother, but at a very young age, their father had begun calling them Dirty and Foolish, respectively. Their real names were soon forgotten.

The brothers were both attired in denim pants and calico shirts, topped off with well worn, black slouch hats. Dirty carried a double barrel, 10 gauge shotgun loaded with small nails and ball bearings for maximum damage, while Foolish preferred the company of .44 tucked in his waistband.

On Curly's right side were Pete Langford and Wesley Trumont. Langford was a sharp dresser, sporting a black Stetson with a hat band studded with silver coin-sized medallions and a black leather vest over his white cotton shirt. He had an oak-handled Peacemaker in a black polished leather holster. Although no one would say it to his face, most people who knew Langford thought he was a back shooter. No one had ever seen him go up against anyone face to face, but he claimed he was quite the gunfighter.

Wesley Trumont was '*whistling in the graveyard*', as the saying goes. He had no fear of death which made him very dangerous. He got excited at the possibility of gunplay and because of his cavalier attitude, he had been shot several times, but he always managed to survive. He carried two pistols, one in a holster and the other tucked in his belt. When asked which one he drew first, he replied that the answer was a secret. Not knowing kept his opponents guessing and off balance. He had another trick that he used to gain an advantage. When in a fracas, he would remove his Planter's hat and bring it down to waist level. His right hand, hidden by the hat, usually unnerved his adversary.

The posse had formed a single line parallel to the veranda. Hollister was in the middle with Jake Romero, Pat Wilkens, Jim Clemfeld, and Mex Hernandez on his left and Tommy Kulbane, Samuel and Nathaniel Fletcher, and Gus Haines on his right. The two lines of men stared at each other for the longest time, sizing each other up before Hollister spoke up. "I am Colonel Hollister. My men and I represent the White Sands Land and Cattle

Association. Rustlers and horse thieves have been helping themselves to the Association's stock and bringing them down here to sell," he stated.

Hollister could have gone on, but he wanted to see the reaction to what he had already said. There was a long, eerie silence before Curly took one small step forward and said, "Well, Mr. Association, what has that got to do with us?"

"Far as I know, right now, nothing. We have it on good authority that the stock is brought down here somewhere, and we are just checking it out," replied Hollister.

Curly stared at Hollister for a moment and then looked directly at Tommy. "You been tellin' stories again, Tommy?" he asked.

Hollister had a strong feeling that Tommy probably knew these men, but he didn't expect Curly to acknowledge it, so he maintained his composure when he asked, "You know this boy?"

"We sure do, Mr. Association," said Curly, with an undertone of irritation.

Hollister sensed the change in mood and decided to push another button. He leaned forward and said, "We hung his three friends."

Curly's face turned red with anger, his cheeks puffed up, and he exhaled a deep breath. Normally, he would have walked up to his adversary and drawn his knife, or if the odds were against him, he would order his men to deal with the situation. Common sense told him he should do neither. Here were eight well armed men with their weapons pointed at him and his men. He took a moment to compose himself and then asked in a casual tone, "Oh, did you know their names? I'm just asking 'cause I'm hopin' you did the decent Christian thing and said a few words over them before you buried them. Hell, it's only proper you should know a man's name before you kill him!"

Hollister kept pushing. "I agree. What is your name?"

Curly and several of his men caught the inference. Curly became even more agitated, unsure of what to do or say next. He didn't have to make a decision as Wesley Trumont stepped down to the top rung of the stairs. He had his left hand on his pistol and was slowly bringing his hat down with his right hand as he said, "You gonna kill me, Mister? Maybe, you should tell me who you are? We wouldn't want to bury you without knowing your name."

"My name is Colonel Benjamin Hollister. And yours?"

"Name's Wes Trumont."

"Well, Mr. Trumont, if you don't put your hat back on your head and step back up on the porch, my friend Antonio is going to cut you in half with his 12 gauge."

Pat Wilkens wasn't sure who Antonio was, but when Mex cocked the hammers on the shotgun and aimed it directly at Wes, Pat understood whom Hollister was alluding to. Trumont looked around for support from his comrades, but when he saw that nobody was too eager to step up, he put his hat back on and stepped back up onto the porch.

There was an aura of tension in the air. Nobody wanted to make the next move until Tommy spoke up. "It was Stick Duncan and a couple of Apaches, they hung. One of them was just a kid!"

Curly digested what Tommy had said, looked at Hollister, and remarked, "Ah well, no big loss." Changing the subject, he asked, "Colonel, what is it you want from us?"

"Not a thing," replied Hollister, casually. "We are going to feed and water the horses down by the creek, camp for the night, and then be on our way."

Curly said as he smiled, "Well, you have a pleasant stay, Colonel. Everyone on both sides relaxed somewhat until Curly asked, "What are you gonna to do with Tommy?"

Everyone within earshot was surprised when Hollister said, "We are going to hang him, Sir. We caught him red-handed stealing Association cattle, and we hang all rustlers." He paused for effect then added, "And anyone who knowingly buys stolen Association stock can look forward to a rope." Hollister didn't wait for a response from Curly and his men. He reached over and grabbed Tommy's reins, and with the boy in tow, he turned his horse quickly and headed away from the ranch house.

Common sense prevailed and neither side wanted to start something that could escalate into a big shoot out. Hollister's men backed their horses a few paces, and sensing that Curly's bunch weren't going to try anything, they turned their horses and followed Hollister. When they were out of earshot, Charlie Goodnall asked, "You ain't gonna let them hang that kid, are you?"

"Don't you worry, Charlie," replied Curly. "There ain't gonna be any hangin's while I'm around. We'll let those boys get comfy for the night and then maybe we'll come a callin'. It would be the neighborly thing to." He smiled, turned, and went back into the ranch house.

CHAPTER SEVEN

THE GLARE OF the hot afternoon sun was shifting into the softer, less intense light of early evening when Hollister ordered a stop for the day. The troop had traveled a short distance south of the ranch just beyond the small settlement Hollister had observed earlier in the day. The village seemed completely deserted even though there were twenty or so inhabitants who had learned that when strangers rode through their streets it was safer to stay inside, stay quiet, and say a short prayer for protection until they passed. The silence was hauntingly eerie, broken only by the intermittent barking of a dog.

About a mile beyond the village, the trickle of the small stream widened into a large pool fed by what little water there was in the creek and several natural springs emanating from the adjacent hillsides. After Hollister circled the pond, evaluating all that he saw, he ordered the men to set up camp on the far side of the water away from the trail and under a large grove of Pinyon trees where there were both plenty of grass for the horses and shade for the men.

Once everyone was settled, Pat Wilkens approached Hollister and said, "Ya know, Colonel, I'm wonderin' with this much daylight left why we just didn't head back north of the border 'stead of stickin' 'round here. I don't trust them fellas at the ranch house, and I got a strong feelin' we ain't seen the last of 'em." He finished by spitting out a large brown gob and wiping his moustache with the back of his shirt sleeve.

Hollister looked up from where he was sitting and answered, "Pat, I definitely don't trust those people, either. I think they are the ones buying stolen stock, and I wouldn't doubt that a lot of them are doing the rustling. As far as a confrontation, I welcome it. If we are attacked, it will be self defense, and it will give us the justification for enforcing the Association's regulations and cleaning up this den of thieves."

Samuel Fletcher, hearing the exchange between Hollister and Wilkens, decided to put in his own two cents worth, "That's what I like to hear. Let us gather up our arms and return to smite the wicked!" He looked sideways at Tommy and his eyes bulged out as he added, "I think we should start by hanging this one!"

Hollister stood and covered the distance between them in a few long strides. He came close enough to Fletcher, so their noses were only inches apart. He thought Fletcher would back down and take a step backward, but he held his ground. Hollister had met several men in his command during the war, who, like Fletcher, didn't back away. They would follow their commander's orders, but they sure let it be known that they didn't like it. Hollister asked in a calming tone, "What is your plan, Deacon?"

This time Fletcher did take a step back and said, "Same plan as always. Confuse and scatter the enemy, then we have the advantage."

When it appeared there was no more information forthcoming from Fletcher, Hollister asked, "And how do we execute this plan?"

Fletcher couldn't resist the opportunity for a dig at Hollister. He remarked snidely, "You being a big military man and all in the war, I figure you'd know the answer to that question."

Hollister didn't bite. He simply said, "Enlighten me."

Fletcher smiled and glanced at the other men before answering. His tone reeked of condescension when he said, "The three of us have handled a lot more situations like this than you have, Colonel. We know what we are doing" Once more, he paused and looked around for effect and then continued, "We station Gus about five hundred yards from the ranch house, and he starts picking off the heathens with his big rifle. He can get two or three of them before they figure out that inside the house might be a safer place."

Hollister remembered the Sharp's .50 with the telescope. He shook his head in acknowledgement and then asked, "And then?"

Fletcher seemed annoyed at having been interrupted. He continued, "Then, my dear Colonel, we have them right where we want them! We surround the building, and we wait them out. They'll go stir crazy, and when they come out of the house, we put them down like the mongrel curs they are!"

"So, the Association is getting their money's worth; you being the judge, jury, and executioner all rolled into one," countered Hollister.

"Do you have a better idea, Colonel?" asked Nathaniel Fletcher.

Hollister didn't want to repeat himself, so he called for everyone to gather and he waited until everyone was within earshot before he said, "I believe some or all of those men at the ranch house are involved in rustling or selling stolen cattle and horses, or both. We have no proof, but I believe they will show their hand tonight. I think they will attack us in our sleep, but as sure as I am standing here, we will be ready for them. I want everyone to get some shuteye now. When it gets dark, we will build a nice inviting fire and spread our sleeping gear close to it. We will conceal ourselves in the trees, and when they descend upon the camp, we will have them in our trap."

Curly MacTavish had run the Dry Haven operation for over a decade. Over time he had seen all types of men come and go. Some stayed a year or so, others just long enough to catch their wind, recharge, and then move on. Lone lawmen had stopped at the ranch house looking for a particular individual or two, but never a large posse like the one that had shown up earlier in the day. He muttered under his breath, "And who the hell are they? White Sands Cattle—whatever they call themselves—what gives them the right to ride in here and treat me with disrespect?"

He slammed a fist on the table, startling Charlie Goodnall and the Johnston brothers. Charlie turned his head slightly, so that his wandering eye was looking straight ahead and asked, "Jesus, Boss! What are you so mad about?"

Curly stood up and set his knuckles on the table, leaned in, and issued an order. "You three go out and round up the rest of your buddies and get them in here, pronto," he commanded.

It took only a few minutes for everyone to gather in the large kitchen area of the ranch house as most of Curly's crew were either on the veranda or tending to their horses in the nearby corrals. The exception was Too-ah-yay-say. He was seldom close by, and Curly didn't seem to care if he was in attendance for the meeting or not.

"What's up, Boss?" asked Dirty Johnston.

Curly went into a rant. "What's up? What's up is we were scolded like a bunch of young kids by a school marm! And we took it! Nobody, and I mean nobody, comes to my house and pushes me around. No sir! This does not sit well in my craw."

Wes Trumont spoke up, "They didn't go far, Boss. The Apache says they went about a mile south of the village and camped near the big waterhole." He was referring to Too-ah-yay-say who, on his own initiative, had followed Hollister and company at a discrete distance and had reported his findings to several of Curly's men, who were sitting about on the veranda at the time. Trumont added, "We could go down there and put the run on them, Boss."

"No Wes. I think it would a little safer for us to pay a little visit sometime tonight.

I recognized that crazy bastard with the bulging eyes who kept turning his head sideways. He is known as the '*Killing Preacher*' and those two with him are his kin and just as deadly. They're bounty hunters, and if the poster says "Dead or Alive", whoever they're after is usually brought in draped over a saddle. I don't know who the rest of those fellas were, but I think that Colonel is a big rancher from up north somewhere."

Carlos Ruiz Ortega interrupted, "Senor Curly, I know of this man with the shotgun. He is Antonio Hernandez. Most people call him Mex. He is a very mean spirited man and a formidable opponent. If I may venture an opinion, Senor? I think all of these men are not to be taken lightly, and maybe we should let sleeping dogs lie."

Curly stared at Ortega for a moment, and then smiling, he replied, "Carlos, you are a cautious man, and sometimes it's a good thing to be cautious. It's not a good thing to provoke a rattlesnake if you don't like gettin' bit. I don't plan on gettin' myself killed, so we will strike when they least expect it, and the element of surprise will give us the upper hand. Now, you all get some rest. We are gonna to be up all night tendin' to business."

In the waning twilight, Hollister and his crew had just finished their evening meal. While Hollister had told them to get some rest, none of the men felt much like sleeping. Mex and Jim Clemfeld sat on one side of the fire, staring into the flames, while several yards away from the fire, the Deacon and his two cronies sat on a log facing Pat Wilkens who was telling them one of his tall tales between spits of brown tobacco juice. Hollister sat with young Tommy Kulbane opposite the fire from Mex and Jim.

"It's time we had a long talk, son" said Hollister.

Tommy lifted his head, and with a look of stern defiance, he replied, "I ain't your son, and I've done all the talking I'm gonna do!"

Hollister very quickly leapt to his feet and backhanded Tommy as hard as he could, knocking the kid over backwards. Before Tommy could gain his senses, Hollister was on top of him, lifting him up with one hand by the shirt front while he delivered another hard backhand. He let Tommy's body slump to the ground and stood over him until the boy was coherent enough to listen, and then he said, "I'm only going to say this one more time. I need to know who is buying the stolen stock. If it is that bunch back at the ranch house, then tell me now. If you don't want to talk to me, I am done with you. I will turn you over to that crazy preacher, and he can do what he wants with you. My guess is he'll have some fun with you before he hangs you." Hollister left it up to Tommy's imagination as to what the '*fun*' might be. Hollister waited a moment and then said, "Well?"

The threat worked. Tommy whimpered, "Curly—Curly MacTavish—he buys anything we can bring to him."

"Who does he sell the stock to?" continued Hollister.

"Mostly the Mexican army," replied Tommy.

Hollister glared at Tommy for a long time and then said through clenched teeth, "I think you're lying! No matter, I found out what I needed to know."

Hollister got up and turned to walk away when Tommy asked, "What happens to me now?"

"I'm not going to hang you. I'll turn you loose soon, but I want you to know two things: one, if I ever see or hear of you back in our part of the country stealing cattle again, I will hang you on the spot and no questions asked, and secondly I want you to tell every one of your cow-stealing amigos about the Association and the Regulators and how they are better off staying out of Association territory."

A couple of hours before dawn, Curly MacTavish stood in the bright moonlight on a small knoll a hundred feet west of the waterhole. From his vantage point, he could see Hollister and his men sleeping around a blazing campfire. He felt a surge of confidence, and he smiled as he thought, "*this is gonna be like shootin' fish in a barrel*".

The nearly dry creek, on Curly's left, ran west to east and emptied into the large pool roughly a hundred feet long and thirty feet wide. A well-worn trail ran parallel to the creek bed, following it to the pool. The path turned south and went along the pond's western shoreline, which was closest to Curly, and then continued to follow the creek from where it poured out of the south end of the pool. The thick grove of Pinyon trees in which Hollister had set up camp was on the far side of the pool. A hundred feet south of the small rise from where Curly was stationed, was another vantage point; a small knoll topped with numerous shale rock formations intermixed with granite boulders of all sizes.

Curly's plan was to come at Hollister from both sides of the pool, and to that end, he sent Carlos Ortega and Pete Langford to the north end of the pool to his left, while the Johnston brothers, Too-ah-yay-say, and Wes Trumont waited on the small, rocky knoll for the signal to attack from the south end of the pool to his right. He had left Charlie Goodnall holding the horses at the bottom of the hill directly behind him. Curly had no sense of fair play, so it didn't bother him to shoot men while they were in their blankets on the ground.

Unbeknownst to Curly, Hollister had stood on the same knoll just before dark and had surveyed the lay of the land, as well. He had come to the conclusion that if an attack was forthcoming, Curly would try and hit them from both sides while they slept. An hour after sunset, Hollister's men cut pine branches and bushes which they stuffed under their blankets, carefully shaping the bundles to look like a sleeping man. A hat, strategically place at one end of the bundle, added validity to the deception.

Jim Clemfeld volunteered to be the visible body, the decoy walking about the camp and adding wood to the fire. Around midnight, Hollister deployed his forces. Jim Clemfeld continued to be the bait, Jake was designated to the back of the grove where he was to guard the horses and baby-sit Tommy, and the rest of the men were ordered to find large trees, boulders, or windfall to hide behind. Mex and Pat were sent to find cover at the north end of the waterhole, while Hollister, the two Fletchers, and Gus Haines would deploy at the south end of the pool which Hollister surmised was the mostly likely spot where Curly would strike in force.

Hollister was certain MacTavish and his band would strike, but he just wasn't sure when. He had lectured the men that it could be a long wait, and they should be patient, keep still and quiet, and most important, listen for his command to fire. He didn't want anyone shooting too soon and letting Curly and his gang out of the trap. Also, he didn't want them to shoot randomly into a crowd, so he carefully instructed them to select a target closest to their position and to keep firing until their quarry was down before moving on to the next target.

It was a long, cold wait. Samuel Fletcher was beginning to doubt if Curly was coming. Some of the other men were getting restless as well, so Hollister made his way from man to man, encouraging them to stay alert. Shortly before the morning sun crept up over the eastern horizon, Gus Haines whispered to Nathaniel, "Lookee, there! See the light?" He was referring to the match Wes Trumont lit to signal the attack to begin. There was no need to point out the light, for everyone had seen it, including Pat and Mex who were well hidden behind a large pile of deadwood at the north end of the pool.

The trap worked like a charm. As soon as he saw the lit match signal, Jim Clemfeld casually headed for the cover of the trees as if he was going for more firewood. Hollister's men had obeyed orders and let Curly's men pass their vantage points. Mex had cocked both hammers on his shotgun and was sorely tempted to fire at the two shadows that passed in front of them, but Pat's hand on his shoulder reminded him to wait for Hollister's command. Nathaniel Fletcher was anxious as well, but when he looked to his right, he saw that his father had stepped out slightly from behind the big pine he was using for cover and put his finger to his lips in the '*keep quiet*' gesture.

From their end of the pool, Ortega and Langford arrived at the campfire area at the same time as the rest of the bushwhackers, who had come from the other end of the pond. Wes Trumont didn't hesitate. He drew his pistol and began firing into what he thought were sleeping men. The rest of Curly's bunch drew their weapons and emptied them, shouting and hollering in delight as flying lead ripped hole after hole in the blankets.

When they stopped to reload, Hollister hollered at the top of his lungs, "Fire!" A barrage of bullets hit the would-be assassins from three sides. Mex's double barrel shotgun blast caught Pete Langford full in the back, and the force knocked him face first into the campfire. He was dead before he hit the ground. Pat had fired at Ortega a split second after Mex let go with the shotgun. In that short time, Ortega had turned, crouched down, and was headed back the way he had come. Consequently, Pat's shot missed its mark and caught Ortega in the hip rather than higher up the body where Pat had intended. Before Pat could take aim for another shot, Ortega had reached cover.

On the other side of the night fire, Trumont stood admiring his work. The smirk on his face disappeared when he heard someone yell '*Fire*'. He never had time to react, as Samuel Fletcher's well placed shot went through his forehead and out the back of his skull. Foolish Johnson was riddled with bullets. He was the closest man to Hollister and Jim Clemfeld, so they both had picked him as their target. After Samuel shot Trumont, he levered another shell into the chamber of his Winchester and also picked Foolish as his next target. Dirty Johnston had reacted quickly. Nathaniel had selected him as his target, and because he was somewhat nervous, Nathaniel fired low and wide. Consequently, the bullet hit Dirty on his right side, just below the rib cage and went clean through, missing any vital organs or blood vessels. Dirty barely felt the sting as he ran for his life to the safety of the boulders at south end of the pool. As he ran, he randomly threw his last two shots in the direction of the trees. Purely by accident, one of the shots bounced off the top of Nathaniel Fletcher's shoulder.

Too-ah-yay-say was a very intuitive individual and unlike many people who exhibited the same trait, he listened to his instincts. Feeling something was wrong and that this present situation could be a trap, he hung back and didn't participate in the shooting of the blankets, and when he heard Hollister yell 'Fire', he turned and sprinted back the way he had come. Gus Haines had him lined up as a target, but the Apache moved so quickly, Haines didn't have time to get a bead, so he just fired the big Sharp's .50, hoping to hit something. He got lucky. The large bullet hit Too-ah-yay-say in the left wrist, nearly severing his hand.

Although visibility was good in the bright moonlight, which was reinforced with the sparse light of the approaching sunrise, Curly's vantage point on the knoll was too far away to see things clearly. Curly didn't know what had transpired, but the second barrage of gunfire made him think something was wrong. He spent a minute or two trying to decide what his next course of action should be. He was interrupted by Charlie Goodnall who had left the horses because he couldn't contain his curiosity any longer, and he wanted to know how things were progressing.

"I told you to watch the horses!" Curly said angrily.

Ignoring Curly, Charlie said, "Horses are fine." He paused a moment before asking, "What's goin' on?"

Curly thought it was a dumb question, so he answered sternly, "Right now, Charlie, you know about as much as I do."

Charlie didn't know what to say next, so he added another comment, "Sure is a lot of shootin'."

Curly imagined walking over to Charlie and choking the life out of him, but before he could act out his fantasy, he heard Carlos Ortega's voice off to his left. "Curly don't shoot! It's Carlos!" A moment later Carlos came into view, dragging his left leg and grunting in pain with every step.

"You hurt bad?" asked Charlie?

Ortega looked at Curly when he answered, "I was shot in the hip. It hurts something awful, Senor."

Before Ortega could explain any further, Too-ah-yay-say, with Dirty Johnston in tow, appeared from Curly's right side. Curly saw Johnston's blood-soaked shirt and assumed the worst. He also noticed the Apache's mangled hand, but because the man was an Indian, and mainly because it was only a hand injury, Curly didn't seem to care. He asked Johnston, "You hit pretty bad?"

"Nothin' serious, Boss. Looks worse than it is," replied Johnston.

"What about the rest?" asked Curly.

"I don't think anyone else got out of there alive. They was waitin' for us. It was a goddamn trap!" Realization set in and he added, "Jesus, they killed Foolish! They killed my little brother!"

Curly turned his attention back to Ortega. "Langford was with you. I'm assuming he didn't make it, either."

"Si, Senor," replied Ortega, shaking his head as he spoke.

Curly stood looking at the waterhole for a moment and then went into a tirade. He kicked at the dirt a couple of times and screamed, "Son-of-a-bitch" as he wrenched the Winchester out of Dirty Johnson's hand and fired three shots in the direction of the pool.

The lead flying over his head from the return fire brought Curly out of his temper tantrum. "Let's get back to the ranch," he shouted.

The three shots surprised Hollister and his men, sending them diving for cover. Pat Wilkens yelled out that the shooters were up on the small hill on the other side of the waterhole. Everyone took aim and directed a volley toward the top of the knoll. Hollister called a ceasefire, and they stayed behind cover and listened for a short time. Fairly certain the bushwhackers had left, Hollister called everyone out and asked if anyone was hit. Other than Nathaniel Fletcher, the only other casualty was Jim Clemfeld. One of Curly's wild shots had creased Jim's temple. Pat Wilkens teased him, telling him it was a good thing he had such a thick skull.

Hollister hollered, "Jake, bring up the mounts." A moment later Jake appeared with Tommy Kulbane and all the horses. "Let's finish this," Hollister said as he mounted.

CHAPTER EIGHT

"WHAT THE HELL happened?" Curly asked, directing the question to no one in particular. Charlie Goodnall, Dirty Johnston, Carlos Ortega, and Too-ah-yay-say sat in the kitchen, grouped at one end of a long plank table that was cluttered with dirty dishes and kitchen garbage. The four men exchanged glances as if they were trying to decide who should respond to Curly's question, but Curly, not expecting an answer, continued with his rant. "They were ready for us! Welcome to the party! Suckered us!" he shouted. There was a momentary pause before Curly concluded in a less volatile, more calculating tone. "I swear I'm gonna cut that bastard's heart out while he watches me do it!" he said, referring to Hollister.

"Boss, what are we gonna do now?" asked Charlie.

Curly's mind raced. He didn't know how to answer Charlie's question because he wasn't sure what his next move should be. The sound of breaking glass diverted his attention. Curly felt momentarily reprieved from having to answer Charlie, but his sense of relief was quickly replaced by confusion. His initial thought was that someone had thrown a rock through one of the windows, but as clearer thinking took over, Curly realized that whoever tossed the rock, threw it mighty hard, for it went through one of the front windows, all the way across the main room, through the kitchen, finally hitting a cupboard hanging on the back wall

A half second later, the distant boom of Gus Haines' Sharp's .50 caliber clarified things for Curly; someone was shooting at them and from quite a distance. Charlie, Carlos, Dirty, and Too-ah-yay-say had already taken up defensive positions against the front wall, facing the direction of the shot; Dirty and the Apache were on the right side of the room in the saloon area, and Charlie and Carlos Ortega were on the left side by the desk. Curly stayed in the kitchen area, oblivious to the potential of more bullets coming through the windows.

"What the hell was that?" screamed Charlie.

Dirty Johnston answered him, "Sounds like a big buffalo gun. The way the bullet hit first and then we heard the shot, means he ain't all that close."

Another shot shattered the glass of the window by Charlie. He heard the bullet whiz by a few inches from his nose, and he could almost follow it as it made its way across the open space, hitting the adobe partition.

"Stay away from the windows!" ordered Curly.

As if in defiance, another chunk of lead came through the clapboard front door which prompted Charlie to add, "And the front door!"

The interior of the *'ranch house'* consisted of one huge room essentially the size of the outer dimensions of the building. It was divided into three smaller areas, using adobe brick walls as partitions. The main living area ran parallel to the front wall. Two windows, one on each side of the main door, were the only source of natural light. Facing the front door from the inside, in the left hand corner was a well-worn wooden desk with a matching chair and two book cases filled with pottery, loose papers, and knick-knacks of all sorts, and not surprisingly, only a couple of books. The right front side of the interior served as a small saloon. Against the adjacent outside wall was a polished oak bar that looked completely out of place. There were three round tables with a collection of chairs of various shapes and sizes randomly scattered around them where men would wile away the hours drinking tequila and playing cards.

The back half of the right side of the interior served as the kitchen area. There were no doors or partitions separating the saloon area from the kitchen. There was a large wood burning stove on the back wall with counters and cupboards on either side of it. The long, bench style, plank table occupied most of the remaining free space.

An adobe divider ran parallel to the front wall. Halfway across the room, it made a ninety degree turn to the right and then continued to the back wall, running parallel to the kitchen area. The result was an enclosed area which occupied about one quarter of the interior space. A framed doorway provided access to the room. Inside were four double bunk beds against three walls, enough to sleep eight and plenty of floor space to accommodate any overflow, if they didn't mind sleeping on the floor. A man could get up in the morning, go out the doorway, and he would find himself in the kitchen where he could fix himself something to eat, or he could walk a few feet to the saloon area if a liquid breakfast was more to his liking.

Hollister didn't know where the survivors of the bushwhacking attempt were, but it was a good bet they had run with their tails between their legs to familiar ground, namely the house. As they approached the buildings, Hollister called a halt before they got too close. He turned in his saddle, twice looking in all directions. The creek bed was about a quarter mile directly in front of the dwelling. On the far side of the creek was a collection of boulders large enough to provide a good blind for a shooter. Facing the ranch house, Hollister could see there was no cover on the left side, but two small storage buildings on the right side of the dwelling provided excellent concealment.

Hollister began to shout orders, "Mr. Haines, take your long gun to those boulders across the creek. Keep firing at the house every few minutes. Vary your targets between the windows and the door. Do you think you can hit them from there? Do you have enough ammunition to keep this up for while?"

Gus Haines replied, "No problem, Colonel. Put a fly on that door, and I can hit it from there." He showed Hollister a canvas shoulder bag full of cartridges and then added, "I can keep them busy all day."

Hollister continued, "Jake, you are babysitting the kid and the horses again. Take them behind the boulders with Mr. Haines." He turned to Pat Wilkens and said, "Pat, find out if this place has a back door, and if it does, you and Mex cover it. Make sure nobody leaves."

Pat spat out a big brown gob before answering, "Sure thing, Boss."

Two of the three smaller buildings offered a good vantage point to the front of the house. After asking if his head was alright, Hollister instructed Jim Clemfeld to take up residence behind the shack closest to the ranch house, surmising that it would be within pistol range. Although the bullet had bounced off the bone on top of Nathaniel Fletcher's right shoulder, the wound was very painful and still bleeding. Hollister suggested Samuel tend to his son's wound and then join him behind the second shack.

Hollister gave everyone ample time to get into position and then waved his hat to signal Gus Haines to start shooting. He let Gus fire three shots and then signaled him to stop. He shouted as loud as he could, "Curly! Curly MacTavish!

This is Colonel Hollister. Come out of the house, so we can talk. I give you my word, you will not be hurt."

Inside the house, Charlie and Curly's three other men all shot questioning looks at Curly, wondering what he was going to do. Curly returned their gazes and asked, "Well, what do you think I should do?" Nobody answered him, so he remarked, "You bastards are a big help," as he headed for the door. He opened the door very slowly and gingerly stepped out on the veranda with his arms raised to show he was unarmed.

Hollister took two steps out from behind the shed, stood where Curly could see him, and said, "My man has got his big buffalo rifle trained on your chest. One shot from inside and you die. Is that clear?"

Curly turned his head back toward the door and shouted, "Nobody shoots! You hear me! Nobody shoots!" He turned back to Hollister and asked, "What do you want?"

Hollister came forward about thirty feet to where he could converse with Curly without having to shout. "You and whoever is left of your bushwhackers surrender your weapons and come out with your hands over your head, and we will discuss your future."

"And if we don't?" asked Curly.

Hollister took a couple of steps toward Curly and looked him in the eyes before speaking, "Then we wait for you to come out, I guess. But you know, my men are not very patient, so we won't wait too long before we burn you out. Your choice."

As Curly turned and took one step back toward the door, he said, "I'll go discuss it with the boys."

Hollister drew his pistol from the shoulder holster and said, "You are not going anywhere until I say so."

The sound of the pistol's cylinder clicking into position, stopped Curly in his tracks, and he turned back to face Hollister who was backing up slowly to the cover of the shed. When Hollister was at arm's length from the structure, he said, "Alright, you can go in now."

Curly rushed back into the house and once inside a few steps, he stopped and put his hands on his knees to catch his breath. He was so nervous that he had held his breath for most of the confrontation with Hollister.

"You okay, Boss?" inquired Charlie.

Curly straightened up. He didn't respond to Charlie's question. Instead, he went into a rage, "Who in hell does he think he is, ordering me around like that?" He stood with his hands on his hips, breathing heavily. He looked at the men in the room as if he was looking to them for an answer.

Dirty Johnston broke the tension when he asked, "What are we gonna do? What's he gonna do to us, if'n we surrender?"

"I don't know," Curly replied. "Why don't we ask him." He went to the window closest to the shed, very carefully knocked out the broken glass out of one of the panes with his knuckles, and yelled, "Hey you, Mr. Association, why don't you just go away? We promise we won't buy any more stolen cattle."

Hollister didn't soften his position when he replied, "You heard what I said. Come out unarmed, and then we'll talk."

Curly turned back to the four men in the room. "What do you fellas want to do?"

Charlie Goodnall replied with a bit of panic in his voice, "They aren't going to let us go. Hell, we tried to kill them. If I'm gonna die, I'm going down fighting."

Dirty Johnston shook his head in agreement. Carlos Ortega didn't say anything. Too-ah-yay-say was thinking to himself about how he was going to get out of this situation. He made a quick decision and headed through the kitchen area to the back door. As he opened it slowly, Pat Wilkens fired his rifle, the bullet hitting the door frame inches from the Apache's head, forcing him to quickly close the door.

Hollister called out, "The back door is covered. You gentlemen are not going anywhere. Are you coming out or not?" He waited briefly for a response and when none came, he told the Fletchers and Jim Clemfeld to open fire. Hearing the shots, Pat and Mex opened up on the back door, and Gus Haines let go with the .50 again. All five men in the ranch house hit the floor and lay prone amidst the flying glass, wood splinters, and pieces of adobe brick flying overhead. After a lengthy time of inactivity, Curly and his men were fairly confident the shooting had stopped for the moment, and they all stood up with the exception of Too-ah-yay-say, who was being a lot more cautious.

Hollister, after ordering a cease-fire, waited briefly before he said, "One minute. You have one minute, and then we burn you out."

In response, Curly took Charlie's pistol from him and fried a couple of shots at the shed, and then he shouted, "You go to hell! Adobe bricks don't burn all that well."

"No, but the smoke will kill you quick," Hollister yelled back.

"Do your best," countered Curly.

"Pat, put a torch to the place!" commanded Hollister, hollering loud enough for Pat to hear him at the back of the house.

Dried tumbleweed tied to a three foot stick makes a good, hot burning torch. Earlier, Mex and Pat had constructed half a dozen such torches and now, on Hollister's command, lit them up, and while Pat covered the back door of the ranch house, Mex tossed them onto different locations on the roof. The patchwork of wooden shingles and planks quickly caught fire, and a moment later the entire roof was ablaze. It wasn't long before Curly and what was left of his crew came coughing and stumbling out of the smoked filled house onto the veranda.

Hollister made his move while Curly and company were disoriented. He stepped out from behind the shed with Jim Clemfeld and the Fletchers right behind him. As soon as Hollister confirmed for himself that the five men on the veranda were unarmed, he asked, "Is that all of you?"

"No, my dear ole mother is still in there just sittin' in her rocker, knittin' me a new sweater," answered Curly, as sarcastic as he could make it.

Hollister decided there wasn't anyone left in the house, so he called Pat and Mex to the front and signaled Gus Haines that the siege was over. He ordered Curly and the rest to come off the veranda and into the yard. They shuffled slowly down the stairs and lined up with Curly in the middle, Too-ah-yay-say and Ortega on his left and Charlie Goodnall and Dirty Johnston on his right. Hollister and his men formed an opposing line, with Hollister in the middle, Jim Clemfeld, Pat and Mex on his right and Nathaniel and Samuel Fletcher on his left. With Azul in the lead, Jake, Gus Haines, and Tommy Kulbane made their way across the creek with the horses in tow. There was an awkward silence that seemed to go on forever. Charlie Goodnall broke the stillness by asking, "What now, Mr. Colonel, Sir?

Hollister smiled and replied, "Well, let me see; cattle rustling, horse thieving, attempted murder. All hanging offenses."

Maybe it was Hollister's smile, or perhaps it was because Too-ah-yay-say didn't have a full grasp of the English language, but he panicked, pulled his knife, and charged at Hollister. Pat Wilkens never took his eye off the Apache, and when he charged, Pat shot him twice in the chest. In that instant, all hell broke loose and everything happened at once. Carlos Ortega bolted to his left and headed for the corner of the veranda only to be cut down by both barrels of Mex's shotgun. Samuel Fletcher, amidst shouts of 'Hallelujah', pumped three shots into Dirty Johnston, and Nathaniel did the same to Charlie Goodnall. Curly had turned and started up the stairs to the veranda, when Hollister screamed, "Stop where you are, or we'll cut you in half!"

Hollister had fully expected Curly to stop, and when he didn't, the momentary lapse in attention was enough time to allow Curly to make it to the front door and back inside the house. Three steps inside, Curly realized his error in judgment. The thick smoke was suffocating, and when he tried to take a breath, he sucked in a lungful of toxic gases. He coughed violently, but could get no air, for every time he took a breath in, he filled his lungs with smoke. He turned and tried to make it back to the front, but it was too late. He collapsed where he stood, and a minute later his heart stopped.

Hollister waited a full ten minutes before deciding Curly wasn't going to come out of the burning house. He called his men together and barked out orders to burn all the buildings to the ground, but to first make sure all the stock was out of harm's way. He told Jake and Tommy to gather the horses, as they would take them along. One could always use extra horses. There were four head of cattle in one of the pens, and Hollister told Pat and Jim Clemfeld to release them and chase them towards the village where the people could claim them once they realized Curly and his outfit weren't around to offer any objections.

An hour later, the out buildings had been reduced to smoldering rubble, and the only thing left of the ranch house was the adobe brick walls. The men had all gathered around Hollister, waiting for further orders.

"What's next, Colonel," asked Pat?

"We make our way back to White Sands country looking for more rustlers and horse thieves, and we keep on doing it until we're sure they've got the message that plying their trade in our territory is not a profitable venture," was Hollister's curt reply.

"Sounds like a full time job to me," remarked Tommy Kulbane.

Hollister, who had been extremely patient with the youngster up to this point, lost his temper. He walked over to Tommy, grabbed him by the shirt front, and when they were nose to nose, Hollister said through clenched teeth, "Listen to me you little sack of horse shit. You are lucky to be alive, but that can change in a hurry. You know more then you are telling, and I know it! You are coming with us. If you tell me what you are hiding, we just might not turn you over to Mr. Thornsbury." He paused for effect and then added, "He'll hang you for sure, boy."

CHAPTER NINE

THE REGULATORS WERE several miles north of the border when they made camp the night before. The morning sun wasn't quite peeking over the eastern horizon, and in the dim light of pre-dawn everyone was still out cold, snoring in their blankets, with the exception of Jake Romero and Samuel Fletcher; Jake because he slept differently than most white men and Samuel because God chose to talk to him at night when things were quiet.

Part of Jake's training as a Lipan Scout was the ability to sleep in short stretches, yet wake up feeling rested and energized. Even in a state of deep sleep, part of his mind was ever alert for any changes in the environment; a new odor, the snorting of a horse, a sound that shouldn't be there, or the cessation of the usual night noises such as chirping birds or singing crickets. Jake opened his eyes, closed them again, and listened. The horses were snorting and stomping. Something was agitating them, so Jake arose and with Azul by his side, he made his way to the grove of trees at the back of the camp where the mounts were tethered.

Samuel Fletcher had risen a moment after Jake, stretching his arms skyward and shouting, "Praise be to the Lord! He has given us the gift of another day in his servitude." He was so focused on his celebration that he failed to notice the shadowy figures encircling the camp.

Jake was amongst the horses, stroking and patting them, trying to settle them down. He wasn't sure what had spooked them, perhaps a wandering coyote or a crawling rattlesnake. The horses had gotten used to Azul and had learned he was no threat. Out of the corner of his eye, Jake caught a quick glimpse of movement back in the direction of the camp. His first thought was someone else had risen and when he heard Samuel praising his god, his tensions eased somewhat, but when he looked in the Preacher's direction, he froze. There was enough light to make out the camp, and he saw a dark silhouette come up behind Samuel and plant a rifle butt in the back of the Deacon's head.

Over two dozen weapons fired almost simultaneously into the air. All of Hollister's men were on their feet at the same time, confused and wondering who was doing all the shooting. Mex brought up his shotgun as a bullet whizzed past his ear, and he immediately dropped the scatter gun and raised his arms. Hollister, assessing the situation, determined the invaders had the advantage. To save his men from getting shot, he shouted for them to drop their weapons and not resist. In the increasing morning light he could make out a large group of well armed men. Hollister kept his nerves in check and in a commanding tone he asked, "Who the hell are you, and what do you want?"

One of the intruders replied in a deep, raspy voice. He spoke broken English with a heavy Spanish accent when he said, "I am Enrique Esparza, and I want to know why you are killing all my friends."

Hollister had to think for a moment before he figured out who Esparza was referring to. He chose his words carefully when he replied, "The only people we killed were a bunch of cattle thieves who ambushed us in the dark. It was self defense."

"After you kill my friends, you burn the rancho. Tell me, Senor, was that self defense?"

When Esparza saw that Hollister wasn't going to answer the question, he looked at Tommy and said, "Senor Kulbane, I think maybe you tell me what I want to know, si?"

Hollister looked stunned when he stammered, "Tommy—you—you know this man?"

Tommy grinned as he replied, "Mr. Esparza is a friend of my father. They do business together." He turned his attention to Esparza and said, "Colonel's mostly right. Curly did try to dry gulch him a couple of nights ago. The Colonel set a trap for Curly and his men and got about half of them. He followed Curly back to the ranch and gave him a chance to surrender, but Curly and the boys would have no part of that deal, so they ended up dead. Then the

Colonel burnt the place down as a message. Just like he hung Stick and couple of his boys; to send a message, he says."

Esparza stared at Hollister for a long time before he said, "So, Senor Cor-a-nell, what is this message you wish to send?"

Hollister took on an authoritative air and answered, "We are duly appointed officers of the law, and we dealt with some cattle and horse thieves and the people who buy their stolen stock, in an appropriate manner. The message—the message is if you don't want to face us again, then don't steal our stock."

Esparza laughed boisterously. He waved his pistol he in a small circle, indicating the men all around him. "Senor, most of these men are horse thieves. Are you going to hang them all? I don't think they got your message."

Samuel Fletcher had regained consciousness and had risen to his feet. He rubbed the back of his aching neck as he looked around. He said to no one in particular, "The Lord sayeth there is a special place in Hell for cowards and back shooters."

Esparza feigned confusion when he asked, "Is this man your priest? He sounds like a padre to me."

"He's no priest. Him and his son and that fella there," Tommy said, pointing to Gus Haines, "are hired killers."

Esparza asked Tommy, "What do you think we should do with them, Senor Kulbane?" This completely surprised Hollister and his men. Here was a bandit leader asking a kid for advice, and it sure sounded like he was serious.

Tommy's response was just as surprising when he said, "Take them to my father. He will know what to do with them."

Esparza countered with a suggestion of his own, "Maybe we kill these gringos to send a message of our own, eh?"

"No, take them to my father. He needs men, and he will appreciate your gift, Enrique." Tommy said it like he was issuing a command which intrigued Hollister even more.

"As you say, Senor." Esparza started barking orders concerning the disarming and securing of Hollister and his men.

When the bandits first fired their weapons, Jake had made his way to a large creosote bush closer to the camp where he could see and hear everything that transpired. When Esparza began shouting orders, Jake snuck back to the horses. His intent was to pick a couple of the sturdier mounts and leave when he noticed two of the bandits. They had been left behind to watch their own horses and had brought their mounts up to where Hollister's horses were tethered. Neither one of them heard or saw a thing. All the first man felt was

Jake's hand as it clamped over his mouth to keep him from screaming as Jake hit him rapidly three times in the temple as hard as he could with the butt end of his knife handle. The second one thought he heard something, and turned around just in time to receive the same knife butt in the middle of his forehead. Jake hit him a couple more times, as the bandit went down, to make sure he was unconscious.

Jake quickly untied all of their mounts, saddled his own horse as well as Hollister's big bay, cut a branch from the nearest bush, grasped the reins of his own horse, and mounted the bay. He hollered at the top of his lungs at the same time swatting several horses on the rump with the branch, driving them toward the camp. As a result, the entire herd, Hollister's and Esparza's mounts included, galloped through the campsite. Men scattered to the left and to the right, diving for cover as the horses charged. Jake rode away in the opposite direction, putting some distance between him and the bandits.

Esparza quickly regained control. He fired two shots into the air to get everyone's attention. A second later Hollister shouted to his men, not to do anything stupid that would get them shot. Esparza asked Tommy, "Who did this?"

Tommy thought for a moment and when realization came to him, he replied, "We forgot all about him. He's an old man called Jake. He's dressed like an Apache, but he's a white man.

Esparza turned to Hollister and asked, "Who is this hombre?"

Hollister didn't see the need to hide anything from Esparza, so he told the truth when he said, "He's our tracker. Name's Jake Romero. Apache raised and he thinks just like them."

Esparza laughed out loud and said, "Jake—I know Jake. Well, I don't know him, but I have heard of this white Apache. It is said he can track a scorpion across a dry rock. Good for you, Senor Cor-a-nell. He is a good man to have."

When the horses charged through the encampment, a couple of Esparza's men had managed to stop three of them. Esparza quickly ordered three of his men to mount and catch the rest of the runaway horses. He looked around and not seeing the two men who were supposed to be watching the horses he shouted, *"Miguel y Fernando, dionde esta usted? Venido aqui immediateamente!"* He waited momentarily and when he got no response, he repeated his command and waited, and again he got no reply. He was about to send someone to check on the two guards when another one of his men rushed into the camp area and reported that someone had knocked both Miguel and Fernando unconscious, and it didn't look like Miguel was going to live.

It took nearly two hours to round up all the runaway horses. During the wait, Esparza issued orders that Hollister and his men have their hands securely tied behind their backs. No one seemed to be saying much of anything, and Hollister saw an opportunity to fish for information. "Where are we going?" he asked.

"We are going on a little ride, two days maybe. This is where General Kulbane has his big rancho," replied Esparza.

Hollister still wasn't getting a clear picture of Esparza's intent, so he continued questioning, "For what purpose?" he asked.

Esparza smiled and replied with a malicious tone, "Business, Senor Cor-a-nell. Just business."

The three bandits had caught all of the runaway horses, including the extra mounts. After taking the time to bury Miguel, who had died of the hits to the temple Jake had inflicted, Esparza had Hollister's and his men's hands untied. A four foot piece of rope was tied to each of their right ankles and once they were aboard their mounts, the other end of the rope was brought under the horse's belly and tied securely to their left ankle. This gave the prisoners the freedom to manage their mounts, but prevented any escape attempts. Also, Esparza had indicated that any attempt at escape would be met with several bullets in the back.

After stampeding all the horses, Jake rode at full gallop due west for the better part of ten minutes and then changed direction, so he was traveling south, paralleling the same route he assumed Esparza was going to take. When he first lit out, he thought he would just keep going. This job was over. He wouldn't collect any pay, but he decided he could cut his loses and besides, the two fine horses he had were payment enough. It wasn't a sense of loyalty or responsibility that prompted him to turn south. Jake didn't care one way or another about what fate awaited the Regulators. He strongly disliked Gus Haines, but at the same time, he had grown fond of Colonel Hollister and Pat Wilkens. He thought Samuel Fletcher was an odd man, a dangerous novelty, not unlike the rattlesnakes he played with.

Jake usually didn't pick sides in a dispute unless one side or the other affected him in some way. In this instant, his loyalty (what there was of it) lay with Hollister and his men, primarily because he liked the Colonel. Hollister had treated him fairly and Jake respected him for it. His plan was to parallel Esparza's route, timing it so that at regular intervals he could get closer and confirm the group was still moving south.

It was a scorcher of a day and Esparza pushed them hard. At one point, Hollister asked for water for himself and his men. The bandit leader refused, saying he only had enough water for himself until Tommy reminded him that his father would most likely want Hollister alive, and Esparza reluctantly relented which made Hollister wonder again what power Tommy Kulbane had over Esparza that he would listen to the young man.

Samuel Fletcher was doing some pondering of his own. Colonel Hollister had enforced his authority over the Regulators during the entire expedition. Samuel, who liked to be in charge of any circumstances in which he was involved, had taken a back seat and for the most part, had kept his mouth shut. Now, the circumstances had changed. They had been waylaid and taken captive by a gang of Mexican bandits, and Samuel had no idea what their intent was. During a rest stop, he decided it was time to speak up for himself. He rubbed the back of his head to ease the stiffness that had set in after being hit by the rifle butt, turned his head sideways, and with bulging eyes said to Esparza, "Give and it shall be given to you. For whatever measure you deal out to others, it will be dealt to you in return."

Esparza stared at Samuel for the longest time as did most of the men within earshot. At first, the bandit leader thought Fletcher had threatened him and then the thought occurred to him that the crazy man might be asking for mercy. He chose his words carefully and replied, "Ah, I see you are a man of God and you quote the Good Book well, my friend. I, too, am a man of faith. I have sinned in the name of my business, but sometimes you have to work with what God has given you, which in my case wasn't very much. I and my compadres, we take what we need where we find it. We are — how do you say — men of opportunity. God provides the opportunity, and we take it."

Fletcher looked back at his son Nathaniel and threw out another quote, "Be strong and of good courage, fear not, nor be afraid — for the Lord, thy God, he is that doth go with thee; he will not fail thee, nor forsake thee."

Esparza smiled as he said, "Very true, Senor. Very true. He has not forsaken us, for he has delivered you gringos into my hands. General Kulbane shall fill our pockets with mucho pesos when we bring you to him."

Samuel Fletcher came to the conclusion that his *'raging preacher'* routine wasn't working on Esparza. His mind was racing, and he was at a loss as to what to say next. Luckily, he was saved by Hollister's interjection, who asked, "Just what is it this General, as you call him, would want from us?"

All he got from Esparza was, "I am sure the General will explain it all to you, Senor."

Later that evening, after a late day meal, Hollister found his way to where young Tommy Kulbane was seated. Hollister motioned to a spot on the ground near Tommy, indicating that he would like to sit down. Tommy made some snide remark about it being a free country which Hollister ignored. When he was comfortable, Hollister turned to Tommy and said, "Tell me about your father. I am really curious about him."

"You'll see him soon enough," Tommy replied.

Hollister countered with a demanding tone in his voice, "What is the big secret? Who is your father and want does he want with us?" Tommy didn't respond. Hollister waited several more seconds before saying, "Well — I'm waiting?"

Tommy seemed agitated, unsure when he responded, "I don't know! He was some big shot General in the war. He says he never surrendered, and he thinks he is going to build an army to go start the war again. All I know is he needs men and money."

It was around midnight when Pat Wilkens woke up in terror. Something was clamped over his mouth and nose, and he couldn't breathe. As full consciousness cleared away the fog of slumber, he realized it was a human hand pressed tight against his face. He started to struggle, but when he heard the voice of Jake Romero, he relaxed and Jake released his hold. Pat sat up; momentarily excited about seeing the scout, then he realized Jake was in the bandit camp with him. He was about to ask how this could be, but Jake anticipated his question and explained to Pat that he was there to rescue him.

Pat had bedded down a few yards away from the picket lines. He liked going to sleep listening to the night sounds the horses made; the snorts, the whinnies, the stamping of the hooves. He had also learned the horses were always a good early warning system if a nosey coyote or a wandering cougar came too close. One of the bandit sentries ordered him to go back amongst the other captives, but Esparza had intervened and asked the sentry where he thought Pat might go with no water, food or transportation. He also stated that if it looked like Pat was trying to leave their glorious company, he should shoot Pat down like the mangy dog he was. The sentry grinned at Pat as if he was hoping he would try something.

As Pat rose into a crouched position, he reached into his shirt pocket and brought out his chewing tobacco, and after taking a big chaw, he followed Jake to the cover of the trees where he stepped over the sentry, who was face down in the dirt. "Is he dead?" Pat asked in a whisper.

Jake waited until they were a fair distance into the grove of Ponderosa Pine before he stopped and answered. "I think he is still alive, but sometimes I hit too many times and too hard," he explained.

Pat paused with his hands on his knees to catch his breathe and then asked, "What's the plan, Jake?"

The question caught Jake off guard because he seldom formulated any long range plans. It was not in his nature. He dealt with situations of the moment and based each subsequent decision on the outcome of his previous action. He said, "I got you away because it was not hard to do. The one you call Mex sleeps close to a couple of large boulders. It would be easy for him to leave unseen. As far as the others, we shall have to wait for a better time."

Pat was going to suggest he come along and help get Mex out, but before he could speak, Jake was gone, and Pat didn't hear so much as a rustle when he left. He didn't have to wait long before Jake reappeared with Mex not far behind. Pat, who was usually quite talkative, didn't say anything. He merely turned his head sideways, spat out a big gob of brown tobacco juice, and stared at Jake who sensed that Pat was waiting for something, so he explained, "We scatter the horses again. Slow them down some more."

Before they could implement Jake's plan, Esparza's booming voice filled the night air. "Apache, I know you can hear me. If you hurt one more of my men, I shall begin killing your friends one by one until you get the message," he shouted. He paused momentarily as if waiting for the breeze to carry his message to Jake and then continued, "We do not wish to harm your friends, Senor. Si, they are becoming our friends, too. Mañana, we shall arrive at General Kulbane's rancho, and then you can come and visit your friends as often as you like. Maybe we could have a drink of mescal together, eh?"

Colonel Hollister resigned himself to the inevitability that they were not going to escape before they got to see this General Kulbane. First of all, there wasn't enough time to formulate and implement an escape plan because according to Esparza, they were going to arrive at their destination some time today and secondly, although Jake had managed to sneak Pat and Mex out from under Esparza's nose last night, Hollister was sure that Jake would take the bandit's warning seriously and stay away.

Now, his thoughts centered on General Kulbane. Many questions raced through his mind. As a result of a long and rather uninformative conversation with Tommy Kulbane the night before, all Hollister learned was that although everyone referred to Tommy's father as 'General', he was not in the Mexican army. It set Hollister to wondering what army Kulbane was affiliated with and what the hell he might want with the Regulators. All attempts at trying to coax more information out of Tommy proved futile.

Jake, Pat, and Mex had spent the rest of the night within eyesight of the bandit's camp. Pat was anxious to go in shooting, hoping to scatter the bandits, making it relatively easy to get the rest of their men out. Jake told him that he would bow to Pat's wishes if that is what he truly wanted to do, but the smarter move would be to wait it out and see where Esparza was taking the Colonel and the rest of the men. Jake argued that if Esparza had intentions of killing the Regulators, he would have done so by now. In Jake's mind, the most pressing issue at the moment was to get another horse as they only had two and he said so to his two companions. Before Pat could protest, Jake was off to do just that.

CHAPTER TEN

THE DEEP, NARROW basin was well hidden from view. Hollister was mildly surprised when one minute it seemed as if the scrub-brush prairie and desert terrain stretched as far as the eye could see, and suddenly, without any warning, they were on the top edge of a ridge, looking down into a small valley. Esparza pulled his horse up next to Hollister's, and indicating the myriad of structures below, he said, "We are here, Senor Cor-a-nell. This is General Kulbane's hacienda."

Hollister looked from one side of the small valley to the other, soaking in all there was to see. A wide but very shallow, rocky creek cut the small valley symmetrically in half. To the east, on the far side of the basin, set against a backdrop of a two hundred foot sandstone cliff, was a large, two level, brick, plantation house. It was a fine example of Southern architecture that Hollister would have sworn on a stack of Bibles had been somehow transported brick by brick from somewhere in Virginia. To the left of the house were at least half a dozen other two-story structures that, as Hollister would learn later, served as barracks for Kulbane's men. There was a courtyard in front of the plantation house with a circular fountain set in the middle. Three large barns and several partitioned corrals, with horses in all of them, occupied the space to the right of the house.

Closer to the creek were dozens of small adobe and wooden shacks where Hollister surmised the workers lived. On the near side of the creek, directly below and to his left, Hollister could see several acres of growing corn while to his right there were several more acres of grassland, where a small herd of cattle grazed.

"There she is, Senor Cor-a-nell, El Rancho de General Kulbane," said Esparza, rather proudly.

Hollister was not about to show his amazement at seeing the plantation house out in the middle of a Mexican desert. He replied, nonchalantly, "Very nice. I am looking forward to meeting this General."

It was far easier on their horses for the men to dismount and lead them down the switchbacks leading down the steep hillside to the valley floor below. Once on level ground, a well traveled road took them across the pastures and the creek and up to the courtyard in front of the mansion. Once there, Esparza had Hollister and his men dismount and form a horizontal line, facing the veranda of the mansion.

They stood for the longest time in the hot sun, waiting for someone or something. Just as everyone was growing restless, a tall, slender man dressed in Confederate grey stepped out onto the veranda and walked forward. He moved down a couple of steps, stopped in the middle of the stairway, and scrutinized Hollister and his men very carefully before he said to Esparza, "Enrique, what have you brought me today?"

Esparza moved directly behind Hollister, pushed him forward and took up a position, standing next to him. He put his hand on Hollister's shoulder and said to Kulbane, "This hombre calls himself Cor-a-nell Hollister, and the rest of these hombres are his amigos."

"Why did you bring them to me?" asked Kulbane.

Esparza was stuck for an answer. He glanced at Tommy, looked back at the General, and said, "Senor Tommy say we should bring them to you."

Kulbane glanced at his son and remarked snidely, "Ah, the prodigal returns. Explain yourself, boy!"

Tommy knew from experience that his father did not tolerate long winded explanations, so he summarized, "These fellas are from some cattle association or something from somewhere in New Mexico. They caught me and three of my friends with a few head of range steers. They claimed we stole them, and they hung my three friends. They made me tell them where we sold our cattle, and then these bastards killed Curly MacTavish and his whole outfit. Murdered them in cold blood! Then Enrique came along and jumped them, and we brought them here to you."

General George Kulbane walked slowly and deliberately down the remaining stairs and the few feet over to Hollister's position, where he stopped and faced Hollister, looking him up and down several times. Hollister scrutinized Kulbane as well. Almost as surprising as it was to find a Virginia style plantation house in the middle of the badlands, it was equally astonishing for Hollister to see a man in a full Confederate Army General's uniform. Kulbane had it all, from the Confederate Stag hat with a yellow hatband tied off in two tassels, to the Three Gold Stars and Wreath on a General's collar. He sported a cadet-grey long coat and sky blue wool trousers with a yellow stripe running up the side of each leg. Around his waist was a black leather belt with a CSA belt buckle, proudly displayed. An Army .44 Colt was tucked in the belt and a Calvary Saber was attached to his right hip.

Kulbane spoke, "Colonel, eh? In whose army?"

Hollister replied with a sarcastic tone, "General, eh? In whose army?"

The two men glared at one another for the longest time. Hollister thought he had better not push this man too far until he found out what Kulbane wanted, so he broke the stalemate and said, "I ended the war as a full Colonel with the 6th Virginia Cavalry Regiment."

Kulbane thought for a moment and then replied, cordially, "Yes, I recall hearing of the 6th — Shenandoah Valley, wasn't it?"

"Yes, and other battles, as well," replied Hollister.

"Myself, I was with the 1st North Carolina Cavalry," offered Kulbane.

Hollister thought a moment and then answered, "I don't ever recall ever hearing of a General Kulbane, and I thought I knew all the Generals in the Confederacy."

Kulbane lost his composure and stammered, "I—well—I—you see, I wasn't a General during the war. I only reached the rank of Sergeant, but I have my own command now. We call ourselves, *'The Sons of the South'*. Changing the subject, he added, "It's too hot out here to be jawing. Let us continue our discussion in my quarters with a drink and a cigar." He turned and promptly marched up the stairs, stopped at the top, turned, and said to Hollister, "Well, are you coming?"

Hollister took a step forward before half turning back to look over his shoulder. He asked, "What about my men?"

Kulbane replied, "Spoken like a true leader. The men must come first. Not to fear, Colonel, your men will be dealt with."

Hollister didn't like Kulbane's inference or tone. He pushed the issue by asking, "What do you mean, *dealt* with?"

Kulbane didn't answer as he continued on into the house. Hollister followed, and as he entered, a flood of memories of many southern mansions filled his mind. The scene before him looked very similar: the tall ceiling, the double staircase leading to the upper floor, the French doors to his left that separated the kitchen and dining area from the parlor, the spacious sitting area to his right, complete with five comfortable looking chairs and a huge granite fire place. Kulbane made his way to a large liquor cabinet to the left of the fire place, removed a carafe of brandy, and poured two generous drinks into two sifters. He turned and handed one of the drinks to Hollister and motioned for him to take a seat. Hollister sat down without taking his eyes off Kulbane who, in turn, sat down directly across from Hollister, raised his glass, and said, "Here's to the glorious Southland. May she live forever!"

Hollister watched as Kulbane took a sip of his brandy and then set the glass down on the table in front of them. Hollister didn't take a drink, opting to hold the glass in his hand while waiting for Kulbane to make his next move. There was an uneasy silence for what seemed an eternity until Kulbane cleared his throat and said, "So, Colonel, what did you do during the conflict?"

Without any hesitation, Hollister replied, "It was a war, Mr. Kulbane and my involvement, frankly Sir, is none of your business."

Kulbane was holding his rage in. Consequently, his face turned red and his hands were shaking when he pointed at Hollister and shouted, "That's General Kulbane! And I am making it my business to get to know you!" He soften his tone when he added, "It will help me decide if you are of any use to me, or if I will have to hang you."

Hollister was taken aback by the threat, but he didn't show it outwardly. He collected his thoughts and replied, "General, or whatever you want to call yourself, the war has been over for a long time. Whatever ideals or cause I and my neighbours fought to protect are all gone. I am in the cattle business in New Mexico and have no desire to join some misguided lunatic in his quest to resurrect a dead way of life." He paused to catch his breath and then continued, "Sons of the South? They did nothing for our cause. In fact, the violent and illegal tactics employed by them before the war in Kansas outraged northerner sympathizers and intensified northern antislavery sentiment —"

Cutting Hollister off, Kulbane got to his feet and uttered through clenched teeth, "Don't you dare badmouth the Sons of the South. We were doing what we thought was right to preserve a way of life. It was our right, damn it."

Hollister realized he was dealing with a man of conviction, no matter how misguided, and he decided not to antagonize him any further. He asked in a friendly, non-confrontational tone, "What do you want of us?"

Kulbane wanted to choke the life out of Hollister, but the Colonel's question made him pause and gain his composure. He stared at Hollister for a long moment, took a drink of his brandy, and sat back down. He took another sip, set the glass on the table, leaned forward in his chair, and said, "I need good leaders. I've hundreds of men who are good fighters and can take orders, but not a one that can think for themselves. That is where you come in, Colonel."

"And what is your primary objective, General?" asked Hollister, feigning interest.

"Why, to continue the war between the North and the South, of course!" answered Kulbane. After a short pause and a questioning look in Hollister's direction, he continued, "To that end, I need weapons and a well trained army. Unfortunately, I have neither due to lack of funds, but I am rectifying that. I have several enterprises going that are proving quite lucrative."

Hollister couldn't help it when he asked, "Would cattle rustling be one of them?"

"I am not going to sit here and let you judge me," spat Kulbane. He stood and continued, "You can join me and be part of something great, or you can occupy a six by four plot of fine Mexican desert sand for the rest of eternity."

"Maybe he is worth something, father," suggested Tommy Kulbane. Neither Hollister nor the older Kulbane had seen or heard Tommy enter the room.

"What do mean, Tommy?" asked his father.

"I'm thinking this association he belongs to has a lot of rich ranchers, and maybe they will pay a ransom to have him back"

The older Kulbane rubbed his chin as he contemplated the suggestion. He thought for a long moment, turned to Hollister, and said, "Well, there you have it, Colonel. You can join our noble cause, or take a chance that your friends back in New Mexico want you back badly enough to pay for your return."

"I would like to see to my men," replied Hollister.

"By all means," said Kulbane. Directing his attention to Tommy, he said, "See to the Colonel's wishes." He paused for effect then added, "Ten should do."

While Hollister was inside exchanging dialogue with Kulbane, Enrique Esparza escorted Jim Clemfeld, the Fletchers, and Gus Haines to an enclosed compound to the right and to the rear of the mansion. A half acre plot was encompassed on three sides with six foot adobe walls with the cliff face serving as the fourth wall. A three-pole gate, complete with a well armed sentry, served as an entrance to the enclosure. Inside the compound, against the cliff, was a small adobe brick building about the size of a tool shed that served as a refuge from the heat for the guards on duty. Scattered about the compound were half a dozen hitching rails, not intended to tether horses but to chain prisoners. Each rail had three iron rings firmly embedded in the cross piece. One of the structures had two occupants seated on the ground with their arms over their heads and their wrists chained to the iron loops. Their heads were slumped into their chests, and they both looked like they were on death's doorstep. In the center of the enclosure was a ten foot pole with a crosspiece nailed across it at shoulder height that was used to dole out punishment to insubordinates, or whoever else General Kulbane decreed needed a few lashes with a bullwhip. Off to the left of the small adobe building was a wooden structure about twenty five feet in height. It looked like the framework that would normally support a windmill or a water tank, but in this case it housed a large bell with the pull rope hanging down one side of the structure.

As Esparza and his captives approached, the sentry quickly slid the three poles out of the gate, allowing them to enter. Esparza called out a name, and two armed men emerged from the small building. One was a heavy set, older, white man while the other was a young, dark skinned lad of mixed race. "*Cuatro hombres para ensamblam su partido,*" said Esparza.

The big white man approached and said with a snide grin, "English, Amigo! We speak English around here."

Esparza appeared angered as he replied with a scowl, "These four gentlemen have come to partake of your hospitality — is that enough English for you, or should I have said, 'Four men for you, asshole?'"

Esparza and the jailer exchanged dirty looks, and Esparza turned and strutted out of the compound. The two men from the hut, aided by the sentry from the gate, ushered the four prisoners to two adjacent hitching rails, Gus Haines and Nathaniel Fletcher to one and Samuel Fletcher and Jim Clemfeld to the other. Amid protests and expletives from Gus Haines and biblical quotes from Reverend Fletcher, the four of them were shackled at the wrists, and the chains were looped through the large iron rings attached to the hitching rails.

Reverend Fletcher was engaged in a rant about the sword of justice having no scabbard, when he was interrupted by the entrance of Colonel Hollister and Tommy Kulbane. As the guards approached, Tommy said to the big man, "The General says he gets ten." As a second thought, he added, "And Mr. Curtis, not too hard. I kinda like him."

John Curtis was a vicious man who seized every opportunity to inflict pain on others. Consequently, he didn't pay any attention to Tommy's request for leniency. After Hollister was tied to the cross, facing the pole, Curtis gave him a dozen lashes with all the strength he could muster. The extra two were because he resented the young Kulbane telling him how to do his job. When the whipping was over, Hollister was unconscious, his tied arms holding up his weight and his lacerated back oozing blood. Curtis's two compadres untied him from the whipping pole, dragged him to an empty hitching rail, and chained him to it.

Back inside the main house, General Kulbane was giving three of his men, Corporal Mathew Allen, Trooper Norbert Bigelow, and Trooper Antonio Santos Quillera, some final instructions on where to find Sinclair Thornsbury's ranch. Just before he dismissed them he said, "Corporal Allen, don't let me down. You make this carpetbagger understand Hollister's life depends on him. We want five thousand dollars for his safe return. If he pays, Hollister will come back alive and well, and if he doesn't — well, I'm sure you can make him understand. You can leave in the morning and I'll expect you back in two weeks."

"Sir, what if they won't pay?" asked Allen.

"I told you to use your imagination," exclaimed Kulbane. He mumbled inaudibly, "Maybe that's asking too much," and then he said aloud, "Then tell them the only thing they will get back is Hollister's head in a gunny sack!"

Jake, Pat, and Mex had been trailing Esparza's outfit at a safe distance, so as not to be seen. The gang's sudden disappearance puzzled Jake when he came up on a small rise and expected to see riders some distance ahead of them. Once they were within sight of the basin, Jake understood where the riders had gone. He turned and rode at a right angle to the main trail, heading for a spot on the basin rim, a safe distance off the main trail where he could scout out the valley below.

"What do think we should do, Jake?" asked Pat when they had dismounted.

"We will let the horses eat some grass. We will rest and when the night comes, I shall go and see what has happened to Colonel Hollister." Jake didn't wait for a reply or any further questions. He removed three sets of hobble straps from a saddle bag and tossed two of them to Pat. He hobbled his own horse, took the saddle and blanket off his mount, and using the saddle for a pillow, he lay down and closed his eyes and went to sleep.

Pat gave Mex a funny look, shook his head, spat out a big, brown gob and said, "Well, shithouse mouse, if that don't beat all."

CHAPTER ELEVEN

DARKNESS WAS KNOCKING on the door, and Gus Haines hadn't had anything to eat since yesterday. He was beginning to wonder if he would ever see food again. "Hey you, Bean Stock," he hollered at the tall, lanky man on sentry duty at the gate.

"What do you want?" answered Stanley Hawkins, as he left his post and took three long strides in Gus's direction.

"You plannin' on stravin' us to death?" grumbled Haines.

"You'll eat when they tell me to feed you," replied Hawkins.

Hollister, who had regained consciousness a short time earlier, interjected and said "Sentry, would you please send for Esparza. Tell him Colonel Hollister wants to talk." The hitching rail Hollister occupied was the closest one to Hawkins, so he didn't have any trouble hearing Hollister's request, but he chose to ignore it, anyway.

Curtis heard the commotion and stepped out of the shack, bellowing as he emerged, "What's the problem, Hawkins?"

"Nothing I can't handle," growled Hawkins.

Curtis crossed the small courtyard in the direction of the insubordinate sentry. As he passed Hollister's position, Hollister said, "Corporal, if you please. These men haven't eaten since some time yesterday. We could all use some water."

"Food and water in the morning," was Curtis's curt response.

"Look! Your General has plans for us that entail us being alive to see them through. I am positive I will be talking to him real soon, so if you don't want to be the next one tied to the whipping post, I suggest you get some food and water for my men."

Curtis stood glaring at Hollister, deciding whether or not to believe the Colonel. The image of getting whipped did not sit well with Curtis, so he decided not to take any chances. "Manuel, get your skinny ass out here!" he hollered at the small building.

Manuel Corza came running at full speed, stopped in front of Curtis, and listened intently with his straw hat in his hand while Curtis gave instructions. "You and Hawkins get these prisoners some food and water and bring Angelena. Tell her to bring what she needs to doctor the Colonel up."

While Manuel sprinted away on his assigned task, Hollister looked up at Curtis and said, "Thank you."

Curtis grunted in acknowledgement and headed back to the comfort of the hut. Jim Clemfeld, who was closest to Hollister, asked, "Colonel, what is going on? What are they gonna do with us?"

Hollister replied, "I don't know for sure, Jim. They are going to try and ransom me back to the Association. As for you men, I believe you will be conscripted into Kulbane's army."

Samuel Fletcher interjected, "I have no desire to join this man's or anybody else's army!"

"You might not have a choice, Mr. Fletcher," countered Hollister.

"We are in the service of the Lord. We do no man's bidding unless we chose to do so," pontificated Fletcher.

Surprising Fletcher, Hollister quoted from the Bible, "And to knowledge temperance, and to temperance patience, and to patience godliness, Reverend." Fletcher didn't look like he understood, so Hollister added, "What I am saying, Gentlemen, is we need to be patient and let this thing play out. Pat and Mex are still out there, so we are not out of options just yet. Don't do anything rash. We should wait for an opportunity to present itself."

About the time the Hollister bunch was wolfing down some refried beans and cornbread, Jake had risen from a deep sleep and had dug out some jerky and hardtack from his saddlebags. Pat and Mex had decided if you can't beat 'em, join 'em, and they had bedded down for a few hours of much needed sleep, as well. When he heard Jake up and about, Pat rose, stretched, kicked Mex on the sole of one of his boots, and said "Rise and shine, Pard."

After a bite to eat, Pat bit off a chunk of his chewing tobacco, directed it to his cheek, and offered it to Jake and Mex. He got a dirty look from Mex and a negative shake of the head from Jake. "Suit yourselves," he said. After a short pause, he changed the subject, "I say we go down there and have a looksee."

"Please don't take offence, Mr. Wilkens. It would be better if I went alone," replied Jake. He could see the anger growing in Pat's expression, so he added, "I move much faster and quieter when I work alone. I shall find out what has happened to your companions. When I return, you can decide our next course of action. If I do not return by daylight, you can assume I am either dead or captured, and then you are free to do as you wish."

The smile returned to Pat's face, but before he could tell Jake that he agreed with the plan, the scout was already sprinting down the hillside to the basin below. "Shithouse mouse, but that boy is quick!" Pat remarked.

In thirty minutes, Jake was at the back of Kulbane's mansion. Barely another hour later, he had explored the entire ranch and all its buildings. He made his way back to the stockade, where a short while before, he had observed Curtis and his two cronies watching over the prisoners closely. Hollister and his men had been unchained to empty their bladders before settling down for the night. Once they were reshackled, and Jake was sure that the three men charged with the security of the stockade were comfortably settled for the night, he made his way to Hollister's side. Jake tapped the sleeping Colonel on the shoulder, and Hollister's heart jumped into his throat. "My God, but you scared the life out of me!" he whispered, not wanting to alarm anyone of Jake's presence, especially the Reverend Fletcher who would most undoubtedly utter some biblical quote at the top of his lungs about some demon of the night, and the guards would come running to see what all the fuss was about.

Jake whispered in return, "I am here to get you out."

"What about the men?" asked Hollister.

"I did not think of them," replied Jake.

"If you take me and not them, they will surely be killed when it is discovered that I have escaped," pleaded Hollister.

Jake took a deep breath and said, "I shall return shortly." Before Hollister could reply, Jake was gone. Several minutes later, there was a low guttural groan coming from the front gate, and a short time later Hollister could hear the muffled sounds of a scuffle emanating from the hut.

Not long after, Jake appeared next to Hollister and said, "Now, we can free the others without fear of discovery."

"What did you do, Jake? You didn't kill those men, did you," asked Hollister.

"I tried not to, but sometimes I hit too hard." Jake replied, as he demonstrated how he used the butt end of the handle of his rather large knife to deliver two or three short, hard jabs to the temple. He didn't wait for a reply from the Colonel, as he produced a ring of keys and unshackled Hollister and then proceeded to do the same for the other four members of the group, who were equally and pleasantly surprised to see Jake. Reverend Fletcher uttered a hallelujah and thanked God for his deliverance. Jake had found Gus's .50 caliber Sharps rifle in the hut along with Samuel's and Nathaniel's Winchesters and several pistol rigs. He had also taken two Henry Repeaters and two pistols from the three men he had knocked cold. He tossed the rifles to Samuel and Nathaniel and the pistols he gave to Hollister who in turn passed them out amongst the men. Jake was removing the last of the three rails to the gate, when a voice out of the darkness said, "What the hell do you think you are doing?"

Jake didn't stop to think about who might be speaking. He reacted instinctively by throwing his knife as hard as he could in the direction of the voice. He heard a groan and then silence. He waited a moment for any sounds of movement, and when he heard nothing, he made his way cautiously toward the spot where he thought the intruder had been. Jake looked down and saw that his knife had found its mark; it was buried to the hilt in the man's throat. Jake knelt down on one knee to retrieve his knife, and he was overcome by a momentary feeling of regret, for before him lay the body of Tommy Kulbane!

Jake led the men on a weaving pattern from building to building, which gave them maximum cover until they reached the pastures at the far end of the corrals. Jake already had a horse for Colonel Hollister tethered at the furthest holding pen, nearest the open field. He told them all to wait while he got mounts for everyone. The horses were not guarded, so it was an easy task to gather four more mounts and saddle them up with gear from a small building at the edge of the corral. When Jake returned with the mounts in tow, he said, "Walk your horses quietly across the open space until you get to the other side of the creek. I will meet you there to show you the way out," said Jake as he sprinted away into the darkness.

They reached the creek and crossed it without incident. Apparently, no one was watching the small herd of grazing cattle, either. Jake showed Hollister the animal trail heading up the slope, saying it might be a good idea to walk the horses up the hill to avoid any mishaps in the dark.

It was a happy reunion at the top of the hill. Pat and Mex exchanged handshakes and pats on the shoulder with Jim Clemfeld and greeted the Reverend and his party with a socially expected, shallow *'nice to see ya,'* greeting. Hollister called for everyone's attention and thanked Jake for his rescue which garnered some applause and vocal acknowledgement. Once the men were relatively quiet, Hollister continued, "Our Host, General (as he likes to call himself) Kulbane, planned to conscript you fellas into his army and to ransom me to the Association. I doubt if Sinclair Thornsbury would pay a plugged nickel to have me back."

"What now, Colonel?" asked Pat Wilkens.

Hollister replied, "We make our way back to our side of the border and report back to the Association. They can decide if they want to keep this thing going or not."

"That horseshit bandit and his boys will be coming hard and fast," retorted Pat.

"He won't have the element of surprise on his side this time. I'm sure he'll tire of the chase and lose his motivation quickly," countered Hollister.

"Esparza may not be motivated, but I believe that the General wants very badly to catch me," interjected Jake. No one responded. It appeared they were all listening, waiting to hear more. Jake continued, "I killed his boy, Tommy."

"My God, Jake, why?" pleaded Hollister.

"I did not know it was him. He was the man who challenged us at the gate. I just threw my knife," replied Jake.

"This changes things, men. We have to ride for our lives," said Hollister.

"Colonel, you and the rest of the men head back to New Mexico. I will go a different direction and lead them away. It is me he wants and I am sure it is me he will follow," offered Jake.

Hollister thought long and hard before answering, "Jake, normally I would say, that is not how I do things. We are all in this together. But I like your idea. It will give us a fighting chance."

Pat spat out a big brown gob and wiped his handle bar mustache on his sleeve before he interjected, "I'm goin' with Jake. He don't stand a chance if they decide to go after him and not us."

Jake came closer to Pat and said sincerely, "I do not wish to offend you, my friend, but you would slow me down. Not to worry, they will not catch me. You make sure the Colonel makes it back to his rancho, Pat." He paused briefly and then added, "I will see you again when I come to collect what Mr. Thornsbury owes me." Jake didn't prolong the situation with any goodbyes. He mounted his pony and as he swung up in the saddle he simply said, "Gentlemen," and rode off into the darkness.

Samuel Fletcher saw an opportunity to be heard. "My kin and I shall find our own way back to New Mexico. You're welcome to join us, but if you do, keep in mind that I will be in charge."

Hollister knew there was safety in numbers, but his ego would not let him submit to having the likes of Samuel Fletcher give him orders. "Well, good luck to you, Reverend." Hollister waited to see in what direction the Fletcher clan had taken before he made his move. Strangely, Jake Romero had headed almost due west, parallel to the flow of the basin, while Fletcher and his bunch had headed almost due north. Hollister decided a northwesterly direction was the most direct route back to New Mexico. He gave Fletcher a few minutes to get ahead, got on his horse, and shouted, "Let's ride," as he spurred his horse into action.

About two hours after the Hollister outfit headed out in three different directions, someone vigorously yanked on the bell rope, sounding an alarm. George Kulbane stumbled out of bed, muttering under his breath that if this was some drunk having fun, he was going to get twenty five hard lashes. He got dressed, pulled on his boots, and was almost at the front door when it flew open, and John Curtis came staggering inside. "General, you gotta come quick! The bastards killed Tommy! They killed Tommy, General!" he blurted out through gasps for air.

Kulbane's mind refused to accept the idea that his son was dead. The man before him was either very drunk or badly mistaken. "Where? Show me," shouted the General as he took three long strides past Curtis, grabbing him by the scruff of the neck as he went by and ushered him out the door.

When they got to the gate of the stockade, Esparza and at least a dozen men were gathered around someone on the ground. Kulbane sprinted the last few feet and knelt beside the body. The minute he recognized his son, he looked skyward and let out a heart wrenching wail. He held Tommy close for what seemed like an eternity to the men milling about. He lay the boy's body back down, stood up, glared at Esparza, and said through gritted teeth, "We are going to catch every one of those bastards and I want the man who killed Tommy alive! I am going to skin him slowly over a smoldering fire!"

It took the better part of an hour to saddle and gear up. Esparza had Yuyutsu, his best tracker, read the sign to try and ascertain where the escapees had gone. Yuyutsu, whose Apache name translated to '*eager to fight*', tracked Hollister's party through the pasture, across the creek, and up the hill to the place where the Hollister party had all congregated. Yuyutsu rode out in ever widening circles, starting at the rendezvous point. By the time he was finished, Kulbane and a large group of riders (just about every able bodied man on the ranch) came galloping up the hill.

Reining in his horse hard, Kulbane shouted to the tracker, "What did you find?"

Yuyutsu positioned his horse near Esparza's, so he could relate his findings to Esparza who in turn translated for the General. Esparza and the tracker talked for what seemed like an eternity to the impatient Kulbane. Finally, Esparza spurred his horse closer to Kulbane's and explained what the tracker had found. "It appears to be ocho hombres, Senor." Three go north, four go to the northwest, maybe following the east rim of the basin, and very strange, Senor, one goes west."

Kulbane barked out orders, "I want six outriders, two to go in each direction. Each of you take a spare mount and make sure you have the fastest horses we have. When you catch up to them, one man stays with them and the other man hightails it back here to let me know where they are."

Corporal Mathew Allen asked, "So, we don't do the ransom thing?"

Kulbane's nasty look answered Allen's question. He turned back to the others and said with unbridle hatred, "Not one of those bastards gets away! Is that understood?"

CHAPTER TWELVE

Jacob Romero was never one to follow convention. Once free of the compound, the rest of the men in Jake's party had one objective in mind; to put as much distance between themselves and Kulbane as possible. Jake, on the other hand, had an innate sense of curiosity, and he wanted to see what his adversary was up to. He was not unlike a Pine Martin, a playful creature that would approach a potential dangerous situation, seemingly without fear, to see what was going on, knowing that it had the skill and speed to elude any threat, should one arise. To that end, he rode due west for about a mile then went in a southerly direction for about half a mile, which brought him to the far end of the basin. He rode back down into the valley and let his horse drink in the creek before crossing and going up the hill on the other side. His acute awareness picked up a presence to his right, pacing his horse. It was still too dark to see anything, but Jake knew Azul had decided to tag along.

He turned back north and rode slowly along the tops of the hills that formed the valley. Suddenly, the rolling hills turned into a mesa, and Jake found himself on the cliff overlooking the hacienda. He tied off his horse, removed Hollister's field glass from his saddle bag, and found a comfortable spot to lay and observe the events taking place below.

Wanting to be alone with his thoughts, Samuel Fletcher rode ahead of his son Nathaniel and Gus Haines. He was sullen and feeling sorry for himself. His ego had been badly bruised in the past few weeks. He was always in command and making all the decisions connected to their business, but that damn Colonel Hollister had made it quite clear that he was in charge, and Samuel and party were there to do his bidding. Hollister's men were blasphemers, disrespecting and ridiculing him and his beliefs at every opportunity. That heathen, that white Apache, was surely Satan's spawn, but the salt on the wound was the way they were treated by this self proclaimed General; forced to lie in the dirt, chained to a hitching rail like some common criminal. He would head straight back to Thornsbury's place, collect what was owed him, and give the pompous carpetbagger a piece of this mind before he went on his way.

He looked skyward and shouted, "And they that know thy name will put their trust in thee: for thou, Lord, hast not forsaken them that seek thee."

Nathaniel broke Samuel's reverie when he rode closer to his father and asked, "Father, are you alright?"

Samuel looked at his son, smiled, and said, "The Lord has delivered us from the clutches of our enemies. Now, we shall collect what is owed to us and carry on with the Lord's work."

Nathaniel had learned over the years not to question, or ask for further explanation of his father's outbursts. He had learned that it was safer to keep quiet and just do what the old man asked.

Hollister became nostalgic as he settled into the rhythm of his horse. Seeing Kulbane's mansion had stirred old memories of a forgotten life before the war. He once had felt the same passion as Kulbane, and he had the same zeal to take up arms and defend his way of life. When it was over, the years of killing and destruction had left a bitter taste in Hollister's mouth. He returned home, only to find the occupation forces had commandeered his house and property. He received compensation; five cents on the dollar for what his property was truly worth. The Yankee Major wore a shit-eating grin on his face as he counted out the money and handed it to Hollister. Colonel Hollister empathized with Kulbane, but he had left that life behind and moved on.

Pat Wilkens interrupted Hollister's trip down memory lane when he rode up close and asked, "What's the plan, Colonel?"

Hollister reined in his mount and stepped down, intending to give the horse a breather. Pat, Mex, and Jim did the same. "Home. Home, Pat. We head for the border as quickly as we possibly can. Kulbane is not going to rest until he has all of us on that whipping post of his, especially after Jake killed his son," Hollister replied.

"Speak of the devil, why do you think Jake headed west?" asked Pat.

"I don't know, Pat. We've spent a couple weeks on the trail with him and I don't know a thing about him. Usually, I can figure out what makes a man tick right away, but not him. No Sir —"

Mex, who was within earshot, interrupted the Colonel, "He is Lipan Apache. He is a dangerous man. He goes back to stay close to his enemy."

Hollister asked with complete surprise, "Are you saying that he went back to confront Kulbane?"

Mex thought for a moment and then replied, "I would bet you pay for a week that he is somewhere watching the rancho at this very moment."

Hollister, driven by curiosity, asked, "What do you think he will do next?"

"It is said when a Lipan feels threatened, he would rather carry the fight to the enemy than run. That is what makes him so dangerous," replied Mex.

Pat, not wanting to be left out, interjected, "Never heard of no such thing as a *Leepan*." He spat and wiped his mustache on his sleeve, waiting for contradiction.

Hollister took up the challenge, "I have heard a little about them. They lived in north Texas before the Mexican war. Nobody knows what happened to them after that. Some say they are gone — extinct. Some say they scattered to the mountains of Mexico." He paused and addressed Mex, "You say Jake is a Lipan?"

"There is a legend among my people that comes from the mountains," replied Mex as he began a narrative. "Many years ago Apaches moved into the canyons and mountains to the west of my family's village. They were not Chiricahua or Mescalero. Some say they came from Texas. The story says that often a young white boy was seen among these Apaches, and that he was raised by them. When the boy was older, he left to find his people back in Texas and was taken by the Comanche. Several years later a rancher called Pancho Romero bought a young girl from the Comanche that he believed to be his daughter. Seeing the white boy, he bought him also. Many believe this boy was Jake Romero, Senor."

Pat listened intently to Mex's account, and when the opportunity presented itself, he asked, "And why do you say that Jake is dangerous?"

"He grew up as a Lipan scout. I do not mean following horse tracks for ten dollars a month for the Calvary. It is said a Lipan scout can track a scorpion over solid rock and even tell you what it had for dinner. Some say they use magic. People have sworn that they have the ability to disappear right before your very eyes." Hollister recalled the time he had watched Jake go after the rustler's horses and how Jake had appeared to momentarily vanish.

Mex was still talking and Hollister focused on what he was saying. "They practice, ummm — how you say it — sneak up — Yes, they can come up on a deer or bear so quietly that they can touch it before the animal knows they are there. They can steal horses right from under the night guard's nose. The warriors are fierce fighters and have no fear. It is said that one of their favourite games is to sneak into an enemy's camp and take something from his person while he sleeps without waking him up."

"Ah, horseshit!" uttered Pat as he spat out a big brown gob. "I don't believe a word of it!"

Jim Clemfeld, who had been quiet up to this point, said with conviction. "First time we saw him, Pat, he was playing tag with a rattle snake. You recall that? Well sir, I have seen some characters in my time and faced some pretty tough hombres, but to tell you the truth, Colonel, I would not want to be on the wrong side of that man."

Mex continued his narrative, "The locals call this one '*Sombra Del Diablo*'. I believe, Senor, that Jake Romero is this '*Devil's Shadow*'.

To change the subject, Pat asked, "What do you think the preacher and his bunch are up to, Colonel?"

Hollister replied with confidence, "Him I understand, Pat. He needs to be in charge. Right now he's on his way back to Thornsbury to tell him I completely failed in the mission and he should have been in charge in the first place. He will most likely ask for more money to put things right."

"How come he headed north?" asked Jim.

"He is taking the long way around. I imagine, in his mind, he thinks that Kulbane and his men will be more interested in us and pursue us rather than him," answered Hollister.

Azul was becoming impatient at having to wait, and he showed his displeasure with several low growls combined with forlorn looks at Jake. "Go, if you want. I must stay," Jake told him. Azul gave him one last growl, set his head back down in his paws, and closed his eyes. About an hour later things began to happen at the main house. Jake could hear a man shouting, but what he was saying was unintelligible. The barracks were illuminated like the fourth of July as lanterns were lit, orders were being shouted, and to Jake, on his lofty perch, the scurrying men far below looked like ants in a colony hill after an intruder had been discovered.

Jake watched intently as events unfolded far below. Trackers had found Hollister's trail and a large group of men mounted and galloped across the pastures, across the creek, and up the hill on the other side, to the place where Hollister's entire group had rendezvoused two hours previously. Jake assumed Kulbane had taken most of the fighting men from the compound in pursuit of Hollister.

Jake waited half an hour, and then following his instincts, he discovered a crevice down the face of the sandstone cliff. He told Azul to wait and climbed quickly but careful down the cliff face. He set foot on level ground directly behind what looked like a large storage building situated off to the side of the barracks. He eased inside the clapboard structure between two loose boards. After letting his eyes adjust to the darkness, he saw a lit lantern on a bench that someone had forgotten to extinguish in their haste to depart.

Using the light, Jake explored the interior of the storage facility. It was an ammo dump. With one sweep of the interior, he could see dozens of cases that look like they could contain rifles, hundreds of boxes of ammunition of various calibres, several large barrels of gun powder, and cannon balls stacked in neat pyramids. That instant, Jake knew exactly what he was going to do. He commandeered three more lanterns from the shelf where he had found the original lit one. He stealthily made his way behind the barracks and to the rear of the mansion. Working methodically but quickly, he sprinkled the fuel from one lantern, saturating the back wall of the mansion. He set fire to it and then sprinted to the barracks. There were six, two-storey buildings, so Jake had to be somewhat conservative with his fuel, but the buildings were very dry wooden structures, and with a minimum of coaxing with a little kerosene, they were ablaze very quickly.

Lastly, Jake saturated the guns and ammo boxes with kerosene, lit it up, and then ran as fast as he had ever run to the base of the cliff and to the crevice that would lead to safety. He was several feet from the top, when the ammo dump exploded, lighting up the entire compound and the night sky. Jake climbed the rest of the way to the mesa top, turned and sat to watch the fireworks. A whimpering Azul came near, afraid of the loud noises still echoing throughout the valley as case after case of ammunition heated and exploded. Jake petted him, gave him a hard scratching behind the ears, and assured his friend that there was nothing to be afraid of.

By this time, the mansion and the barracks were well ablaze. The fire had spread to some of the roof tops of nearby adobe huts, sheds, and living quarters of the field workers. Without Kulbane or any of his men to give them orders, the workers concentrated on saving their homes and belongings and didn't pay any attention to the General's house or the men's barracks. Several of the field workers had sense enough to turn the horses and livestock loose that were penned in the corrals close to the burning buildings.

George Kulbane could not get the seething anger out of his brain. Tommy was dead! His son was gone! He just wanted to get his hands on the throat of the person responsible for Tommy's death. He didn't care who had wielded the knife. As far he was concerned, they were all responsible, and he would hunt every last one of them down, even if it took the rest of his life. If he had to chase them to the ends of the earth, they were all going to pay!

Kulbane's men had built several campfires for warmth at the rendezvous spot. No one had given any orders or indications as to how long they were going to be waiting on top of the ridge. If they were waiting for the outriders to return with news, it could be a long wait. Some of Esparza's men were beginning to grumble. They could just as easily have waited for news in their nice warm barracks, instead of out here in the cold night air.

Esparza was reluctant to approach Kulbane, given the General's state of mind. Just as he had mustered up the courage to go and talk to Kulbane, one of his men came running towards them, yelling "El Rancho se arde! El Rancho se arde!"

Kulbane bellowed, "What does he mean, *'the ranch is on fire'*?"

Esparza didn't realize the question was rhetorical which wouldn't have mattered anyway because the bandit leader didn't have an answer other than to repeat what his man had said. Kulbane gave him a dirty look as he hurried to the rim of the hill to where he could see the valley below.

When he saw the majority of the buildings, including the mansion in flames, he went into a rage. He clenched his fists and grimaced his face so intently that Esparza thought the General's head was going to explode which was ironically well timed, for as the thought of Kulbane's head coming apart like a melon hit with a sledge hammer passed through Esparza's mind, the first explosion interrupted in the ammo shed.

"Jesus Christ, now what?" asked Kulbane, with a hint of disbelief in his voice. He could not wrap his mind around who could possibly be doing this to him and more importantly, why? Intuitively, he knew it had to be connected to the men who had just escaped and killed his son in the process, but he couldn't fathom how?

Corky O'Halloran and Sebastian Medina were recruits in Kulbane's army. Corky's real name was Patrick, but because he was always bragging up the county of Cork, where he had come from in Ireland, he got the nickname of Corky. As far as Corky was concerned, he and Sebastian had been sent on a fool's errand. The real action was going to be when and where the General's men caught up to that bunch that had killed the General's kid. Maybe they could find this lone rider they were tracking quickly enough to either capture him or kill him, and they could hurry and get back into the scrap.

For nearly a year, he had dug latrines, weeded rows of corn, shovelled horse manure, and did marching drills until his feet hurt. He hadn't seen any action. This is not what he signed up for. Hell, that goddamn greaser Esparza and his band of walking garlic sacks were the ones doing all the fighting. He resented Esparza and his bandits because they never seemed to have to do any of the dirty work, and he didn't hide his distain in his daily dealings with them.

As the two men rode, gaining elevation, the valley below came into view. By this time the buildings were well ablaze and the first of the explosions from the ammo shed had just occurred. Corky shouted excitedly, "Hey greaser. The whole place is on fire!" Both of them watched the blaze below for several moments. They were as uncertain about who might be responsible for the calamity as Kulbane was.

Corky turned his attention back to the task at hand. After he recognized where they were, Corky grumbled to Medina, "Christ, we're on the cliff above the ranch. You dumb greaser, you been followin' some outrider's trail. Jesus, you __"

He didn't have time to finish his sentence. A shadow leapt out of the darkness and as it passed over Corky, the hilt of a knife handle hit him in the temple and knocked him off his horse. He was unconscious as he hit the ground. Sebastian Medina drew his pistol and fired three shots in three different directions, hoping to hit something. He knew he had missed when he felt someone leap up in the saddle behind him. The last thing Sebastian Medina felt in his life was the cold steel of Jake Romero's knife as it cut his throat from ear to ear.

CHAPTER THIRTEEN

KULBANE SHOUTED AS loud as he could, "Everybody back to the ranch! Ride hard! Ride hard!" He was hoping to get back in time to save the mansion. In his heart he knew it was futile, but he had to do something. An hour later, with the remnants of the ranch house, all the barracks, and several of the storage sheds, including the ammo dump, lying in smoldering heaps, Esparza had some of the men go through the ruins, looking for anybody who might have perished in the blazes. As far as he could tell, everyone was accounted for. He had the rest of the men set up several camps along the creek, where they would wait while General Kulbane decided on the next course of action.

The loose stock had been rounded up and penned in a makeshift corral, and crying women and children were comforted and assured the danger was over. Esparza had just sat down near Kulbane with intentions of asking the General about his plans when one of his men came riding into view of the campfire light. He was leading another horse, and it seemed to Esparza there was a body draped across the saddle. Kulbane leapt to his feet, and with three long strides, he was face to face with the man leading the macabre cargo.

"I thought you said no one was hurt?" asked Kulbane in a tone that signified there had better be an explanation coming.

The man leading the horse, unable to speak English, didn't want to deal directly with Kulbane, so he addressed Esparza in Spanish. The bandit leader listened carefully without interruption, and when the man was done talking, Esparza stepped closer to Kulbane and related what the man had said. "He says he found the body at the back of the barracks, or what's left of the barracks, I mean." Esparza laughed nervously because of his little faux pas and continued, "He says the man did not die in the fire. He is named Corky and my man thinks he is one of the men you sent out after the escaped prisoners."

Kulbane had a look of total confusion on his face and he expressed his inner thoughts verbally, "Make sense! How could a man who is supposed to be out on the trail, end up back here? How did he die?"

"My man thinks he was beaten to death and then left here," answered Esparza, fully believing that was the answer.

Kulbane had Esparza's man remove the body from the horse and lay it face up on the ground. He knelt down beside the dead man and turned, poked, and prodded the corpse.

Esparza mustered up the courage to ask, "What do think, Senor General?"

Kulbane rose to his feet, removed his hat, ran his left hand through his hair, put his hat back in place, and said, "I don't know, Enrique. I just don't know. It looks like he was stomped by a dozen horses."

"If I may, General?" Esparza waited for a nod before he knelt and examined the body. After a moment he stood and said, "I have seen this before, General. My cousin fell from a cliff, and when we recovered his body it looked just like Corky here. I believe he fell from the cliff behind us, Senor."

Kulbane turned and his eyes scanned the top edge of the mesa. For a split second he could have sworn he had seen the silhouette of a man accompanied by a big dog, but he blinked and it was gone. "No, my friend, I think he was thrown off that cliff," he replied, knowingly.

Esparza was reluctant to accept Kulbane's conclusion because in his mind he could not fathom who could have done the deed. "I do not understand, General. Who would do such a thing?"

Kulbane answered with definite hatred in his voice, "The same scum of the earth who killed my son, set those prisoners free, and burned my place." He took a very deep breath and let it out very slowly before he continued, "Enrique, pick three of your best men who can follow sign. Tell them they can pick up the trail at the top of the cliff. They are to capture the man who left that trail and wait for the rest of us to catch up. Tell them I want this man alive! I will skin all three of them until they scream for me to end their miserable lives, if they kill him. Make that clearly understood! Then assemble the rest of the men with weapons and provisions for several weeks in the field."

Anyone who didn't know Jeb and Virgil Morgan would assume they were brothers after watching them interact with each other for a short time, but the truth was the inseparable pair were first cousins on the paternal side. They had been following the Fletcher party's trail half the night, and now that daylight was breaking, they picked up the pace. The trail was easy to follow, for the Fletchers were not doing anything to hide their tracks. "Whoa, Virgil. I think I see somethin' just ahead, there," Jeb commanded. When it came to decision making, Jeb was the leader and Virgil the follower. Virgil stopped, and using his hand as a visor he scanned the horizon. He could barely make out two riders.

When Gus Haines fired the Sharps .50, Vigil Morgan actually heard the bullet whistle past him before it blew out Jeb's spine and knocked him off his mount. As soon as Jeb hit the ground, Virgil was off his horse and running toward his cousin. His quick action saved his life, for a second shot from the big rifle whizzed over his head the instant he began to dismount. With one glance he could see Jeb was dead. He hit the ground, lying face down next to Jeb's body, putting it between the shooter and himself. Two more shots about thirty seconds apart took out both their horses. Another two shots came in rapid succession. One hit Jeb again and the other raised a small cloud of dust a few feet to Virgil's left. He lay perfectly still, not daring to move a muscle. After, what he figured to be at least an hour, Virgil could not fight the urge to flee any longer, so he leapt to his feet and sprinted across the prairie in a zigzagging pattern. He could have just as easily walked because Gus Haines had made the assumption he had killed both his targets and had moved on. On foot, it would be another four days before Virgil got back to the ranch.

The morning sun was creeping over the eastern horizon when Jake left the cliff-top and doubled back on his own trail across the valley. Once he was back atop the other side, memory reminded him that Hollister had gone in a northwesterly direction, so he headed that way, hoping to pick up some sign. What Jake didn't know was that five minutes after he had crossed the valley floor, three riders galloped up the same trail in the opposite direction, heading for the top of the mesa where Kulbane swore he had seen Jake standing.

Nacoma, a half breed of Comanche and German mix, was also one of Esparza's best trackers. He spent the better part of an hour riding back and forth in ever widening arcs parallel to the spot where they had found Sebastian Medina's body. He had carefully searched the ground for any sign for a couple hundred yards from the edge of the cliff. Satisfied, he joined his partners, who had been waiting patiently while he scoured the area. Nacoma addressed the other two men, "This devil has doubled back on his own trail. He has gone back to the other side of the valley. That is where we must go."

"Looks like two riders been doggin' us all morning, Colonel," Pat said as a point of fact. He assumed Hollister had already seen the tag-alongs, and he was right.

"Yes, and they are keeping their distance, Pat. Almost like they just want to see where we are going," replied Hollister.

"You want Mex and Jim to drop back and maybe ask them their business?" asked Pat.

"No Pat. Leave them be. I am sure they are Kulbane's men. If we push the horses a little, I don't think Kulbane can catch up to us before we cross the border, and even if they do, I don't believe they will cross the border after us," explained Hollister.

Pat wasn't so sure. The bandits had already crossed the border to catch them the first time. An hour or so later, Jim Clemfeld remarked, "Now there is only one rider. Wonder where the other one is?"

The two riders trailing Hollister's foursome were Georgio Castoro and Ricardo Mastal. A couple of hours after sunrise, Georgio said to Ricardo, "These men are headed for the border. You ride like the wind, Ricardo and tell Esparza what I have said. Now, go!" Ricardo never returned to the ranch, for on his way back he crossed paths with Jake Romero.

All through the day, Kulbane was like a bear with a sore rear end. He paced. He kicked things out of his way. He yelled at servants. He yelled at Esparza. He yelled at the dogs. He continued in this foulest of moods until noon the following day, when his impatience got the better of him. He called Esparza and his men together for a planning session. "Where the hell are those outriders you sent out? They should have been back by now," Kulbane asked the bandit leader.

Esparza thought for a moment before answering. He concluded that the straight truth would be best at the moment. He felt Kulbane was on the edge and would not tolerate anything less. He said, "Senor Kulbane, I strongly believe that if the men have not returned by now that they are not coming back. We have — how you say it —underestimated this Colonel and his men."

"Where do you think they are headed, Enrique?" asked Kulbane. He did not wait for a reply, but instead answered his own question. "They have split up to make it more difficult for us to catch them, but I think they are all headed back to the same place. What baffles me, is this lone rider that came back to burn me out? That one I can't figure. Who the hell is he?"

Esparza did not answer immediately. He stood looking at Kulbane until the General shrugged his shoulders and made a gesture that said, '*Tell me something*'.

Esparza spoke slowly and carefully, fully expecting a tirade from Kulbane, "There are not many men who would do what this hombre dares to do. I believe this man is one they call '*sombra del diablo*'. He could tell that Kulbane did not understand, so he added, '*the shadow of the devil*' is how you say it in English, I believe.

Esparza was about to offer a further explanation, but Kulbane cut him off, shouting, "I don't give two hoots about your goddamn, ignorant, superstitious myths. I am going to catch him and his cohorts if it is the last thing I do, so help me God! Gather all the men together and be ready to ride in twenty minutes." As an afterthought, he added, "And bring plenty of ammunition."

The sun had just gone down when Georgio Castoro felt the knife blade on his throat as it cut just deep enough to draw blood. A quiet voice whispered in his ear, "Go back to where you came from, or the next time you sing, it will be your death song." The pressure from the cold steel disappeared. Georgio quickly drew his pistol and emptied it, firing in all directions. He didn't take time to reload, but sprinted for his horse, mounted and galloped off. Every night for months to come, it would take Georgio a long time to fall asleep.

"Did you smite the Philistines, Brother Haines?" asked Samuel Fletcher.
"Yes Sir, I did," replied Gus Haines, proudly.
Nathaniel Fletcher wanted to get his two cents worth in and he interjected with, "Sure a lot of shooting for just two men, don't you think, cousin?"
Gus, not wanting to get drawn into a pissing contest about who was the better shot, replied casually, "One extra shot for sighting in and two others for the horses. Don't want them wandering back to that make-believe General."
The mention of General Kulbane brought Samuel back into the conversation and he quoted from Psalms, "The wicked watcheth the righteous, and seeketh

to slay him. The Lord will not leave him in his hand, nor condemn him when he is judged. And the Lord shall help them, and deliver them: he shall deliver them from the wicked, and save them, because they trust in him."

Nathaniel Fletcher had learned over the years to not worry a whole lot about what his father meant when he quoted scripture. The elder Fletcher's quotes were accurate, but what they meant or whether they were applicable to the situation, Nathaniel was never sure. In his earlier years, Nathaniel had foolishly asked his father for clarification only to become the object of his father's wrath, so he learned quickly not to ask questions.

Samuel Fletcher truly believed he was doing God's work and his constant rants and quotes were his way of reinforcing his commitment when his faith began to waver as it was at the moment. When he had been hired by Thornsbury and company to catch horse thieves and cattle rustlers, there was a clear objective in mind. When they had caught up with the rustlers and dispensed their own brand of justice and then wiped out Curly Mactavish's den of iniquity, it was clearly part of the plan. But now, running for his life from a man whose motives he did not understand, he felt confused and without purpose. What did this self proclaimed General want with him? What had he done to offend God, so that he should be punished? Samuel said aloud, "And without faith it is impossible to please him, for whoever would draw near to God must believe that he exists and that he rewards those who seek him."

Gus Haines interrupted Samuel's sojourn into doubt when he asked, "Where are we headed, Reverend?"

Samuel reined in and leaning across the saddle horn, he replied, "We are going to collect the pay that is owned us and then move on to do the Lord's work. I think our business is finished here."

"Hallelujah!" shouted Nathaniel.

At about the same time that Kulbane, Esparza, and a host of riders were galloping out of the hidden valley, Pat Wilkens pulled up beside Hollister and said, "I don't see nobody trailin' us any more. Must've got tired and gone home."

"Maybe, Pat. Maybe," mused Hollister.

"What's got ya thinkin', Boss?" asked Pat.

"Something's not right here, Pat. Kulbane did exactly what I would have done. Send two outriders after us and when they pick up our trail, one follows at a distance and the other rides hell bent for leather back to the main group to relay our position. We should still be seeing one rider on our back trail, but we don't and that bothers me."

Pat interrupted, "I don't understand, Boss. Why is that a problem? I figure he just gave up and turned back."

Hollister replied somewhat more animated, "No, Pat. Kulbane will not give up easily. We killed his son, and he's going to make someone pay. I got a bad feeling that this is not over, not by a long shot."

CHAPTER FOURTEEN

SINCLAIR THORNSBURY HAD just finished his breakfast of a half dozen fried eggs, a dozen rashes of bacon, the plate wiped clean with several thick slices of sourdough bread, and all washed down with several cups of coffee, heavily laden with fresh cream. "Where are Hollister and the rest of the Regulators?" he asked Jake Romero, in an impatient, overbearing tone.

Jake paused a moment before answering, not for effect or dramatic pause, it was just his way. If he decided to reply or comment, he always thought about what was being asked or said before responding. Most people engaged in a conversation continue the exchange with small talk, or they add superfluous comments to what the other person has just said. Jake never did. He replied, "Don't know. They were behind me."

"And why is that, my friend?"

Again, a pause before Jake replied, "Don't know. Slower horses? You owe me forty dollars."

Thornsbury harrumphed and replied, "Forty dollars? For what?" knowing full well the arrangement he had made with Jake. It was said Thornsbury didn't have the first dollar he ever made, but he knew where he spent it. Jake played along and replied, "Two dollars a day for three weeks. I'll settle for forty dollars."

"I'll talk to Colonel Hollister and then decide what you have coming. Come see me in a few weeks, and we'll settle up," stated Thornsbury with a haughty dismissive tone.

Two hours later events began to quickly unfold. Connor Muldoon was a young Irish lad straight off the boat from Ireland. He had headed west to make his fortune, but had ended up as a wrangler's helper, shovelling horse manure, and feeding and caring for Thornsbury's wagon horses, working mules, and extra mounts that the men who worked the cattle wouldn't or couldn't look after. The cowboys on the ranch took good care of their own horses, but tending of the spare mounts usually fell to the wranglers and their helpers. Thornsbury had given young Connor a special task; complete responsibility for the well being of his most prized possession, his pure bred Spanish Andalusian stallion.

Young Connor stood before Thornsbury with his hat in his hand, his legs shaking, and a quiver in his voice when he said, "Sir, beg your pardon, Sir— uh —"

Thornsbury displayed his impatience when he interrupted, "Spit it out, boy! What is the matter?"

"Well Sir, that white Indian fella, he took your stallion. Twern't my fault, Sir. He had this big knife — said he wouldn't hurt me if I didn't get in his way. Said to tell you he was just takin' the horse 'cause you owed him some money, and you could buy it back for forty dollars."

Thornsbury held his breath, gritted his teeth, and clenched his fists. His face turned rhubarb red, and he began to shake. Just as Connor thought the boss's head was going to explode, Thornsbury inhaled, coughed, cleared his throat, and shouted, "Get me Pat Wilkens!"

In his rage he had forgotten Pat was with Hollister. Connor, with great trepidation, tried to tell him so and Thornsbury, trying to save face, said, "Yes, yes! It slipped my mind for a moment. Go get me whoever is in charge." He was hoping the young lad hadn't noticed he didn't know the foreman's name.

Fifteen minutes later Connor was back with an old hand, Morley Gruber, in tow. Morley's hair was greying, while his whiskers had already completed the transformation. He walked with a limp in his left leg from a bad crash back when he saddle broke wild mustangs to earn his keep. At his age, he still held on to a job, partly out of homage to his years of loyal service, and partly because of his wealth of knowledge that most ranch foremen considered invaluable.

Connor could see the disappointed look on Thornsbury's face when he laid eyes on Morley Gruber. In Thornsbury's opinion, Morley was not the man he had envisioned as his foreman. "You're in charge while Pat Wilkens is away?" Thornsbury asked, secretly hoping Connor had made a mistaken and had brought him the wrong man.

"Yes Sir," replied Morley.

"A man by the name of Jake Romero has stolen my stallion, and you need to go after him as quickly as possible," explained Thornsbury.

"Jake — that white Apache — you mean him? No Sir! Not if you gave me a posse of a hundred men would I go after that man," stammered Morley.

Thornsbury went into a rage again, "You coward! He's a horse thief! Now, do your goddamn job and go and get my horse back!"

Connor interrupted, "Mr. Thornsbury, I don't mean to butt in, but Pat and the Colonel can't be far behind. They'll get your horse back, for sure. Don't ya think?"

Connor had just given Thornsbury a way out of having to deal with the loveable Morley. Thornsbury thought momentarily and said, "Fine. We'll wait a few hours and see what transpires."

Things didn't quite come to pass as Thornsbury had expected. Shortly after his conversation with Morley Gruber and Connor Muldoon, Reverend Fletcher and his two cronies rode in. Samuel Fletcher got straight to the point when he, not unlike Jake Romero, demanded payment for services rendered. He stated that he, his son, and nephew were in a hurry to be on their way to continue their never ending struggle against the evil besieging the land. Thornsbury argued they had been contracted to rid the area of rustlers and horse thieves, and he wasn't sure the job had been completed. He stated in no uncertain terms that he would wait to confer with Colonel Hollister before making any decisions.

Samuel Fletcher ranted, "Do not take advantage of a hired man who is poor and needy, whether he is a brother Israelite or an alien living in one of your towns. Pay him his wages each day before sunset, because he is poor and is counting on it. Otherwise, he may cry to the Lord against you, and you will be guilty of sin."

"I am guilty of a lot worse sins than not paying men what they think they are due, *Mister* Fletcher," Thornsbury spat out the words, emphasizing the word *Mister* to make the point that he didn't regard the self-proclaimed preacher with any reverence. "Quote the Bible all you want, we are still waiting for Ben Hollister, and then I'll assess the situation. At that time, Mister Fletcher, you shall get what is coming to you."

Samuel Fletcher's head turned sideways, and his eyes bulged out of their sockets. He was about to go into a tirade when Nathaniel intervened. "Father, I am sure Colonel Hollister won't be far behind us. Why don't we partake of

Mr. Thornsbury's hospitality for a few days and rest up before we continue on with our work?"

Samuel noticed Thornsbury's scowl at Nathaniel's suggestion and threw out another quote, "It is a sin against hospitality, to open your doors and darken your countenance."

Thornsbury took a step as if he was about to leave the room but stopped and said, "Well then, it is settled. Now, if you'll excuse me I have more important matters needing my attention. Stay as long as you like. You can take a bed in the same bunkhouse you occupied before you left, and you can take your meals with the rest of the hired help." He continued to make his way out of the room, dismissing the Fletcher bunch with a wave of his hand.

For most of the afternoon, Thornsbury went out for several walks around the ranch yard on the pretence of being interested in the everyday workings of the ranch. He was a *'final results'* man and could have cared less how his employees went about their daily chores, but he had to work the nervous energy off somehow. Thinking about Jake taking his stallion turned his stomach into a hard knot, and if there weren't repercussions, he would have choked the first human being he had his eyes on.

Thornsbury was back in his study, sipping on a brandy and waiting for his supper, when a ranch hand raced into the house, mud and cow dung all over his boots, shouting that four riders were approaching. Thornsbury calmly put on his boots, stuffed his pipe, and went out to the veranda, where he lit the pipe and stood waiting while the four dots on the southern horizon came closer and closer. By the time Hollister and company made it to the ranch yard, Thornsbury had grown quite impatient, and it showed when he said to Hollister, "Nice to see you, Colonel. Now, I need to discuss something with you, if you would be so kind as to join me in the study."

As Thornsbury turned to go, Hollister said, "We have horses that need looking after and myself and the men haven't eaten for nearly four days. I think we will attend to that first and clean up a little before we talk." He didn't wait for a reply from Thornsbury. Instead, he turned his horse and headed towards the stables, with Mex, Pat, and Jim close behind. Thornsbury huffed twice and headed back inside the ranch house.

Two hours later, in Thornsbury's study, Hollister gave the head of the Association a full report of everything that had transpired during the past three weeks. Thornsbury mulled over the information and then offered Hollister some brandy and a cigar. After a sip of the liquor, Thornsbury said, "Well Ben, that's a good start. Take a couple of days and then gear up and go out again. The first thing I want you do is find that cursed white Apache you brought into our midst and hang him. Make sure he chokes slowly for a long time before he dies. Better yet, bring him to me so I can do it."

"Sinclair, you sound quite upset with Jake," Hollister remarked, finding it hard to hold back a smirk that was fighting to come out. "What did he do that is making you so angry?"

"It appears to me, you have taken a liking for this savage, Colonel. He is nothing but a common horse thief, and there is nothing amusing about it," grumbled Thornsbury.

"Whose horse did he steal?" asked Hollister.

"He took my prize stallion!"

"Why would he do that?"

Thornsbury hemmed and hawed then admitted, "He claims I owe him forty dollars. I don't see it that way. It would appear he has taken my horse in lieu of payment."

Hollister feigned sympathy while inside he was thinking that it was something Jake would do. Finishing the conversation they had started, Hollister had another surprise for Thornsbury. "No Sinclair, you'll have to find someone else. I have had enough. Tomorrow bright and early, I am headed back to my place to focus on building up a profitable cattle business. I hope to find a couple of good men like Pat or Mex to help me." He paused briefly and added almost under his breath, "I wonder if they want a job?"

"You can't do that! We have a job to finish," bellowed Thornsbury.

"I'm sure there are plenty of men out there who, for the right price, will do the job for you. I'll tell you one thing, and this is just friendly advice, but don't send anyone after Jake. They won't come back alive. Just give him his forty dollars and save yourself a lot of grief," replied Hollister.

Thornsbury was visibly angry. His face had turned red, his breathing became shallow, and his demeanour changed. "That will be all, Colonel Hollister. Finish your brandy quickly and leave my premises. Like you say, I don't need you."

Hollister didn't bother finishing his drink. He headed for the door as quickly as he could. Behaving like the gentleman he was, he said, "Good luck to you Sinclair," as he closed the door behind him.

Fifteen minutes later Samuel Fletcher, having been sent for, was standing before Thornsbury in his study. Unlike Hollister, he was not offered any expensive brandy or a hand rolled cigar. Thornsbury simply came to the point. He asked Fletcher what he thought he was owed and then counted the money out on the big oak desktop. Just as Samuel Fletcher reached for the cash,

Thornsbury scooped it up and waving it in Fletcher's face, he asked, "Reverend, how would you like to make three times this for a couple days work?"

"People who want to get rich fall into temptation and a trap and into many foolish and harmful desires that plunge men into ruin and destruction. For the love of money is a root of all kinds of evil. Some people, eager for money, have wandered from the faith and pierced themselves with many grieves," replied Fletcher.

"You don't have to pierce yourself with anything — Hell — can't — can't you just once, talk in plain English?" stammered Thornsbury. "I am going to pay you a lot of money to catch one horse thief. A hundred dollars if he is draped over a horse, five hundred if you bring him back to me alive and coherent. What you do with the money is none of my concern. Now, do you want the job or not, Mr. Fletcher?"

Samuel Fletcher had been called and he folded. He took the cash from Thornsbury's hand and asked, "Who is this horse thief you want so badly, Mr. Thornsbury?"

"Jake Romero, the man you rode with. He stole my prize stallion and by God he is going to pay dearly!" was Thornsbury's curt reply.

"The robbery of the wicked shall destroy them; because they refuse to do judgment," quoted Fletcher.

"Enough! I have had enough bloody biblical quotes to last a life time. Now, get your two cohorts and catch that damn savage," bellowed Thornsbury.

Samuel Fletcher strutted to the bunkhouse to get his son Nathaniel and Gus Haines. He was proud of himself. He had made a deal for more money than they had seen in a long time, and all they had to do was catch a middle-aged Apache. Yes, the Lord was indeed looking after him.

As he approached the corral next to the bunkhouses, Samuel noticed Gus Haines sitting on the top rail with a pair of field glasses up to his eyes. He seemed to be focused on the crest of the row of hills about a half mile west of their position. "Let us get outfitted for a ride, Brother Haines. We have a job to do. We are to catch Jake Romero and bring him and Mr. Thornsbury's horse back in good condition," said Samuel.

Gus lowered the glasses and turned to face Fletcher. "No need to hurry, Reverend," he said. He pointed to the row of hills and added, "I believe that is our quarry atop that hill, just sitting there as pleased as punch. Call me loco, but it is as if he is sitting there waiting for us."

Samuel took the glasses from Gus and surveyed the hilltop. It was hard to see in the hazy late afternoon light, but it was just as Gus had said: Jake was sitting cross-legged on top of his mustang, holding a lead rope attached to Thornsbury's stallion. Suddenly, Jake turned his head and looked right at Samuel. It startled the preacher. It was as if Jake knew he was being watched. It reminded Samuel of an incident a long time ago when Nathaniel was a little boy. They had been camped in a well wooded area, and in a tall pine tree about a hundred yards away, sat two big hoot owls. As soon as Samuel put the glasses on them, they turned their heads simultaneously and stared right back at him. Samuel said with excitement in his voice, "Go and fetch Nathaniel. I will be at the cook shack getting some provisions. Bring the big gun and lots of ammunition. This is going to be the easiest five hundred dollars we have ever made." He looked up to the heavens and added, "Praise be to the Lord!"

Shortly after his evening meal, Sinclair Thornsbury stood leaning against one of the ranch house veranda posts with a freshly lit pipe of tobacco in one hand and a lukewarm coffee in the other, enjoying the evening breeze. He watched with mild amusement as Ben Hollister brushed and saddled his horse before giving it a handful of oats from a bag hanging on the nearby fence post. His focus on Hollister's activities was interrupted when one of the wranglers galloped into the yard, stopping within a couple of feet of the veranda

The cowboy said with a hint of panic in his voice, "Mr. Thornsbury, there's a whole passel of riders ridin' hell bent for leather, and they are comin' this way! Me and Billie thought it was Calvary or somethin' at first on accounta the lead man is in this here fancy uniform, or somethin'. But then we looked closer and well Sir, a whole bunch of 'em is Mexicans. What you want us to do, Mr. Thornsbury?"

"Tell Pat Wilkens to round up every able bodied man in and around home base, arm them and station them strategically behind cover, so they can see the yard," instructed Thornsbury.

Hollister, having heard the entire thing, tied off his horse and approached Thornsbury. As he came within earshot, Thornsbury asked, "Any idea who our approaching guests might be?"

"Oh, I have a fair idea, Sinclair. I have a fair idea."

"Well, for God's sake, man, spit it out."

"I strongly believe the man in the uniform is General George Kulbane, and the men with him are his vagabond army. He must have nearly killed his horses catching up to us. I don't think he is here for a social call. Best arm yourself, Sinclair."

With that having been said, Hollister walked to his horse, drew his rifle, levered one in the chamber, and stood rifle in hand with his horse between himself and the yard. Thornsbury had gone back into the house, and a few seconds later he reemerged, checking a long barreled shotgun to make sure it was loaded. A short time later, the large group of approaching men entered the yard in front of the ranch house. Thornsbury was the first to speak. "To whom do I owe the pleasure?"

Kulbane came right to the point, "Sinclair Thornsbury, I presume? Are you the man responsible for sending the band of wanton killers to murder my son and destroy my business enterprises?"

Thornsbury didn't back down. He showed no sign of fear when he answered, "I sent a group of deputized men to track down horse thieves and cattle rustlers that were preying upon the ranchers in this valley. There were some men killed in the process, and if your son was one of them, you have my deepest sympathy. If your business is dealing in stolen livestock then I would consider it a good thing you are out of business. What is it you want?"

"I want — I want the man who killed my son and the man who burned my place. I'll see them both suffer long and hard before they die," retorted Kulbane.

"They are one in the same," replied Hollister. No one had seen him behind the horse. Esparza, as well as half a dozen of his men, drew their weapons at the sound of Hollister's voice. "Ah, Colonel Hollister, it is good to see you alive and well," remarked Kulbane. "What do you mean *'one in the same'*?"

"The same man did both."

"Where is —" Kulbane was about to say.

Hollister cut him off and finished saying what he wanted to say, "Your son was killed during our escape from your clutches. No one knew it was your son. It just happened that way. As far as burning down your place, he did that on his own. He was not following any orders."

"Who is this man and where is he?" growled Kulbane through gritted teeth.

"Not my place to say," answered Hollister.

"Burn it down!" shouted Kulbane.

"Not so fast, General," interjected Thornsbury. "There are at least a dozen rifles pointed at you right now. Pat! Pat, if these men don't holster their weapons and ride out of here, shoot the General first and then cut loose on the rest of them. You hear me, Pat?"

"Yeah Boss!" came the muffled reply from the corner of the tool shed.

The bluff worked. There were actually only five rifles, but Kulbane didn't know that, so he had his men holster their pistols. He said to Thornsbury as he was about to leave, "I will destroy every place and kill every man in this valley, if you don't give me the man who killed my son!"

Thornsbury knew Kulbane meant it. Since Jake meant nothing to him, he said, "His name is Jake Romero. He was hired to do some scouting for us. In fact, I have three men out looking for him right now. He stole one of my horses and I am going to hang him for it. You are free to join the festivities when we catch him."

Kulbane replied, "Thank you for the invitation, Mr. Thornsbury, but I may just hang you right beside him, and then I am going to seek retribution from any man who had a hand in invading my domain! Good day to you, Sir!" He turned his horse sharply and his men parted, letting him through.

Hollister sheathed his rifle in its scabbard and approached Thornsbury. When he was within earshot he said, "Mr. Thornsbury, I have changed my mind. I will stick around long enough to see this thing through, and then I am done with you and your association.

As soon as Kulbane and company were well on their way, Thornsbury called Pat in and instructed him to send a man to trail Kulbane's posse and report back as to where they were headed. The man didn't have to go far. He was back in just over an hour to report that Kulbane and company had made camp near a natural spring, barely a mile south of the ranch. The man was of the opinion that by the look of the camp, it wasn't going to be a short stay.

CHAPTER FIFTEEN

"HE WAS JUST there! I saw him!" snorted Gus Haines.

"Look around you, Cousin. Do you see him now?" responded Nathaniel Fletcher.

"Hell Nate, he was only a hundred yards ahead of me. I went down into a little ravine and back up, and now he is nowhere in sight," insisted Gus.

"Do not use profanity in my presence! As he loved cursing, so let it come unto him: as he delighted not in blessing, so let it be far from him," quoted Reverend Fletcher with his usual cocked head, bulging eyes, and sermonizing voice. He added, "Brothers, stop thinking like children. In regard to evil be infants, but in your thinking be adults."

There wasn't much daylight left, perhaps an hour or an hour and a half at most, when Reverend Fletcher and company had set out after Jake Romero. The preacher seemed excited with anticipation of an immediate solution to the '*Romero*' problem, as Thornsbury had referred to it. The horse thief was in plain sight, maintaining the same distance between them. If Fletcher sped up, so did Jake. Likewise, if Fletcher slowed down, or let his horses blow, so did Jake. Samuel Fletcher was becoming increasingly annoyed at the cat and mouse game.

Just before dark, the terrain changed to a series of small rolling hills, separated by deep gullies. It was here that Gus Haines almost caught up to Jake. He was tracking ahead of his uncle and cousin when he saw Jake sitting on top of a small knoll as if he were waiting for the Fletchers to catch up. Gus saw how close Jake was and with several whoops and hollers, he spurred his horse hard, raced down one knoll, through the gully and up the next hill where he had spotted Jake. When he got to the top, he fully expected to see the horse thief galloping up the next knoll. Gus figured he'd take a shot with the Sharp's .50 and try to knock Jake's horse down since the boss rancher wanted the man alive, but Jake was nowhere in sight!

"Well, where do you think he got to, Gus?" asked Nathaniel, mockingly.

Gus, paying no heed to Nathaniel's sarcasm, said, "It's like he just vanished."

Nathaniel wouldn't let up, "Oooohh, like a ghostie in the night?"

Samuel interjected with another quote, "Do not resort to ghosts and spirits, nor make yourselves unclean by seeking them out."

"Sorry Pa. I was just having a little fun with Cousin Gus," apologized Nathaniel.

"But the Lord laughs at the wicked, for he sees that his day is coming," retorted Samuel.

Not everything that came out of Samuel's mouth was a biblical quote. He could and would carry on a normal conversation on occasion, if the situation called for it. To all those who didn't know him well, it appeared he was just blowing hot air, and they thought most of what he said was made up and not even in the Bible. Gus, when he was a young man, decided to test Samuel, and for the longest time Gus carried a Bible around, and when Samuel spouted something Gus would ask him where in the Good Book he could find that particular quote. The game grew tiresome after about a dozen such forays into the scriptures proved Samuel correct.

"Getting too dark to see anything, Pa. Maybe we should camp for the night?" suggested Nathaniel.

"The ravine we just come through has water and some grass for the horses," remarked Gus.

"Then that is where we shall camp for the night," decided Samuel.

The Fletchers made a simple camp. Accustomed to spending nights out in the open because of their line of work, their first order of business was to water, brush down, feed, and tether the horses. If there was ample grass in the camp area, they used hobbles. If there was no grass, they were afraid the horses would wander too far, searching for something to eat even thought they were hobbled. In that case, they would set up a tether rope and tie the horses securely to it.

After the mounts were taken care of, they built a small cooking fire and prepared whatever food they had at the time. Today, it was hardtack and jerky, no need for a fire, but Samuel liked it for his coffee and the light allowed him to read his Bible, a nightly ritual. Conversation was scarce and usually consisted of small talk about the weather or the day's activities. Once in awhile, Samuel would go off on a tangent, wanting to get into a debate about some dogmatic religious point, which neither Gus nor Nathaniel wanted any part of, but participated because to not do so would have sent Samuel into a tirade of finger pointing, name calling, and character assassinations. Participation consisted of Gus and Nathaniel agreeing to everything Samuel said with a lot of head nodding, 'yes sirs', 'praise the Lords' and 'amens'.

The events of the past few days had left the three men exhausted. As a result, soon after a bite to eat, listening to Samuel read from Psalms, and one final check on the horses, sleep came as a welcome relief, and all three were producing a chorus of snorts and snores that made a nearby coyote turn his head in wonderment.

It was a couple hours before dawn, the darkest part of the night, when Samuel was awakened by something licking his face. He opened his eyes to look right in the snarling teeth of what he thought was a large grey wolf. Suddenly, a human hand brushed the creature aside and Jake Romero, with his knee on Samuel's chest, lowered his face until it was only a couple of inches above Samuel's. The point of Jake's big knife nearly breaking the skin right next to Samuel's jugular vein, kept him from any movement. Jake patted down the preacher, looking for any hidden weapons, and finding none, he released the pressure on the knife and removed his knee from Samuel's chest.

Samuel seized the opportunity and shouted as loud as he could, "Nathaniel! Gus! Get this heathen! Nathaniel!"

There was a long pause. Jake looked around then *he* hollered, "Nathaniel? Gus?" He waited for a response and when none was forthcoming, he added, "It looks like they are not here."

"What have you done with my son and my nephew?"

"I hit them with the knife handle, but not very hard." As a side comment, he added, "I have been hitting too hard lately."

Samuel's eyes bulged out, and as he stared into Jake's face, he quoted, "Submit yourselves therefore to God. Resist the devil, and he will flee from you."

Jake feigned bewilderment when he asked, "Who are you talking to? I don't understand. Do you think I am a demon?" Using his knife, Jake nicked the back of his hand. He squeezed out some blood and smeared it on Samuel's cheek, asking the preacher, "Does a demon bleed?"

Samuel was becoming visibly upset. He had an overwhelming urge to get up and run off into the night. Jake softened his tone and asked, "Tell me about your demons and gods. I would like to know."

Samuel's confidence returned as he stated emphatically, "God, not gods! There is only one god!"

"What do you call this god?"

The question confused Samuel momentarily, but he recovered and replied, "He has many names, but we usually refer to him as *God*."

Jake had a basic understanding of the Christian religion, having spent a few years with the Romero family, who were practising Catholics, but Samuel had no knowledge of this fact. "Is one of his names Jesus?" asked Jake in contrived sincerity.

"No! Jesus is the son of God."

"So there are two gods?"

Samuel took the bait. "In our faith we believe in the holy trinity: God the father, the Son, and the Holy Spirit."

"I have been taught by the People that there are many spirits and one Great Spirit. We have Mother Earth, Father Sun and the Great Spirit sees over all of the People," explained Jake, knowing full well that Samuel could care less. Jake continued, "This god of yours, he has commanded you to hunt down and kill men who take cattle and horses?"

Samuel paused for a long time, trying to think of a way to explain to Jake that God had told him he was to be an instrument to rid the country of evil. "God has commanded me to hunt down and eradicate evil wherever I find it."

"You hunt me because you have decided I am evil?" asked Jake.

"You are a horse thief! You need to be punished for your sin."

"I did not steal the horse. The stallion is payment for the scouting I have done," stated Jake strongly. "The fat cattleman decided I did wrong, and now he has sent you to kill me for taking what was owed to me? I do not understand."

"It is the law of the land. You cannot just help yourself to another man's property just because you think he owes you something," expounded Samuel.

"And who punishes the one who owes something and will not pay?" queried Jake.

"There are courts of law for that purpose," explained the preacher.

"If I took his horse in payment, and he thinks it is not right, should he not go to the same court of law," asked Jake. Reverend Fletcher never had to justify his actions to anyone before and this debate was frustrating him, especially when Jake asked him, "Does your god not see the fat cattleman as evil, or do you make that decision?"

Fletcher had reached his limit, and he reverted to the slanted head, bulged eye, scripture quoting creature when he said, "Blessed are they which are persecuted for righteousness' sake: for theirs is the kingdom of heaven. Blessed are ye, when men shall revile you, and persecute you, and shall say all manner of evil against you falsely." Jake was tired of the game, as well. Before Samuel could blink, Jake swung his knife butt-end catching Samuel in the temple.

The morning sun caught Sinclair Thornsbury on his front veranda in his favourite repose, leaning against one of the pillars with a coffee in one hand and a lit pipe in the other. He was as nervous as a trapped cat, for he knew Kulbane and his army were camped nearby, but he had no idea what their next move was going to be. Before sunrise, he had sent riders to the other prominent members of the Association with instructions to come at once and to bring as many men who were willing and able to handle a gun. He knew Patrick Dunnigan and Michael Conklin had some hands who could account for themselves if it came down to gunplay. Conrad Mueller's, Joseph DeLarosa's, and Ben Hollister's men were ranch hands in the truest sense and seldom, if ever, got involved in anything that might require the exchange of gunfire. Counting his own men and Ben Hollister, who had remained at Thornsbury's place overnight, Thornsbury calculated he had around twenty men to back his play against Kulbane.

Whether it was intuition or not, Thornsbury just happened to look up at the row of hills to the west where Gus Haines had previously observed Jake, and he noticed a peculiar sight. There were four horses atop the rise, all bearing occupants. The strange thing was that two of the men were belly down across the saddle, and another one was upright in the saddle, but he seemed to have his arms spread out at his shoulders. He looked like he was attempting to fly. The fourth rider was leading the other three.

Thornsbury nudged Hollister who had just joined him with coffee in hand on the veranda. "Take a look to the west, Colonel. Looks like riders coming."

Both of them watched as the lead man escorted the other three along the top of the hill until they came to the crest, where he slapped the horse carrying the flying man on the rump. It took off down the slope towards the ranch house with the horses carrying the prone men in tow.

Thornsbury hollered for Pat, who showed up in the yard a couple minutes later accompanied by Mex and Jim. "What do you make of that, Pat?" asked Thornsbury, pointing in the direction of the approaching riders.

Pat looked quizzical. As the horses got closer, he thought he recognized Reverend Fletcher in the lead. As to what he was doing, with his arms spread out like that, Pat wasn't sure. "Don't rightly know, Boss. Wait 'til they get a little closer," he replied.

Not one of the dozen men milling about in the yard seemed concerned that the approaching riders might be a threat. When Fletcher was a hundred yards away, Pat instructed a couple of the hands, who had their horses nearby, to mount up and check out the situation. Within minutes they were back in the courtyard. Pat couldn't contain himself. He went into an immediate fit of laughter. Pat's reaction was contagious and the rest of the men began to smile and smirk. Even Thornsbury cracked a grin. Hollister was the only one who didn't see the humour in the situation. Someone had tied the Reverend Fletcher to a makeshift cross, and had lashed it to the back of his saddle. The man was unconscious as were Gus and Nathaniel who were a little less conspicuous, merely draped belly down across their saddles.

Nathaniel was just coming to. The two hands eased him off the horse and laid him on his back on the ground. Pat, who had gained his composure, issued instructions to cut the rope around Nathaniel's wrist and then to do the same for Gus Haines, freeing him as well. It was Hollister who had to give the order to get Samuel down. When Hollister spoke he looked at Pat, who spit out a big brown gob and grinned. He shook his head and said, "That Jake sure has a funny bone. Yes Sir, he makes me laugh."

Thornsbury became defensive when he asked, "What makes you think the goddamn horse thief did this."

Pat shrugged his shoulders and replied, "I don't know for sure. I was just thinkin', is all."

Thornsbury remarked, very cuttingly, "You should leave the thinking to those more capable."

Pat thought someday soon he was going to quit this job, and just before he left, he was going to punch the fat English son-of-a-bitch square on the nose.

Hollister interjected, "I think pretty clearly, Mr. Thornsbury, and I think Pat is right."

Pat spit, smiled, and looked to Thornsbury for a reply.

"Nonsense! One horse thief does not get the drop on three men who hunt men like him for a living. It was that Kulbane fellow and his bloody Mexican army," said Thornsbury, almost shouting.

Almost as if in answer, an Apache yell was heard coming from the hill crest where the Fletcher bunch had just come from. Everyone's eyes focused on the figure atop the hill. Although no one could make the man out clearly, everyone in the yard, with perhaps the exception of Thornsbury, thought the man on the horse was Jake and that he was taunting them. Thornsbury became enraged. He snatched a Winchester rifle out of the nearest man's hand, and as quickly as he could, he lever shells into the chamber and fired at the figure on the hill. When the rifle was empty, Thornsbury still tried to fire another couple of rounds. Hollister gently took the rifle from Thornsbury's hands and simply said, "He's out of range."

Suddenly a loud report came from the top of the hill. A hollow, whizzing sound passed just over their heads. Something struck the wind chimes hanging from the veranda a few feet above Thornsbury's head. "Good lord, what the hell was that? He just missed me," whined Thornsbury.

Nathaniel Fletcher, who was fully conscious and on his feet, answered Thornsbury's question. "That was Gus's .50, and if that's who I think it is, he didn't miss. That was a warning."

Thornsbury's face was so red it looked like it could burst at any moment. He was literally screaming, his spittle spraying anyone unfortunate enough to be close to him. "Saddle up all of you! Get that bloody bastard and bring him to me this minute! This minute, I tell you!" One of the cowhands wasn't moving quickly enough for Thornsbury's liking, so the ranch boss helped him along with a well placed boot to the rear end.

Mex, who had been watching intently without saying anything, stepped forward and said, "Senor, you don't want to do that."

Thornsbury turned in his direction and in the most condescending tone he could muster, he replied, "And pray tell, my Mexican friend, why shouldn't I?"

"That man is a Lipan Apache. You send these cowhands out after him, not many will return," answered Mex.

"Alright, then you and Pat go and get him," commanded Thornsbury.

Before Mex could respond, Pat stepped forward, spat, and said, "You want him so bad, Boss, you go get 'im. I quit!"

A split second later Mex followed his partner's lead and said, "Me too."

"You're both a pair of cowards," bellowed Thornsbury. He glanced over the rest of the men in the yard and said in a more subdued tone, "One hundred dollars to the man who gets me that goddamn horse thief. Make it five hundred, if you bring him back to me alive, so I can watch him swing."

"Would that be on top of what you are already paying us?" asked Nathaniel Fletcher. He was speaking for Samuel and Gus as Samuel was still unconscious and Gus was just coming to his senses.

Although Gus was barely conscious, he had a gist of what was going on from the conversations. He snorted, "Count me in. That heathen near killed me. He's got my rifle and I want it back."

Nathaniel looked Thornsbury in the eyes and vowed, "We will get that demon for you, Mr. Thornsbury. I will try and convince my father to bring him back alive, but Papa may be too angry for convincing."

Hollister, who had been listening intently the entire time, said to Nathaniel, "It won't be just a knock on the noggin this time. He will kill you and without mercy."

Gus answered, "He can try."

Thornsbury smiled and turned to go up the veranda stairs. Part of the way up, he turned to Hollister and said, "That's settled then. Good. Care for a brandy and cigar, Colonel?"

CHAPTER SIXTEEN

REGINALD "RED" COCHRANE, Tommy Kulbane's slightly older cousin, was one of the half dozen men Esparza had sent out to various lookout points where they could watch the comings and goings to and from the Thornsbury ranch. Shortly after the exchange of gunfire between Thornsbury and Jake, all of Esparza's lookouts headed back to base to report. Red was the first to arrive, and when asked if he knew what all the shooting was about, he related the strange events he had witnessed. "I was watching from the boulders just below the rise west of the ranch. Right above me, this Apache lookin' fella is leadin' three horses, all with men on them. Two was belly down, and General, I swear on a stack o' Bibles he had the third fella lashed to a cross, like he was Jesus or somethin'. He smacks the lead horse, and it takes off for the ranch, draggin' the other two hombres with it."

Esparza interrupted the narrative when he asked, "What was all the shooting?"

Red continued his story, "Well, this Apache fella, he started it all by yelling like they do just before they come at ya', and this made this rancher fella real mad. I was watching him through the field glasses, and he looked near ready to burst. He empties a Winchester at the fella on the hill. Must have been six — seven shots, maybe. The Apache, he fired one shot back. I don't know what kinda rifle he had, but it sounded like a cannon went off."

"What do you make of that, Enrique?" Kulbane asked Esparza.

"General, I think this hombre on the hill — I think he is the man we want."

Kulbane thought for a moment and then began reasoning out loud. "And now he is on the outs with his employer. Who were the three men he sent packing? Too many questions. Not enough answers." He raised his voice and said to Esparza, "Then, Enrique my friend, will shall have to pay this carpetbagger a visit, and maybe he can give us some answers. Have everyone ready to ride in fifteen minutes."

'Chatter' Toliver spoke up. His companions all called him 'Chatter' because he stuttered when he was nervous. If he couldn't get the words out right away, his lower jaw would move up and down in rapid succession, causing his teeth to chatter as if he were freezing to death. "– – – Gen – Gen - General, I – I saw – I –

Con Ferguson, who had been on lookout with Chatter, intervened, "Oh Christ, Chatter, let me tell it, or we will be here until next Tuesday." He took a breath and went on to explain, "Awhile after the rifle shots, two groups of men rode into the ranch about a half an hour apart. There was about a half dozen in each bunch, and they looked well armed, General. Just thought you should know."

Kulbane did some quick addition in his head. By his calculations, he still had the advantage of numbers. Thornsbury's forces numbered about twenty to twenty five men, while he had nearly forty well armed combatants. The time for a confrontation was now, while he still had the upper hand. He shouted, "Saddle up! Time to pay our respects to the White Sands Land and Cattle Association."

Less than an hour later, there was a summit conference in front of Sinclair Thornsbury's ranch house. Two armed camps faced each other in the open space between the ranch house and the surrounding buildings. On one side was General Kulbane, Enrique Esparza, and at last count, about thirty five pistoleros from all walks of life; mostly drifters who had no particular place to go and nothing in particular to do, so they hooked up with Esparza and the General for awhile. The work wasn't difficult, and the fringe benefits were pretty good: lots of food, all the bad tequila you could drink, and an occasional Senorita to bed.

On the other side, were Sinclair Thornsbury and the other major members of the Association, which included Patrick Dunnigan, Joseph DeLarosa,

Michael Conklin, and John Ballard with about fifteen of their ranch hands. Conrad Mueller had refused to come, stating that he didn't want any part of this business, and he didn't care if Thornsbury and the rest bounced him out of the association. Out of all the hired hands, there were perhaps three or four men who could hit the broad side of a barn door when it came to shooting. Mex and Pat were the most capable with a firearm, but they had just quit Thornsbury, and along with Ben Hollister, they were in the saddle and ready to depart when the Kulbane bunch had shown up.

Kulbane recognized Hollister and asked, "Going somewhere, Colonel?"

Hollister didn't show any fear when he replied, "Yes I was, Mr. Kulbane," emphasizing the '*Mister*'.

Hollister had produced the effect he wanted, for Kulbane replied through gritted teeth. "That's '*General*' to you, Sir!"

"As you wish," conceded Hollister. "You and '*General*' Thornsbury can work things out. I am done with this business."

Kulbane caught the '*General*' inference, which only made him angrier. "Nobody goes anywhere until I get some answers!" he roared.

You could cut the tension in the air with a dull butter knife. No one on either side knew what they should do. The whizzing sound of a fifty caliber bullet, as it sailed over their heads and ricocheted off the wind chime again, caught everyone's attention. Unfortunately, one of the nervous cowhands thought that someone in Esparza's band had taken the shot, so he drew his pistol and started firing erratically. He didn't hit anything, but he was peppered with at least a dozen shots a second later. It could have been an all out free-for-all, but cooler heads prevailed. Hollister and Kulbane, almost simultaneously, shouted "Hold your fire! Hold your fire!"

In the awkward silence that followed, the familiar whizzing sound was heard again. Everyone instinctively ducked, even though the shot was well over their heads. The wind chimes on Thornsbury's porch rang out once more, followed closely by an Apache yell.

All eyes turned to the knoll, where Jake stood with rifle in hand, taunting the accumulation of humanity in Thornsbury's yard. "There's the man you want! He's the one! He is to blame for all of this!" Thornsbury was almost in hysterics as he continued ranting and pointing to the hilltop.

Kulbane nodded to Esparza, who in turn shouted to the men nearest him, "Go and fetch me that Apache dog!"

Two men broke ranks and galloped towards the knoll where Jake calmly waited. Jake casually sighted the long gun on the lead rider's mount and fired. The shot caught the horse right between the eyes, and it dropped like a stone, throwing its rider head over heels onto the ground. The second rider pulled up. He looked at Jake and then glanced back at Esparza, trying to decide what to do. He made the wrong decision. As he spurred his horse towards Jake, the .50 rang out again, and the man was knocked backwards off the horse with a fist sized hole in his chest.

"Get that son-of-a-bitch!" hollered Kulbane. Esparza and his men turned and spurred their horses towards the knoll. In a matter of minutes, they were at the top of the hill where Jake had been a moment before. One of the first men to arrive at the spot did not see any sign of Jake or in which direction he might have gone, so he began to circle, looking for any tracks that would indicate which way Jake had gone. Esparza reined up and let his tracker do his work while he waited patiently.

After what seemed an eternity, the man approached Esparza and explained the situation. There were tracks everywhere, at least a dozen trails leading off into the trees and brush in all directions. It seemed Jake had been very busy while waiting for things to develop in the yard down below. "Senor Esparza, there is no way of telling which direction he may have gone," the man explained and then stood waiting for instructions from his boss.

Esparza didn't reply. He simply turned his horse and headed back to the ranch house and the others all followed suit. Kulbane was waiting for him with anticipation, though somewhat confused by the bandit leader's quick return. "Well, did you get him?" Kulbane asked.

"No Senor! This is a very — how you say it — clever man. He leaves us many trails to follow. He will be miles away before we can tell which way he went."

Thornsbury, who was listening in on the conversation, interrupted. Not quite sure of what Esparza was referring to, he asked for clarification. Esparza gave Thornsbury a funny look, and then he glanced at Kulbane as if he were seeking permission to speak to Thornsbury. After a nod from Kulbane, Esparza, very slowly and very deliberately, explained how Jake, with lots of time on his hands, had walked the two horses in every direction, leaving hundreds of tracks and dozens of trails. He had even alternated between the two horses, making it difficult to tell which one he was riding at any particular time, Thornsbury's stallion or his own mustang. It would take many hours to sort it all out. The better solution would be to try and outthink Jake, guess which direction he would go, and then follow up on their hunch.

Sinclair Thornsbury had picked one of the best spots in the basin to build his ranch house. It was situated in a small vale encircled on three sides by rising hills with the open end facing south. The configuration was ideal for sheltering the small valley from the prevailing northwest winds. A spring-fed creek ran north to south, providing enough water for all the ranch's needs. Jake Romero had taken up a position on the western row of hills.

"Then what is your best guess?" Thornsbury asked Esparza.

Esparza ignored Thornsbury, but answered his question by talking directly to Kulbane. "I do not think he will go to the west. That is nothing but desert. It is — how you say it — hell on earth. I think he wants to go south, but I do not think he will go there right away. Too open and he would be too easy to catch. He will circle around us and go to the east and then cut south."

"Very well, Enrique, I trust your judgment," replied Kulbane. He looked directly at Thornsbury and asked, "Are you going to join the party, Mr. Carpetbagger?"

Thornsbury was offended, but he didn't let it show when he replied, "I would like to come along — to protect my interests, so to speak. I want my stallion back in one piece." He paused and then added, "If any of my contemporaries and their men wishes to tag along, their support would be appreciated." The words sounded like he was asking, but his tone strongly suggested they should accompany him.

Searching for Jake's possible route and the discussion in the ranch yard had taken the better part of half an hour. There was a pause in the action, and in that brief moment when no one was doing or saying anything, they heard the unmistakable whizzing sound of another chunk of lead as it came towards them. The bullet hit Esparza's horse in the head, and the animal dropped like a stone, but Esparza, thinking quickly, leapt to the side and wasn't injured. A split second after the horse fell, everyone heard the report of the big rifle. However, this time the shot had come from the east side hills. The shooter had circled behind the ranch house and was now on the opposite side of the vale.

Everyone on a horse dismounted and hid behind their animals, putting their mounts between themselves and the hill. Anyone near cover took advantage of it and hid themselves from view. Nothing stirred for a good five minutes. One of Patrick Dunnigan's men asked Pat if he thought Jake was gone, and Pat suggested the man step out from behind cover and find out. Pat laughed, spit, stepped into the open, and waved to the hill top. It was a show of bravado, but Pat had calculated he would have lots of time to duck back behind his horse if he saw a small puff of smoke from the hilltop. Pat looked at Gus Haines, spat out a wad of brown juice, wiped his big mustache with his left sleeve and asked, "How much ammunition has he got for that cannon?"

Without pausing to think, Gus replied, "Twenty four in the ammunition belt and about the same in a leather pouch, and he's got them both."

"Christ!" spat Pat. He looked at the men all around him and then added, "Well, I wish you fellas luck. You're gonna need it. You go after that man and a lot of you aren't coming back alive." And just for emphasis he added, "A lot of you."

"The wicked man flees though no one pursues, but the righteous are as bold as a lion. Fear of man will prove to be a snare, but whoever trusts in the Lord is kept safe," spouted a now conscious, wide-eyed Samuel Fletcher.

"Well, there it is," responded Pat, mockingly. "You are all safe now. Reverend Fletcher will protect you. He has God on his side. Hell, you won't even need any guns. The good Reverend here will just talk ole Jake to death."

Thornsbury took command. "Wilkens, you and your greaser friend have quit me. You have thirty minutes to get off my property. If you leave right now, you might just make it. The same goes for any of the rest of you, only if anybody leaves, don't ever come to me if you ever need anything." He waited for any reaction. Jim Clemfeld mounted and joined Mex and Pat and when Hollister mounted and joined the three of them, Thornsbury felt a swell of anger rising in his gut.

"Good luck, Mr. Thornsbury. I mean that. We had the right idea to begin with, cleaning out the rustlers and horse thieves. Now it has become a fool's errand. Why didn't you just pay the man what you owe him?" said Hollister.

"Oh, he'll get what's coming to him. Don't you worry about that," snorted Thornsbury.

As Hollister, Pat, Mex, and Jim Clemfeld started their horses, Kulbane shouted orders. "These men are not going anywhere! They were somehow involved in the death of my son and the destruction of my property, and I will deal with them after we catch the renegade. I want him alive! He is going to tell me what really happened even if I have to peel every inch of his hide off slowly with a hot knife!" He looked Hollister in the eyes and added, "If he tells me you four were involved, you can die with him. Until then you are staying with me."

"Now see here," interrupted Thornsbury. "I think—"

Kulbane cut him off and said, "I don't care what you think, or do, for that matter, Mr. Thornsbury, I've changed my mind. You are all going to join us!" After a short pause, he added, "I want you to remember two things; one, I am in charge and two, don't get in my way."

"What about us? I mean my father, my cousin Gus and me. Are we included?" asked Nathaniel Fletcher.

"No, Mr. Bounty Hunter, you can go your separate way, but if I find out you were involved in my son's death, all the faith and prayers in the world won't save you," answered Kulbane. Glaring at Reverend Fletcher, he added, "Just one more thing and this is for everybody here, I want that murdering bastard alive. Anybody kills him either by design or by accident will wish he hadn't been born. I hope I have made myself clear."

Kulbane ordered Thornsbury to gather gear and provisions for at least a week in the field. Thornsbury wasn't very pleased with the turn of events and he voiced his displeasure to the other members of the Association. "I am not footing the bill for everything! When this is all said and done, all of you are going to reimburse me for your share of the expenses."

Pat, after hearing Thornsbury's rant, spat, smiled, and remarked, "I sure hope everybody gets what's comin' to them, 'specially you, Mr. Thornsbury. 'Specially you."

CHAPTER SEVENTEEN

THE MAJORITY OF men under General George Kulbane's command consisted of Enrique Esparza and his rag-tag group of misfits. For Kulbane, the key to controlling the bandits was to make sure Esparza was content with his status in the organization. By including Esparza in all decisions, Kulbane made him feel important. Little did Esparza know he was being manipulated by the self-proclaimed general. Sergeant Willie Herrington was Kulbane's second in command, in charge of a dozen men who had served with Kulbane during the war and had stayed with him out of loyalty. Kulbane valued Herrington's input much more than he did Esparza's, but he never let it show when the bandit leader was around.

Pat Wilkens smiled at Mex, spat out a big brown gob, shook his head, and laughed. "What is so funny, amigo?" asked Mex.

Pat wiped his mustache with the back of his sleeve and replied, "Ya know, Mex, the first time I laid eyes on ole Jake I thought to myself, '*here's trouble*'. And you know what, Pard? I was right. Why just look at all the fuss he's caused. Look around, Mex. You gotta laugh."

What Pat alluded to was the collection of men separated into five distinct groups atop the hillside about a half mile east of Thornsbury's ranch house. Kulbane and his soldiers formed one tight party, Esparza and his bandits another, Thornsbury and the other members of the Association along with their men formed the third large contingent. The Fletcher trio, who had separated themselves from everyone else, and Hollister, accompanied by Pat, Mex, and Jim Clemfeld, formed the last two groups.

Yuyutsu and Nacoma, the two trackers, had been riding in expanding circles for about an hour, scouring the ground. Everyone was getting impatient. Thornsbury was the first one to lose control, "Hell's bells, what is taking so long?" he asked of no one in particular.

Kulbane motioned the trackers to come closer and questioned them as to their findings. They explained it was just like on the hilltop to the west of the ranch house where there were tracks everywhere, leading in all different directions. Kulbane wondered when the Apache would have had the time to do all this. Then the realization hit him like a school marm's slap. Jake had set up all the tracks on both sides of the glen before he'd taken any action against Thornsbury. But what was he up to now?

Kulbane made a decision. Speaking loud enough for everyone to hear, he said with a hint of sarcasm, "My God, there is a small army gathered here, and we can't figure out how to find one man, an old man at that!" Softening his tone, he continued, "We need to decide our course of action, and I need to hear from you ranchers. What is the terrain like? Where is he most likely to go?" He paused for the questions to sink in and then created a new train of thought when he asked, "Is there anyone here who knows this man? We need to know everything we can about him."

Samuel Fletcher rolled his eyes, tilted his head, pointed skyward, and shouted, "He repays a man for what he has done; he brings upon him what his conduct deserves."

Kulbane considered Fletcher a fool, and his tone indicated as much when he said, "Listen you pretentious windbag! You take your inbred kin and all of you get out of my sight before I have Esparza's men burn you at the stake for the hypocrites you are."

Fletcher didn't have to be told twice. As he was leaving, he rode close to Thornsbury's position and asked, "I assume our agreement is still binding?"

Thornsbury didn't answer one way or the other. He simply lowered his head and ignored the question. Samuel hadn't determined which would be the best direction to go. Since his horse was pointed north, that was the way he went. After a few minutes of riding at a brisk pace, Samuel slowed his mount, allowing Nathaniel and Gus to catch up. Nathaniel asked, "Father, where do you think we should start looking for the heathen?"

Samuel didn't answer immediately, for he seemed in deep contemplation over Nathaniel's question, almost as if he were looking for some divine inspiration. Gus Haines took the opportunity to put in his two cents worth. "If I know anything about Apaches — and I do — he's going to want to head for home, or in other words, straight south."

Nathaniel argued, "If he'd headed south, we would've seen him!"

"Not if he cut back to the west first and then south," retorted Gus.

"That is pure desert out west. Nothing survives out there for long," argued Nathaniel.

"He's Apache! Those heathens love the desert," stipulated Gus.

Samuel wasn't sure how long the argument was going to continue, so he intervened and stated, "Nathaniel, I think your cousin is right. That is just what that Son of Satan would do."

There was an uneasy moment of silence, and Nathaniel broke it when he asked, "Are you telling me that we are going to chase him into the desert?"

"That's exactly what we are going to do! This time he will be the one tied to a cross!" barked Samuel as he turned his horse westward.

Kulbane and Esparza sat in the saddle facing each other, so they could converse. "What do you think he will do next, Enrique?" asked Kulbane.

"He will go to the country he knows best. I believe he will head back across the border and hide in the mountains and canyons. He will be very difficult to find, Senor," replied Esparza.

"Then we must get him before he gets to those mountains and canyons!" snarled Kulbane. He softened his tone and spoke slowly and deliberately as he issued orders to Esparza, "Enrique, I believe it is as you suggested. Our nemesis is headed south to familiar territory. He is going to head straight east or maybe back to the west for a few miles to throw us off his trail, and then he is going to turn south and head for home. Send six men due south to see if they can cut his trail. After five miles or so, three men head east for about five miles and the other three head west looking for his trail. If they don't find anything, they will backtrack, wait a few hours, and then head east and west again. I want them to keep doing this until he crosses their trail, or until sundown tomorrow, then they can rejoin us, and we will have to think of something else if we don't cut his trail. We will be heading south at a reasonable pace, so as to not wear out our mounts." Esparza picked the men as requested and sent them on their way, spare horses and all.

Samuel Fletcher truly believed God was talking to him when he got these ideas that his life's work was to track down evil men and vanquish them for their sins. The bounty paid well, either as prepayment for a predetermined objective, or collecting the money offered on a wanted poster, which in most cases read *'Dead or Alive'*, and the good deacon preferred to bring them in draped belly down over the saddle. It didn't matter to him if the man was guilty or not, or that his petty crime might not warrant a death penalty. He'd had no pangs of guilt over the killing of a young lad of fifteen. Even though the poster had said dead or alive for three brothers who had robbed a stagecoach, the youngster in question didn't participate in the hold-up. He simply had the misfortune of associating with the other two and was basically wanted for questioning. That didn't matter to the Fletcher group. His name was on a poster that read *'Dead or Alive'*, so Gus Haines put a bullet through the young man's chest from a great distance.

The Fletcher standard operating procedure was to find the wanted man and follow him until an opportunity presented itself where Gus could set up and take a shot. The rest was easy; no fuss, no bother. This time, however, Gus didn't have his long gun. In fact, their quarry had it. They would have to come up with a different method to take Jake Romero. Samuel was at a loss as to how they were going to accomplish the task, especially if they had to take him alive like that crazy General had insisted, but he found comfort in his faith that God would give him a sign.

Fifteen miles and several sets of rolling hills later, the sun was setting, and the Fletchers found themselves on the edge of another world, the land the Apache called *'the journey of the dead man'*. The name said it all, for there were hundreds of square miles of sand, sun, and sorrow awaiting any man foolish enough to venture there.

"Where to now, Pa?" asked Nathaniel.

"We'll camp for the night. At first light, we will start again. We will stick close to the hills here. If the heathen has come this way, we should cut his trail," answered Samuel.

"But what if he don't come this way?" questioned Nathaniel.

To save them from another biblical blast, Gus interrupted before Samuel could say anything. "I'll bet a year's pay on it, Cousin. You just gotta keep the faith," he said. His last remark brought a scowl from Nathaniel and a cheesy grin from Samuel.

Gus was correct. At short time after daybreak, about six miles south of where they had entered the desert, they found the tracks of two horses, one set not as deep as the other, indicating one horse had a rider and the other did not. The trail was easy to follow. The rider certainly didn't care about hiding his tracks, which bothered Gus. He had a tight feeling in his gut that something was not right. If this trail was Jake's, it sure looked like he was pretty confident no one was following him, or he just didn't care. The thing that didn't sit right with Gus wasn't so much that Jake didn't care about being followed, but *why* he didn't care.

Another two miles brought the trio to an ancient, dry riverbed with high sandy embankments on each side. Jake's tracks lead down the middle of the riverbed for a hundred feet and then completely disappeared. Both Gus and Nathaniel dismounted and began scrutinizing the ground for anything that might indicate which way their quarry had gone. As they moved slowly down the rocky riverbed, Nathaniel happened to glance up. There, atop a three foot sand dune was what appeared to be Gus's .50 calibre rifle, resting against a Skunkbush Sumac. Nathaniel nudged Gus and pointed to what he had seen. "Well, I'll be a monkey's uncle. What in hell? Is that my rifle?" Gus asked without expecting an answer.

Gus started quickly towards his weapon, but a shout from Nathaniel slowed him down. "It's a trap, Cousin. He's waiting for you to climb up the bank, and then he'll shoot you when you pick up your rifle."

Usually Gus didn't listen very intently to what his younger cousin had to say, but this time he made sense. In fact, it made a lot of sense. Gus made his way cautiously to the embankment just below the small mount of white sand that the Skunkbush had saved from the eroding winds. With his back to the old river bank, Gus reached up over his head and took a good hold of the rifle up the stock just below the trigger guard and gave a good pull. He was quite pleased with himself for having outsmarted Jake, but when the rattlesnake sank its deadly fangs into his cheek and pumped its lethal venom into his face, he screamed in terror. Instinctively, he grabbed the snake behind the head and ripped it from his face, tearing the fang holes in his cheeks into long gashes. He threw the snake as hard as he could, but to his shocking surprise, it didn't go anywhere. It flew right back at him, burying its fangs into the side of his neck. Again, he tore the snake away from his body and threw it to the ground. The rattler hit the sand and started to crawl away as fast as it could, but then it suddenly changed direction and sank its fangs into Gus's calf, expending what little venom it had left. As Gus looked down, he saw that the snake had been tied tail first to the rifle just above the trigger guard, and someone had cut off its warning rattle.

Gus's screams brought Nathaniel running. Seeing the rattlesnake at Gus's feet, and quickly realizing he was unarmed, Nathaniel swiftly removed Gus's pistol from its holster. While keeping a constant eye on the snake, he got as close as he dared and with one shot blew the snake's head off. By this time Gus had collapsed. The toxin was doing its damage, and Gus lapsed into unconsciousness. Nathaniel picked up Gus's rifle with the dead snake still attached. In a fit of raging anger, he took the rifle by the barrel and swung it as hard as he could over his head and down towards a large rock a few feet away, aiming it so that the dead rattler was smashed against the rock with each swing, but the rifle didn't sustain any damage.

Samuel Fletcher's voice interrupted Nathaniel's tirade, "That's enough! A hot-tempered man stirs up dissension, but a patient man calms a quarrel."

Nathaniel stopped his outburst, and with his knife he cut the piece of rawhide holding the snake to the rifle. He held the dead rattler in his hands, and presented it to his father as if it were an offering and then asked, "Why does God allow the heathen Apache to use one of his creatures to kill Cousin Gus? Why?"

"It is not for us to question his will," retorted Samuel.

"His will? His will?" Nathaniel was still in a rage. "Is it his will for us to follow a demon into the desert, a spawn of the Devil who has bested us once before? His will? No father, I think it is your will and nothing to do with God! You and the white Apache can settle your differences. I've had enough."

Samuel started to protest only to be cut off by Nathaniel when he stated very emphatically, "I'll stay with Gus until he passes, and then I'll bury him and say a prayer over him."

Again Samuel protested, "It is not your place. I shall see to my nephew's spiritual needs."

Nathaniel, who had been kneeling over Gus, rose to his feet, his face clearly displaying the anger he felt. He spoke through clenched teeth, "I think you have done enough. I am sick of your hypocrisy, and I am sick of you! It ends here! Stay if you want, but when Gus is in the ground, I am done with you. I'll go my way, and you go yours."

For the first time in his life Samuel was at a loss for words. His son's outburst and the hateful things he was saying had taken him by complete surprise. He responded the only way he knew how, "There is a place in hell waiting for you, blasphemer!"

"I am sure there is, Papa, but I think you will be waiting for me when I get there," Nathaniel shot right back.

Samuel had no more to say. He was hurt beyond words, so he turned his face away to hide the tears that had begun to run down his cheek. His attention was drawn to a spot about a hundred yards down the riverbed. There, sitting cross-legged on his horse, was Jake, bold as brass as if he were dropping by for afternoon tea. When Jake was sure Samuel had seen him, he waved his right arm in greeting.

Samuel shouted to his son, "Nathaniel, do you see the heathen? There he is!"

Nathaniel looked up, and when he saw Jake, he picked up Gus's big rifle and opened the sliding breech to see if it was loaded. It wasn't! He dropped the big gun in the sand and picked up his Winchester from where he had leaned it against a nearby rock. Nathaniel took careful aim and fired. There was a thunderous bang and a huge flash as the rifle exploded in Nathaniel's face, knocking him flat on his back several feet away from his original position.

The suddenness of the explosion shocked Samuel momentarily, but he quickly regained his senses, and his first thought was to raise his Winchester and kill the heathen before tending to Nathaniel. As he brought his rifle up and took aim, he realized there was nothing to shoot at. There was nothing down the riverbed, for Jake had vanished as quietly and as quickly as he had come.

Samuel turned his attention to his injured son. He knelt down beside Nathaniel and with his hand gently brushed the hair from Nathaniel's face. What he saw sank his heart into despair. The explosion had turned the rifle into a grenade with shrapnel flying in all directions. A shard of metal had penetrated Nathaniel's temple, and it was obvious it had caused major damage as he was going into convulsions. Samuel watched helplessly as his son's body shook violently and foam came from his mouth, and then he gave one last breath and died.

Samuel was trying to understand what had happened, and he realized that somehow the heathen had snuck into their camp during the night and jammed the Winchester. He quickly checked his own rifle and sure enough, the end of the barrel was plugged tight. It looked like it had been packed with wet sandstone that had dried as hard as cement over night. Samuel got to his knees and began pulling his hair out and waling in despair to the heavens. He began chanting, "Why? Why? Why?" over and over again. Someone passing by who heard him but didn't see him might even think it was some Apache singing a death song over a lost loved one.

He didn't know how long he had been lost in his agony when Gus's groans caught his attention. He got to his feet and still sobbing uncontrollably, he half stumbled and half ran to where Gus lay, a few feet away. Gus's face and throat had swollen to the point that he was unrecognizable, and he was having difficulty breathing. As Samuel approached, Gus turned his head in the preacher's direction. His eyes widened and he smiled as he said to Samuel, "May God forgive you for your arrogance." By the time Samuel got to him and knelt down beside him, Gus had succumbed to the poison.

"I told you not to hunt me, or the next time me met, I would kill you." Jake's voice startled Samuel, and he looked up to see the white Apache standing near by with his knife drawn.

Several days later, two Yuma women, who were searching the desert for medicinal plants, came across a bizarre sight. Beneath a ten foot Saguaro cactus were two stone covered graves side by side, which in itself wasn't very strange, but the man tied to the cactus in a manner not unlike Christ on the cross was definitely material for a good story to tell around the fire later that night.

CHAPTER EIGHTEEN

WHILE THE FLETCHERS were making their way to their fateful reckoning with Jake, Kulbane and company were initiating plans and preparations for the trip south. Ben Hollister could feel Pat's eyes on him, so he turned his head in the grizzled cowboy's direction. When their eyes met, Hollister asked, "What's on your mind, Pat?"

As usual, Pat spat out a big brown gob and wiped his big moustache before speaking, "What's going on, Colonel? Are we prisoners? What's that crazy Reb gonna do with us?"

Hollister didn't answer Pat's questions. Instead, he rode the short distance between himself and Kulbane and said loud enough for Pat, Mex, and Jim to hear, "General Kulbane, I have a ranch needing my attention. My three men and I will be bidding you farewell."

"No, Colonel Hollister, you and your men are not going anywhere. You are going to accompany me," replied Kulbane.

"To what end?" demanded Hollister.

Kulbane answered with a snide grin, "Oh, there are several ways this little scenario could play out. If I find out from your white renegade that you had any involvement, or gave any orders to hurt my son or burn my place, you can die right beside him." He paused long enough for Hollister to absorb what he had just said. After a moment, he continued, "If he acted on his own, you can watch me skin him alive, and then you will be conscripted into my army. I am going to need a good second in command and some strong labour to rebuild."

"And if I refuse?" asked Hollister with confidence.

"Esparza will set you against the nearest wall or wide tree, and his men can use you for target practice. I will give them orders not to kill you right off. We shall have a little lottery to see how many bullets you can take before you die."

"You are insane, Kulbane," responded Hollister. After a short pause he asked, "And what about Thornsbury and the other ranchers and their men?"

"They are in the recruitment program as well. Will there be anything else, Colonel?" asked Kulbane with a dismissive tone.

Hollister returned the short distance back to join Pat, Mex, and Jim. "What'd you find out, Colonel?" asked Pat.

"Looks like we are in the army, boys," was all Hollister had to say.

Much to Kulbane's consternation, it took nearly two hours to gather up all the spare horses and to load a couple of wagons with saddles, tack, gear, and grub for a long haul. Kulbane voiced his displeasure at Thornsbury's men leisurely pace when he said, "You will find, Mr. Thornsbury, if you continue your cavalier attitude towards my authority, it will earn you a session with one of Enrique's men and his bullwhip."

Thornsbury huffed once, snorted twice, and he began to say. "Now, see here —" when Kulbane moved his horse directly next to Thornsbury and backhanded him across the face, nearly knocking the portly rancher from his horse.

Michael Conklin owned a small spread just east of Thornsbury's ranch. He minded his own business and thought other people should do the same. Because he was a member of the Association, he considered the business of the Association his business, so when Thornsbury sent out a message that he was needed, he and his two ranch hands answered the call. He wasn't sure who this Kulbane character was and he didn't care. He came to the conclusion Thornsbury was on some wild goose chase after some Apache who had stolen his stallion. Conklin couldn't figure out why so many men were needed to catch one horse thief, and he decided he wasn't going to be a part of it.

"Sinclair, I don't know what is going on here. I got work to do, and I don't have time to be chasing around the country after some horse thief. Me and my men will be headed back now, if you don't mind," he stated emphatically.

"You're not going anywhere!" bellowed Kulbane.

Conklin was angry when he asked, "Who the hell are you to tell me what I can and can't do?"

"I am your commanding officer!" retorted Kulbane.

"Command — What the hell is this?" stammered Conklin. He paused for a moment, looked all around as if he couldn't believe what he was seeing, turned his horse, and said, "Let's go home boys. We got work needs doing."

Kulbane drew his pistol and fired a shot into the air. When the sound of the report died down he said, "You Sir, are not taking this seriously. The next shot won't be a warning. Do I make myself clear?"

Conklin's wife, before she died of influenza a few years back, had often chided him about how his stubbornness would get him into trouble some day. He had turned his head around and looked back at Kulbane when the General had fired the shot. Now, he turned backed forward, spurred his horse, and began to ride away. Kulbane's second shot caught him square in the back of the head.

Pandemonium broke loose. Cowboys from the ranches drew their weapons simultaneously with Esparza's and Kulbane's men. Nobody wanted to be the first to fire, and nobody was going to until one of Esparza's bandits, who was close to some of Thornsbury's men, panicked and shot the cowboy directly across from him. His friends in turn shot the bandit and his friends, in turn, killed the two cowboys who had returned fire. Luckily, the shooting stopped as quickly as it had begun. Men on both sides looked to their leaders, unsure of what to do next.

Kulbane took charge when he commanded, "Enrique, if another shot is fired upon us, kill them all!" Everyone who heard the order knew in his heart that Kulbane meant it. As a result, the combined force of the ranchers and their hands put away their weapons. Kulbane issued another order, "Disarm them all and put their weapons in one of the supply wagons." He paused momentarily and then added, "And if anyone holds out, shoot them."

Hollister asked, "Does that include us, General?" referring to Pat, Mex, Jim, and himself.

"Especially you four!" responded Kulbane.

It took only a few minutes to collect the arms and ammunition from the ranching contingent, and Kulbane gave the order to move out. Esparza had split his men so half rode in front of and the other half rode behind the ranchers and their men. Hollister and his three friends had been ushered into the middle of the pack.

Shortly after Jake sent Samuel Fletcher to his heavenly home and headed south, Nacoma, who was Esparza's best tracker, along with "Red" Cochrane and Benito Farna turned their horses due west as instructed, hoping to cross Jake's trail as he made his way south. Nacoma was a full blooded Chiricahua Apache. As a young adult he had dreams of working as a scout for the U.S. Cavalry, where he thought he would gain the respect of white people. He was gravely disappointed, for even thought he fought alongside white soldiers and faced the same dangers as everyone else, he was still treated with disrespect. Hell, he would have settled for second class status, but even the dogs were treated better then the Apache scouts. They ate and slept in separate areas of the camps. They were not welcome around the camp fires with the regular soldiers. They were left out of any strategy meetings the NCOs and officers held. They were given direct orders and never asked for input they may have had, even though they were the most knowledgeable people present.

For pulling a knife on a Sergeant, who just didn't like Apaches and thought it was fun to bully the scouts whenever he got drunk, Nacoma was given three months in the stockade, even though the Sergeant had provoked the entire incident. When he had served his sentence, he kissed the army goodbye and headed south, where he hired on as a tracker for the Mexican army, who were engaged in a conflict with the Yaqui Nation and their leader Cajeme.

Nacoma was scouting ahead when Esparza attacked the patrol. When confronted by Esparza, Nacoma denied any association with the soldiers and although Esparza didn't believe him, he conscripted Nacoma into his band of renegades because he was in need of the Apache's skills as a tracker. Nearly five years had passed, and Nacoma was quite content as he had found a place where he was treated as an equal. Although no one showed him any special acknowledgement for his skills as a tracker, he was not disrespected, which was most important.

Red Cochrane had served in the same unit as Kulbane during the war, and after the conflict he joined his uncle in his pipe dream of resurrecting an army to continue the war against the Yankees. Kulbane didn't offer his nephew any special treatment other than respect for him as a soldier. Red had become a source of solace to the General after Tommy died. Red was heartsick over Tommy's demise, but deep down he saw it as an opportunity to fill the void in Kulbane's life left by his son's death. Not that he could ever take Tommy's place, but he thought he could work the situation to his advantage.

Benito Farna had a similar connection to Enrique Esparza as Red Cochrane had to Kulbane. He was Esparza's sister's stepson. Benito was one of those few people who didn't seem to have any talent for anything, including hard work. Esparza loved his sister dearly and would do anything for her, so when she asked him to take Benito off her hands, he agreed. He took the young man aside and told him this was his last chance. No one was going to look after him anymore. He could join Esparza's band, but the bandit leader assured him that if he didn't pull his weight, he would be set loose in the middle of Yaqui country to fend for himself. It seemed Benito had found his calling, provided there was always someone around to tell him exactly what to do. Although Benito could think for himself, being the lazy individual he was, he just didn't bother to do so.

The trio had ridden south and after a short time had turned west. As instructed, they rode toward the western horizon for approximately five miles, turned and headed north for half a mile and then turned back east. They surmised if Jake was travelling south through the desert and because they hadn't cut his trail yet, it meant Jake hadn't made it that far south. As they passed close to a row of small cactus covered knolls, Nacoma felt the hair on the back of his neck bristle. He acknowledged to himself there was something watching them, but he made the mistake of thinking it was nothing more than a coyote or some other curious creature.

Jake Romero lay on the knoll concealed by a creosote bush. He watched intently as the trio rode past him in single file; Nacoma scouring the ground, Red looking all around in every direction for any sign of movement, and Benito picking dirt from under one of his fingernails. He saw Nacoma lift his head and look right at the spot where he was hidden. Jake thought he had been spotted, but when the Apache scout rubbed the back of his neck and went back to scouring the ground, Jake let out the breath he had been holding and concluded that although the Apache tracker was intuitive enough to get the message that danger was near, he had not learned to listen to it.

An hour or so later the trio cut their own trail heading south. They turned back north for a half mile and then headed west again. This time, Nacoma let out a loud yelp when he discovered the tracks of two horses; one with a rider and one without. Red wanted to head back to Kulbane immediately with the news, but Nacoma convinced him they should follow the tracks for a short time to verify it was the man they were looking for and secondly, that he was, indeed, headed south.

Nacoma knew Jake was clever, but he couldn't figure out why the man was heading west. There was absolutely nothing out there but sand and snakes. Nevertheless, the scout followed Jake's tracks for over a mile, when he lost the trail. The tracks just simply disappeared. It was as if two horses and one rider flew off into the air. One minute there were tracks and the next there was nothing. Nacoma dismounted and began walking in ever widening circles, starting at the point where the tracks had disappeared. About thirty yards out from that point, Nacoma noticed a human footprint, barely distinguishable to the layman, but to his trained eye it stood out as plain as day. He walked in the direction the footprint pointed, and he was rewarded with several more well defined prints in the sand. He followed the footprints up and over a sand hill and when he came over the crest of the dune, he discovered the tracks led to an opening in the sand. Edging closer, Nacoma surveyed the landscape. A rock outcropping formed a semi-circle with a hole about ten feet deep in the middle and someone had gone to the trouble of sealing off the open side with loose rock, brush, and sand so the hole was completely encased. It looked like an old, dried up, abandoned well. Nacoma didn't have time to give the puzzle any further thought, for as he bent over slightly to peer into the makeshift well, something or someone pushed him from behind, and he fell headfirst into the hole.

It was nearly a quarter of an hour before Nacoma regained his senses and realized where he was. He explored his prison and discovered it was impossible to climb out. The sandstone walls had been polished smooth by the desert winds. The only way out was to dismantle the man-made barrier. This knowledge elated Nacoma and he began to pull at the debris and rocks that made up the barricade. The distinctive sound of a rattlesnake forced him to back up. Somehow, Jake had pinned the back end of several snakes inside the wall, and digging out was not going to be so easy.

Nacoma began to holler for his two comrades in arms. He shouted several times and waited for a reply. Each time there was no answer. Just when he had given up, a body flew out of the air and if it hadn't been for his quick reflexes, it would have knocked Nacoma into the wall with the snakes. Instead, it landed with a dull thud at his feet. Nacoma wasn't sure if it was Benito Farna or Red Cochrane who had joined him so unceremoniously in the pit. He waited a full minute before moving forward to satisfy his curiosity. He rolled the body over, recognizing Benito Farna, who gave out a painful yelp when Nacoma touched him.

"What happened?" Benito asked in English.

"I do not know. You tell me," snarled Nacoma. Although he was fluent in English, he preferred Spanish.

"Senor Cochrane and I heard you calling, so he told me to go check on you while he watched our backs. The next thing I know someone hits me in the head, and I wake up here with you," explained Benito.

Nacoma's instincts told him to look up to the top of the pit. There, sitting on his haunches was Jake Romero, rifle in hand. "You son of a scorpion, you get us out of here, or I swear if I ever find you, I will squash you like the '*insecto*' you are!" screamed Nacoma.

"My fight is not with you, Apache. If you wait until the cold of the night, the snakes will be slow enough for you to dig your way out, but you must be patient. Dig any sooner, and you could get bitten," Jake said in a pleasant tone, as if he were explaining how something worked to a child.

Nacoma changed the subject, "Where is Cochrane? Did you kill him?"

"If you mean the white man who was with you, he is still running. He is a very frightened man! He was running so fast the buzzards circling overhead were having trouble keeping up." Jake laughed at his own joke about the cowardly Cochrane, but Nacoma didn't find it amusing at all. Jake lost the smile and said firmly, "I will leave your horse for you. You should leave these men, Brother. If we meet again like this, I will kill you," and then he was gone.

Nacoma was prepared to wait like Jake had instructed. He knew enough about snakes and other reptiles of the desert to believe what Jake had told him about the snakes becoming docile in the cold of the desert night. Benito, on the other hand, must have been a bit claustrophobic. He was very anxious and antsy for the better part of two hours, before he finally broke and ran to the wall of debris and stones and began tearing at it with his bare hands. He was in such a state of panic, he didn't feel the snake bites as the rattlers struck at his arms repeatedly, nor did he feel Nacoma trying desperately to pull him away from the wall. A short time later, as he lay dying in Nacoma's arms, he heard the Apache say, "Jake Romero, you are truly a heartless one."

CHAPTER NINETEEN

As THE EARLY morning sun slowly inched its way above the eastern horizon, it illuminated two solitary clouds hanging in the lavender sky. Nobody noticed as the clouds changed color from dark gray to varying shades of bright pink, then orange, then strawberry red, and as the sun showed it's face completely, the crimson hues disappeared, the sky turned a powder blue, and the two clouds took on a fluffy, cotton ball appearance.

Kulbane and the entire posse waited the whole night, anticipating Nacoma's and Benito Farna's return. They were hours overdue and every man in the camp had an empty feeling they would never see the two men again, especially after the story Red Cochrane told. Red had stumbled into the camp just after sunset, completely exhausted and drastically dehydrated. After he drank his fill of water and took the time to catch his breath, he told Kulbane how Jake got the drop on all of them. He related how Jake shot Nacoma right between the eyes with the long rifle from over a mile away, and as he and Farna ran, Jake shot Farna in the back. Red claimed he dove into a shallow gully and crawled on his belly until he was sure Jake couldn't see him, and then using scattered boulders and bushes for cover, he darted from one to the other until he was out of range.

Not many believed Red's story, but he was the General's nephew, and there wasn't a man amongst them brave enough to say anything, except Pat Wilkens, who spat out a brown gob of well chewed tobacco and said under his breath to Mex, "Now, there's a load of horseshit. If Jake was anywhere near that fella, he wouldn't be here waggin' his jaw."

The camp cook brought Kulbane a hot cup of black coffee. He was about to take his first sip when he was interrupted by a sentry's holler, "Rider comin' in."

Everyone within earshot hurried to see who the rider might be and much to Esparza's relief, it was his good friend and tracker, Nacoma. As he entered the camp and dismounted, Nacoma was greeted by vigorous handshakes, pats on the back, and warm smiles. "Is it my birthday, or something?" he asked.

Nephew of the General or not, Red Cochrane had some explaining to do. As soon as he saw Nacoma, he ran forward and shook the tracker's hand and then went into his act. "I thought you were dead. I could have sworn he shot you. Well, I'll be!" he said with a Cheshire smile.

Nobody bought it, especially Nacoma. He began a rant, basically calling Red a coward and a liar, and if he weren't the General's relative, he would cut his lying tongue out where he stood.

"Don't let that stop you," said Kulbane. Nacoma knew the General well enough to know what he meant. He turned to face Cochrane with knife drawn. Red, fearing for his life, turned and ran for the horses. He didn't make it. Kulbane shot him three times in the back. "I don't abide with cowards; I don't care who they are!" he said with conviction.

Esparza wanted to know what happened in the desert. Nacoma related how Jake put him and Benito Farna in the pit with the rattlers and how Benito panicked and was bitten by the agitated snakes. He explained how he waited until the cold desert night subdued the snakes, and then he slowly and carefully dug his way out, all the while calling to Cochrane for help.

Pat Wilkens turned to Mex, spit, wiped his mouth with his sleeve, and then muttered, "Jake and his snakes. Damn!"

Nacoma turned to Esparza and said, "I will go now. I no longer want to track the Lipan. I do not want the General to shoot me, so will you tell him I am not a coward? I no longer wish to make war against the white Apache."

Esparza pleaded Nacoma's case to Kulbane, explaining that even if he didn't give his blessing to the tracker's departure, Nacoma would be gone when the first opportunity presented itself. Kulbane refused, stating everyone present was in for the long haul no matter how long it took, and this included any of Esparza's men. Nacoma didn't believe Kulbane would shoot him, so he walked to his horse and mounted. As he rode past Kulbane, the self-appointed general drew his pistol and took careful aim at Nacoma's back. As he was about to pull the trigger, Kulbane heard Esparza say, "Don't kill him, General! You shoot him and I shoot you!" The dozen or so men completely loyal to Kulbane simultaneously drew their weapons as did most of Esparza's bandits. Kulbane immediately saw the benefit of discretion, and using his best diplomatic tone, he said, "Very well, Senor Esparza, if you feel so strongly about it, the man can leave, but this better not set a precedent."

It was the first time in their long relationship Esparza had gone against Kulbane. There were many occasions when Esparza did not agree with Kulbane's actions or his plans, but he went along with them for the sake of harmony. Thornsbury, who had sat back observing the proceedings, saw an opportunity and asked, "Does that included me and my men, General, or are we free to leave, as well?"

Kulbane turned angry and spoke loudly and precisely, "We have a mission! We have an objective! We will not rest until we achieve that objective! Is that clear?" He softened his tone and then added, "I let the Apache scout go because I know for sure he had nothing to do with killing my son or burning my place." He turned his head to face Esparza and said, "If I thought for one minute he had anything to do with either, I would have shot him on the spot and any man who tried to stop me would be next!" Still making eye contact with Esparza, he paused long enough to let the last statement sink in, dismounted, and began issuing orders regarding his plans for the day.

Two minutes after Thornsbury made the decision to continue his quest for permission to leave, he regretted it. He had taken on an air of indifference to Kulbane's authority and though not speaking directly to Kulbane, he said loud enough for everyone else to hear, "Well, I for one have had enough of this nonsense. I have three very capable men on this horse thief's trail, and I am quite confident they will get the job done. I shall get my stallion back and you, General, can have what is left of Jake Romero when the crazy preacher and his kin are done with him!"

An hour after Nacoma left the company of the maniacal Kulbane and his collection of "*Jake Chasers*", he was riding out of a shallow ravine and up onto a small plateau. He stopped long enough to let his horse catch it's breath after climbing out of the gully. Jake's voice startled him, but not to the point where he jumped or showed any sign that he had been caught off guard. "We meet again, Chiricahua," Jake stated, as a matter of fact.

Nacoma deduced Jake was a few paces behind him, but he didn't show any sign of fear or weakness when he answered, "Yes, we do, *white man who thinks he is a Lipan.*"

Jake didn't often defend himself against anything said about or to him. To Jake, there wasn't a single person in the world whom he cared anything about, so consequently, he felt he didn't need to justify himself or his actions to anyone. Nacoma, whether he knew it or not, hit the one sore spot that would get a rise out of Jake, but still he did not react with any anger or resentment. He merely stated, "I may be white by blood, but my spirit and my magic is Lipan. Why do you make war on me? Chiricahua men are not warriors. They are washer women, good for cooking and washing babies' behinds."

Nacoma didn't take the bait. As if he was bored, he asked, "What do you want of me?"

"I told you, Chiricahua, next time you came after me I would kill you."

"I didn't come after you! I no longer ride with Esparza. I must go to the White Mountains and cleanse my spirit of these white men." Nacoma was referring to a meditative ritual in which he would go for days without food or water, and while in a transcendental state, he would ask his ancestors to rid him of the unnatural things he learned from the white man and to give him guidance on what path to follow next.

There was no reply from Jake, so Nacoma turned around. There was nothing behind him and no sign of Jake anywhere. Nacoma dismounted and searched the sandy ground for any sign. The only thing that had disturbed the sand for yards in all directions was his horse's hoof prints. His right hand began to shake as he edged it towards the handle of his big knife, which rested in a leather scabbard tucked in his belt. He pulled the knife quickly and whirled around, ready to confront anyone or anything directly behind him. Nothing there. He backed up slowly with his left arm outstretched, reaching blindly behind him for his horse's bridal rope while keeping his eyes fixed directly in front. Once he secured the rope, he turned at lighting speed and threw himself up onto his horse, which baulked at the suddenness of its rider's movement. Nacoma took one last quick look around, and feeling a sense of relief mixed with a small dose of uncertainty, he spurred his horse hard several times and galloped away, stopping only when he had put a couple miles between himself and what he believed should have been his death site.

He had heard stories and legends of Lipan invisibility; how they could come into a wickiup or kowa while someone slept and cut their hair, or paint the sleeper's cheeks or nose. The victim would not know anything had taken place until they were asked embarrassing questions about their bad haircut or the paint on their face. When the truth was discovered, the jocularity turned into an atmosphere of wonderment, at first, then into dread and terror, and the next night everyone slept with their hands on their knife handles. He recalled stories he had heard of how a Lipan scout could shape shift and take on any animal form he chose, and how he could trick your mind and make you see things that were not there. He thought these tales were just exaggerations to tell around a night fire to amuse the children, but now he was not as sure.

With Nacoma's hasty departure, Yuyustu, Cameron Bigelow, and Punch Hamner (the trio who had been scouting to the east) were sent on Nacoma's back trail to see if they could cut Jake's trail, while the rest of the troop continued south. Yuyustu was of mixed blood, Mescalero Apache on his mother's side and a mix of English and Irish on his father's. His father was a prospector who had taken an Apache woman for a wife primarily for company and warmth on cold nights. It was a good arrangement for the prospector. He had a cook, someone to do all the camp work, and regular sex when he wasn't too drunk. He had the best of everything until the baby came along. His woman paid more attention to the squalling brat than she did him and even several beatings didn't change her attitude, so he dumped her and the kid with her relatives and went his merry way, leaving mother and child to fend for themselves.

Yuyustu was raised Apache, but he was constantly reminded he was not one of the People. Everyone made it clear he was impure and didn't belong. He learned quickly he had no one to look out for him other than himself, and when he grew to manhood he kept to himself, seldom spoke unless spoken to, and ran away from any confrontation or trouble. In his teens, his uncle, (his mother's brother) took the time to teach the boy some tracking and hunting skills, so he could provide for his mother in her later years. Apache women who had bedded down with a white man seldom found an Apache man who would have anything to do with them. Now, nearly a dozen years later, he found himself a recruit in some crazy army of banditos and misfits.

Cameron Bigelow was a lazy, petty criminal, an opportunist who seldom planned anything in his life, let alone a crime. He would steal anything left lying around. He would hide in the shadows of a back alley behind some saloon, bash some drunken working man in the back of the head, and take what little the man had. He decided joining up with Esparza's bunch was an easy way to make a living. He was wrong. Esparza and the crazy man, Kulbane, rode them hard and long. What the hell were they doing out here in the desert trying to find some damn renegade? It didn't make sense to him; all these men to catch one horse thief.

"Punch" Hamner's nickname had nothing to do with any propensity for punching anybody. Usually, he was the one getting hit, because he wasn't the sharpest knife in the drawer and in an effort to fit in with whatever crowd he was with at the time, he would usually utter something stupid, in a slow drawling tone that made him sound mentally challenged. He would follow it up with a snorting chuckle that added to the perception of idiocy. He was a follower of the highest order. If he got fed a couple of times a day and was warm on cold nights, he was content. Also, the psychological comfort he felt from being a part of something (even thought he didn't know what that something was) made him the happiest he'd ever been in his entire life.

The three of them found Nacoma's back trail and followed the tracks back to the make-shift snake trap. Seeing Farna's venom inflated body, Cameron Bigelow's face showed the horror and fear he felt. He screamed like a debutante after seeing a spider. Yuyutsu and Hamner rushed to see what had alarmed Bigelow. Punch asked, hoping one of his two compadres would answer, "Who would do that to another person?"

A voice from behind them replied, "He did it to himself." All three men turned at once with weapons drawn. They were completely surprised to see a large grey wolf standing twenty five feet away. Yuyustu was transfixed on the wolf's blue eyes. All the stories he had heard as a child about demons and other things not of this world went through his mind. He let out an Apache war cry to the heavens, turned his horse, and galloped away on their back trail just as fast as he could make the horse go. He would not go back to Esparza. He decided to let the bandit leader and the crazy white man face the demon without him. His horse was near exhaustion before Yuyustu was willing to slow down.

Cameron Bigelow was shocked by Yuyustu's reaction to Azul. It was just a goddamn wolf; no reason to be so afraid. Sure, it had the strangest eyes he had ever seen that seemed to look right into your soul and made you feel very uncomfortable, but it was still just a varmint and a well aimed bullet would close those cryptic eyes. Bigelow raised his pistol and took careful aim, but before he could pull the trigger, a fist-sized rock hit him right between the eyes and knocked him off his horse. A split second later, Punch Hamner was pulled off his mount from behind, and a well placed knife handle to his temple sent him into unconsciousness before he hit the ground.

Cameron Bigelow felt like he was waking up from a deep sleep as consciousness returned to him a few minutes after he hit the ground. His right hand went up instinctively to feel the bump on his forehead, and he felt something warm running over his fingers. He lowered his hand and saw that he was bleeding as well. He squinted to clear his vision, and when he opened his eyes the first thing he saw was Jake Romero's face positioned about six inches from his. Before he could move, Cameron felt Jake's knee pressed hard on his chest and the blade of a large knife across his throat.

"You are not going to die, today. You will carry a message to the men who hunt me," said Jake. He stood up and allowed Cameron to do the same, then continued, "Tell these men I do not make war on them. My fight is with the one called Thornsbury. He owes me forty dollars and when he pays me, he will get his horse back."

Jake paused to let that much sink in and then finished by saying, "If it is war they want, I will give them one. Many will die! You tell them that!" Jake turned quickly and sprinted for a small grove of scrub brush a few yards away.

Cameron didn't move until he was sure Jake was gone, and then he loaded the still unconscious Punch Hamner on his horse and rode off at a slow lope back to the main column. An hour later, when they arrived, Punch was barely sitting upright in his saddle. He had suffered a severe concussion and didn't have any idea what happened or where he was. Cameron headed straight for Esparza to give him an update, when he heard Kulbane's voice saying, "You will report to me, soldier!"

Cameron thought, *I'm not a goddamn soldier*, but before he could say anything stupid, his common sense told him to humor the General, so he turned his horse in Kulbane's direction and rode closer.

"Dismount and give me your report," shouted Kulbane.

Cameron looked around nervously, dismounted, and stood before Kulbane, who saluted. Cameron knew enough about military things to know he should return the salute, which he did, and this seemed to please the General. Cameron related the events of the encounter with Jake and concluded the report by stating they would never see Yuyustu again.

This seemed to anger Kulbane, who asked in a threatening tone, "Did he say anything? Tell me, his exact words!"

"No – uh, no – he looked at the wolf and then rode away," replied Cameron.

Kulbane was enraged, "No, you ignorant hillbilly! Not our goddamn scout, the white Apache – Did *he* say anything?"

"Yeah, yeah – he said he didn't want no war with anybody. He just wants the forty dollars the rancher owes him, and he will give the man his horse back."

There was a long pause before Kulbane, who was expecting more from Cameron, asked, "Anything else?"

"No – oh, wait. He said he didn't want no war, but if you did, he would kill everybody," replied Cameron.

"Those were his exact words?" asked Kulbane.

Cameron thought for a moment before replying. "No – no, you're right. He said many would die if we kept chasing him. Yeah, that's what he said."

Kulbane turned to Esparza and began shouting. His speech was directed at Esparza, but it was loud enough for everyone to hear, "We are going to catch this son-of-bitch, if it is the last thing we do! Do you hear me? I want him alive! Any man kills him before I do, will take his place and I'll skin him alive, inch by inch, instead!" He paused long enough to get his emotions under control and then asked Esparza directly, "Do we have any more trackers left who can find him?"

Esparza replied, "Not good ones, but do not worry, Senor General, we do not need to find him. I have a feeling he will find us."

CHAPTER TWENTY

It HAD BEEN an exceptionally cold night, and as the increasing daylight chased away the last remnants of darkness, one could see scattered patches of frost on the Yucca plants and other near-the-ground vegetation. Several blazing fires were scattered throughout the encampment with men crowded around, trying to get some warmth. The tension was as thick as the fog that swirled from the movement of the men as they went about their morning rituals. Kulbane hadn't issued any orders the previous day. It was near nightfall when Bigelow had returned and had given his report. Kulbane told everyone to get some rest, and he would 'settle' things in the morning.

It was the word '*settle*' that bothered Pat Wilkens. When he had to '*settle*' anything, it usually meant confrontation that sometimes escalated into fisticuffs or something worse. As Pat approached, Hollister was drinking a black liquid that was supposed to pass for coffee. "Damn cold morning," Hollister remarked, trying to make conversation.

"Seen worse," replied Pat. He spat and wiped his big mustache with the back of his sleeve before asking, "Colonel, what the hell's going on? Why are we here?"

Hollister paused before answering and said deliberately and slowly, "I don't know for sure, Pat, but if I had to guess, I would say the General has lost his mind. He thinks he's back in the war, and Jake Romero is the enemy. I believe we have been conscripted into his army."

Pat spat, wiped his mustache, and said, "Ah horseshit, I ain't joinin' no army and I ain't goin' up against Jake."

Hollister countered with, "Sit tight, Pat. Let's wait and see how this thing plays out. We should be cautious and wait for an opportunity." Although Pat didn't agree with Hollister's strategy, he did as the Colonel suggested out of respect for the man.

A short time later, Kulbane began to shout, asking everyone to gather together, so he could talk to them all at the same time. Once everyone was assembled, Kulbane cleared his throat and waited a moment until everything was quiet before he spoke. He explained to everyone how his objective had changed. He now wanted to go back to his burnt out headquarters in Mexico and rebuild it and Thornsbury and the rest of the ranchers, which included Hollister and his men, would be accompanying him and Esparza. Once at their destination, they would be put to work rebuilding the mansion and the ranch. No one dared protest or ask what would happen after the rebuilding was completed, except Thornsbury, who began to protest that he had his own ranch to run, and his business would be in ruins if he embarked on this journey.

All Kulbane said in response was, "No exceptions. Now, pack up and let's move out."

Hollister wondered about Kulbane's change in tactics. Was he giving up on catching Jake, or did he simply change his priorities? Hollister concluded Kulbane had lost all sense of reality and he had become very unpredictable in his thinking and consequently, in his actions. Maybe Kulbane believed Esparza when he said Jake would find them. Hollister thought it best not to antagonize the General in any way and he passed those thoughts onto Pat, Mex, and Jim.

Sinclair Thornsbury was not a man to be pushed around. His large ego made him feel he was any man's equal and superior in intellect to most. He felt he could enter any discussion and sway things around to his way of thinking. He was probably right if he was dealing with a sane man, but to Thornsbury's misfortune, Kulbane's mind was far from rational. Thornsbury stepped forward in Kulbane's direction and shouted, "The ranchers, me included, are not going another step further. We have businesses to run, and the work isn't going to get done while we are chasing around the countryside after some old Indian. He can keep the damn horse, for all I care."

"Private! You will not talk to a superior officer in that manner! That is insubordination and a punishable offence," screamed Kulbane.

Thornsbury met Kulbane's tirade with equal energy when he shouted back, "Are you insane? We are not soldiers in some delusional army of yours! And I, for one, have had enough of this nonsense!"

Patrick Dunnigan was a stubborn man who kept his feelings pent up inside until he exploded. He had reached his boiling point, as well. "I agree with Mr. Thornsbury. I've got a ranch to run, and the work is not going to get done with me traipsing around the countryside looking for God-knows-what," he said as he turned and started towards the horses, but he didn't get far. Kulbane ran up behind the angry rancher and clubbed him on the back of the head with a pistol butt, not hard enough to do any serious damage, but with enough force to daze Dunnigan and knock him off his feet.

Kulbane began shouting orders. "Corporal, this man gets ten hard ones, on the spot. We'll see if that doesn't change his attitude!"

Corporal Mathew Allen took charge. He ordered two men to hold Dunnigan upright and had them remove the rancher's suit coat, vest, and shirt. Then each man grabbed an arm and pulled in opposite directions. The Corporal instructed John Curtis (the sadist who had whipped Hollister to unconsciousness) to give Dunnigan ten lashes. Curtis delighted in inflicting pain on others, and he drove the whip as hard as he could on each stroke, smiling with maniacal delight as the hardened leather struck Dunnigan's flesh. Dunnigan screamed like a banshee with the first four strikes, and then he passed out and didn't even feel the rest.

Hollister watched with empathy, counting each stroke and when Curtis got to the twelfth stroke, he had seen enough. "General Kulbane, are you punishing the man or trying to kill him?" he asked.

Kulbane turned in Hollister's direction and asked in a level tone, "Another insubordinate? Would you like to join him?"

Hollister saw an opportunity to open a door to the possibility of earning Kulbane's trust. He played right into Kulbane's delusional world when he replied, "No sir! I am an officer and a gentleman, and I was simply pointing out to the General that the man wielding the whip does not know how to count. He has far exceeded your orders and is likely to kill the man."

Kulbane bit. He shouted at Curtis, "That will be all, soldier. Get that man dressed and in the saddle. We leave in five minutes!" He turned to Hollister and said, "Thank you for input, Colonel. You'll make a good second in command."

About an hour into the day's ride, Patrick Dunnigan regained consciousness. His attention was immediately directed to his stinging back. He descended into a state of self pity. He couldn't understand why he had been singled out for punishment. He hadn't done anything wrong. This Kulbane person was obviously overstepping his authority. What right did he have to give orders to a well respected rancher like himself? Dunnigan still hadn't recognized his error in judgment. He thought Kulbane was making rational decisions, an assumption Hollister did not make.

Dunnigan lifted his head and looked all around. On his right rode Sinclair Thornsbury and another rancher, John Ballard. One of Ballard's men was leading Dunnigan's horse. He looked to his left and there was Jake Romero riding Thornsbury's black stallion. Dunnigan shouted. "Mr. Thornsbury! It's Him!"

Thornsbury glanced in the direction Dunnigan had pointed, and much to his astonishment, there was Jake Romero. Jake smiled and said, "Nice horse you have here, Mr. Thornsbury, but to tell you the truth, I would rather have the forty dollars you owe me."

"Thornsbury began to shout, "It's him! It's him! Shoot him! Somebody shoot him!"

Ballard approached Thornsbury and asked. "What's wrong, Mr. Thornsbury? Shoot who?"

Thornsbury apprehensively turned his gaze back to his left, fully expecting to see a grinning Jake looking back at him. Instead, Morley Gruber, the man Thornsbury had made foreman when Pat quit, was next to him. He had a bewildered look on his face stemming from his concern as to why Thornsbury wanted someone to shoot him. Thornsbury began to apologize, "I'm sorry, Morley. I thought you were — uh — that is to say—" As he stuttered, Thornsbury looked back at Dunnigan on his right. *But it wasn't Dunnigan!*

Jake Romero was now sitting on Dunnigan's horse, still grinning. "Forty dollars, Mr. Ranchman. Forty dollars!" was all Jake said. Thornsbury closed his eyes and tried to convince himself that he was still unconscious and this was just all a bad dream. He waited a few seconds and opened his eyes and much to his relief, Patrick Dunnigan was back in the saddle. For the rest of the day, Thornsbury remained in a state of high anxiety, and on one occasion when he glanced back, there was Jake atop the stallion, grinning and waving to him. He closed his eyes, shook his head, and looked again. As he expected, Jake was gone, which was a good thing because if Jake had still been there, Thornsbury might have begun screaming again. He came to the conclusion that he was seeing things as a result of the stress he had been under the last couple of days.

One thing Thornsbury couldn't explain away, which he found very puzzling, was the pocket watch he had suddenly and miraculously acquired.

He had decided to check the time of day and reached for his pocket watch. He removed the time piece from his vest, opened it, and checked the time. He immediately noticed it was not his watch, but one entirely different from his; one he knew he had never seen before. As he turned the watch over, he noticed an inscription on the back which read: *'A man's heart deviseth his way: but the Lord directeth his steps — Uncle Samuel'.* Realization smacked Thornsbury like a glass of ice cold water in the face; the watch belonged to one of the Fletcher bunch.

Thornsbury fought to control his emotions. He knew another outburst might bring Kulbane's wrath down upon him. He calmly called out, "Hollister! Hollister! Might I speak with you for a moment?"

Hollister heard Thornsbury calling and brought his mount up alongside the rancher's. He could see Thornsbury was frightened. In fact, he seemed almost panic stricken. Hollister asked, "Mr. Thornsbury are you alright? What is it? How can I help?"

Thornsbury looked Hollister in the eyes and said, "Ben, I think I am going insane."

Hollister had always considered his neighbor a man of sound mind. He was as greedy as the day was long, stubborn as a rented mule, and he would stab you in the back at the first opportunity, if he thought there was any profit in it for him, but insane never entered Hollister's mind. "What seems to be the trouble, Mr. Thornsbury?" he asked.

Thornsbury looked up at Hollister with wide, tear filled, puppy eyes and said, "This is not my watch!"

Hollister was at a loss, trying to make any sense out of what Thornsbury had just said, but he played along and asked, "What do you mean, Mr. Thornsbury?"

Thornsbury seemed annoyed that Hollister didn't understand such a simple statement of fact, so he said again through clenched teeth, "I said, this is ***not*** my watch."

Hollister directed the conversation in the right direction by asking, "Whose watch is it?"

"Judging by the inscription on the back, I would say it belongs to one of Samuel Fletcher's henchmen. I believe his nephew was the proud owner of this watch," replied Thornsbury, as if he were answering a simple question a child had asked.

Hollister asked the next obvious question, "How did you come by the watch?"

"Ah, therein lays the mystery. Somehow my own watch has been replaced with this one," replied Thornsbury.

Hollister offered the only plausible explanation he could think of, "Sinclair, you have had dealings with Fletcher and his men. Perhaps, you both had your watches on the table and you picked the wrong one up?" Hollister looked to Thornsbury for a reaction, then another idea struck him and he continued, "Or most likely, Gus Haines is a thief, and he liked your watch better, or perhaps he thought it to be more valuable than his own, so he swapped them out."

Thornsbury didn't hesitated when he answered, "No! I know exactly how this happened. I sent Fletcher and his relatives out after that horse thief. He must have gotten the better of them, and now he has brought me a souvenir to let me know they have failed." He leaned forward in the saddle to get closer to Hollister and said, "I know, because he is here among these men. I have seen him several times."

Hollister considered the possibility of Jake sneaking into camp and swapping out the watches, and he was about to dismiss the idea, when Mex, who had been listening along with Pat and Jim, spoke up. "Senor Hollister, there are many stories told to me as a boy about powerful Lipan Apache Medicine Men. I believe our friend Jake is one such man."

"Powerful? What kind of power?" asked Hollister, genuinely inquisitive.

Mex thought carefully and then replied, "It is said they can come and go as they please and no one hears or sees them. It is said they are very good at — invisi — oh, how you say it in English?"

Pat had an idea of what Mex was trying to say, so he spoke up. "You mean invisible?"

"Si, invisible," Mex confirmed and then continued, "But the most amazing stories are the ones where they can get inside your thinking and make you see and hear things that are not so."

Hollister thought himself to be fairly open minded, and he was giving Mex's explanation some thought in spite of Pat's *'Ah, horseshit'* comment. He was about to offer his own thoughts on the subject when Esparza interrupted the soiree. He seemed tense and on edge when he questioned the group, wanting to know why they had stopped and what the discussion was about. Hollister speculated that Esparza had been ordered to see what the delay was and to get things moving. Hollister didn't believe Esparza was looking for any lengthy explanations, so he commented that Dunnigan wasn't doing too well, and they were just checking on him.

Esparza would have accepted the explanation and been on his way, but Thornsbury shouted at him, "He's going to kill me! I know it!"

Esparza moved his horse closer to Thornsbury and asked. "Who's going to kill you, Senor?

Thornsbury pointed to a man several feet to Esparza's left. The bandit leader turned his horse and crossed the short distance to the man Thornsbury had indicated. "Are you going to kill Senor Thornsbury?" Esparza asked the man?

About the only thing Harley Dunn had ever killed in his entire life was a coyote or two. He looked at Esparza with a bewildered look on his face before he said, "No, Sir!"

Esparza didn't like Thornsbury or what he represented, and he seized the opportunity to have some fun with the man. "Senor, this man claims he is not going to kill you. You cannot go about throwing out false accusations like that. I want you to apologize to this fine young man."

Thornsbury turned his gaze from Esparza to Dunn and apologized. One minute he was saying sorry to Harley Dunn and the next, Jake Romero was sitting on Harley's horse. He said to Thornsbury, "No harm done, Sir. Now, about the forty dollars."

It pushed Thornsbury over the edge. He spurred his horse hard and rode off, nearly knocking Esparza over. He was screaming "Leave me alone!" over and over as he galloped away.

Kulbane saw Thornsbury and assumed he was trying to escape. He spurred his horse hard and caught Thornsbury before he got very far. As he got close to the rancher, he drew his pistol and brought the barrel down across Thornsbury's ear, knocking him from his horse. Kulbane reined up, dismounted, and began pistol whipping Thornsbury about the head and shoulders. Ben Hollister let his anger get the better of him. He rode up to Kulbane and stated, "You murdering bastard! What the hell are you doing? Are you trying to kill him?"

Kulbane looked at Hollister for the longest time before he answered, "Colonel, while I may seek your counsel in matters of strategic warfare, I do not need you to question my actions when it comes to matters of discipline. This man was trying to desert, and he is being punished like all deserters should be." He paused momentarily and then asked, "Anything else on your mind, Colonel?"

CHAPTER TWENTY ONE

CONVERSATIONS AROUND THE night fires were sparse. No one, from either Esparza's band or Kulbane's group, had anything much to talk about, primarily because the strange events of the day occupied the thoughts of most the men. The severe beating of Thornsbury didn't surprise most of them. It was something they had seen several times during the time spent with Kulbane. What bothered them more than anything was Thornsbury's strange behavior just before he had bolted.

The ranchers and their men were certainly not going to say anything for fear of some sort of reprisal, but Pat, Mex, and Jim gathered in a tight group around Hollister, asking all sorts of questions. Hollister explained he did not know any more than they did, after which the conversation died out.

Several hours later, most men in the encampment were sound asleep, positioned around several dying fires for what little warmth they still offered. Ben Hollister was still wide awake. He had nodded off a few times only to open his eyes and look around his immediate area before his eye lids slowly slid shut again, and he dozed for a few seconds only to open his eyes and repeat the entire process over again. His eyelids had just closed for the third time when he felt a sharp pain under his chin. Hollister opened his eyes and there was a squatting Jake Romero with the point of a large knife pressed against his throat, and Jake was applying just enough pressure to let Hollister know it was there but not enough to penetrate the skin.

Hollister tried to sit up, but Jake's left hand on his chest suggested he stay down. Hollister lifted his head and supported his weight on his elbows. He spoke very softly when he asked, "What do want, Jake?"

Jake seemed surprised by Hollister's indifferent tone. "Why do you ride with these men?" he asked.

"Some of us don't have a choice. We can't leave."

"Who is stopping you?"

"Well Jake, if you have been watching us, you must have seen what happened to Thornsbury when he tried to leave."

"Yes, that was not a good thing," commented Jake.

"Oh, now that surprises me; you having sympathy for Thornsbury," said Hollister with a hint of sarcasm.

Jake, ignoring the comment, removed his knife from under Hollister's chin and sat down next to him. "I do not want the man to die. That was his doing. All I want is what he owes me." Jake paused momentarily and then added as an afterthought, "I no longer have need of the big stallion. I give him to you as a gift. You can give it to the Crazy Man, and he will let you and your people leave"

Hollister realized that for all of Jake's survival skills, he was very naïve about the ways of men. Hollister felt like declining the offer, but instead said, "The horse is not yours to give away."

Jake smiled and said, "Then I will sell him to you — for forty dollars!"

Sandy Russell was having trouble sleeping. He hated the goddamn desert at night. In fact, come to think of, he hated the goddamn desert in the daytime, too. He hated shivering at night and baking in the daylight. He had been breaking broncos on ranches from east Texas to southern California for over twenty years and sleeping on the ground constantly aggravated every swollen joint and reminded him of every broken bone he'd ever had. He had decided to go for a little stroll before trying to bed down. His walk took him in the direction of the Hollister campfire. As he got closer, he saw Hollister, who was facing him, and another silhouette of a man with his back to him. In the flickering campfire light, the shadowy figure looked like an Apache. Sandy's first thought was that one of the scouts had returned, but as soon as the man turned to look in his direction, Sandy could see his face, and he knew he didn't recognize the man. Then the thought crashed into his brain as to who this might be. His first instinct was to holler as loud as he could. "It's him! It's him! The Apache is here!"

Jake turned back to face Hollister and said, "We shall talk later, Colonel. I will free you from the Crazy Man." Then he was up like a flash, and before Sandy could utter another word, Jake was gone into the night.

Sandy's shouting brought Mex, Pat, and Jim to their feet. Pat saw a glimpse of Jake as he disappeared into the darkness, and ignoring Sandy's shouts, he asked Hollister if it was Jake he had just seen. Before Hollister could answer, Sandy began shouting again, which brought everyone within earshot running to Hollister's position.

Kulbane, who seldom slept any more, was once of the first to arrive, demanding to know what all the commotion was about. Sandy, in a calmer voice, explained how he had just seen Jake. "And what was he doing?" asked Kulbane.

"He was talking to Colonel Hollister."

"I don't know you. Who are you?" asked Kulbane.

"Name's Sandy Russell. I work for Mr. Ballard."

Kulbane didn't know who this Ballard fellow was, but he assumed it was one of the ranchers. He turned his attention to Hollister, who by this time was on his feet. "Well Colonel, explain yourself," Kulbane said.

"There is nothing to explain, General. The man came to see me in the middle of the night, and when he was discovered he ran off."

Kulbane waited for more and when there was no more information forthcoming, he asked, "What did he want?"

"He came to sell me a horse."

Kulbane was not amused. He thought Hollister was mocking him. He stated, "If you don't want to be the next one to feel the sting of the whip, the next words out of your mouth had better be a straight answer."

"I gave you a straight answer. Jake stole Thornsbury's stallion because Thornsbury owed him forty dollars. He was holding the horse, thinking Thornsbury would buy him back for forty dollars. Since then, it appears Jake has changed his mind, and he doesn't care where he gets his money. He was trying to sell me the horse when the wrangler spotted him and started hollering."

Kulbane was enraged and he shouted, "This sounds like pure poppycock to me! I think you are conspiring with the enemy! I think you are a traitor! Twenty five lashes for this man!"

Mex stepped forward to protest. Kulbane immediately saw the movement and confronted him. He didn't say anything to Mex. Instead, he directed his tirade at Esparza. Kulbane had made the assumption Mex was one of Esparza's men, when he said, "Esparza, you keep your men away from my business, or they will feel the whip as well!"

Esparza listened half heartedly to Kulbane's tirade as the General went on about discipline and men knowing their place and how he was going to whip them all into shape. The bandit leader was intelligent enough to see the psychological change in Kulbane, and how he was losing touch with reality as he slid deeper into his delusional fantasy that he was a General still fighting the Civil War. Esparza's relationship with Kulbane had once been of benefit to both men. Kulbane had his make-believe army and Esparza had a home base from which to run his criminal enterprises. Esparza tolerated Kulbane playing soldier. In fact, at times, he found it humorous and a source of amusement around the night fire as he and his men passed around a bottle of mescal and laughed at the General's latest escapade.

Now that it had stopped being entertaining, Esparza decided it was time to cut his losses and sever ties with Kulbane. He too had mistaken Mex for one of his own men and came to his defense when he said, "My men follow my orders. If you have a problem with one of my men, you will speak to me, and I will deal with it as I see fit, not you, Senor General."

Mex was about to speak up. He had it in mind to tell them both that he was his own man and that he didn't answer to either one of them. Pat discreetly grabbed him by the shirt sleeve and when Mex looked in his direction, Pat shook his head slightly to indicate that he shouldn't say anything, and when he made eye contact with Hollister, Mex saw the same expression on the Colonel's face.

Kulbane addressed Esparza as if he were talking to a recruit. He went on about how a well trained army had to have a chain of command and there could not be two top commanders. One man and one man alone had to have the final say in any matter. He concluded by saying that if Esparza didn't like it, he would be demoted and replaced by someone of the General's choosing.

This was the first time Esparza thought the self-proclaimed General would be a threat. He had always treated Kulbane and his pipe dreams as a bit of a joke, but he played along as long as there was some benefit for himself and his men in doing so. "*Sacar sus armas y disparar el primero de ellos, que va para un arma de fuego!*" he shouted, and in a split second every one of his men within earshot had their weapon cocked and trained on Kulbane and his men.

Kulbane was incensed. "You ordered your men to draw on me? What is the meaning of this?" demanded Kulbane.

Esparza said, "It means we are finished, Senor General. No more business for you and me, eh?" He paused briefly and then hollered, "Mount up amigos.

We leave this place!" As Esparza hurried away, he looked back to see Mex still with Kulbane. He wasn't sure what to make of it, but at the moment, he didn't have time to deal with what he thought was a traitor. Ten minutes later, Esparza and his men were gone with only the distant sound of some whooping and hollering from some of the men who'd had too much to drink before being ordered to leave.

"What now?" asked Hollister in all sincerity.

Kulbane had forgotten he was about to punish Hollister. He treated Hollister with equal respect when he answered the Colonel's question with another question, "What do you think the scoundrel will do?"

Hollister thought for a moment and then replied, "If I were him, I would regroup and hit us hard before dawn."

"Why would he do that, Colonel?"

"Because he fears you and his thinking is to get you before you can get him. Besides, you made him lose face in front of his men, and he has something to prove," theorized Hollister.

Kulbane thought for a moment and then concluded, "Then we have to be ready for them. We have to find a place we can use as a good defensive position."

Pat Wilkens, who had been listening to the conversation, interjected and suggested that Mex knew the country pretty well and might offer some insight. All eyes turned to Mex, who seemed surprised Pat had put him on the spot. "Well, you see," he stammered, stalling for time, "you are right. We do not want to be caught out in the open. A half day's ride to the southwest will take us to the mountains. There are many canyons and many good places to use for cover."

Kulbane, still thinking Mex was one of Esparza's men, said to Hollister, "And why should we trust this man?"

Hollister realized what Kulbane was alluding to and he answered pleasantly, "No, General, Mex is not one of Esparza's men. He is with me! Esparza assumed he was one of his men, and we let him think so."

Kulbane thought for a moment longer and then said, "To the mountains then! We ride in ten minutes."

There was almost a full moon in the cloudless sky. Kulbane's troop of twenty men, which included himself, Hollister, Pat, Mex, and Jim Clemfeld, made their way towards the mountains, following an easy, ancient trail that ran its course through a dried up river bed. The unarmed ranchers along with the dozen hands, who had come with them, rode behind the main body.

Hollister and Kulbane estimated they would reach the mountains a couple of hours after daybreak, plenty of time to elude Esparza, without having to ride their horses into the ground. As they rode, Hollister steered his mount next to Mex's and asked, "Antonio, once we reach the mountains, do you know of a good place to defend against Esparza?"

"You can call me Mex, Senor, just like everybody else. I am fairly certain we will reach the mountains at a place called the Valley of the Hawk. There would be a good place to set a trap for Senor Esparza."

When it appeared Mex wasn't going to say anything more, Hollister prodded him for more information. Mex responded by telling him about the old legend associated with the valley. According to stories passed from generation to generation, there were an ancient people living in the area. Some say they were the forefathers of the Apache, some say they were the original people, while others didn't care because the story was more important. These people were connected to Mother Earth, and they were the guardians of all living things.

One night the village Shaman had a vision. In it, men with metal heads and metal bodies would come and kill the people with sticks that roared like thunder and shot flame out of one end. He also dreamt that he was to lead his people up a certain valley and a hawk would be their guide. The next day the Shaman gathered his people and told them of his dream. As they collected their belongings, they looked up in the sky and there were several hawks soaring above them. With the hawks leading the way, they traveled up the valley to escape the conquering Spaniards.

Although the valley reached a dead end, not unlike a box canyon, there were hidden trails, leading through the boulders and shale to climbable chimneys that led to the top of the ridges on either side of the canyon. The people, having been shown the way by the hawks, made their escape and the Spaniards were dumbfounded. It was as if they had vanished into thin air!

It was not a totally happy ending, however. It seems three men of the village had been out hunting and hadn't left with the others. The hawks said they would return to the village and guide the men. Although the hawks searched everywhere and waited several days, the three hunters were not found. One of the hawks made a huge sacrifice. He asked the Great Spirit to turn him into a beacon for the men to see. To this day, as one begins the journey up the valley, the first landmark one sees is a mountain top that looks exactly like the head of a hawk.

Hollister thought about the story for a moment, and then he realized that, legend or not, they could use the same tactics to outsmart Esparza and his bandits. Hollister approached Kulbane and laid out his plan to scatter their forces among the rocks and boulders of the box canyon. They would let Esparza and his men enter the canyon before opening fire. Using the element of surprise, he thought he could kill or injury a lot of Esparza's gang, thus lessening the odds. They would continue sporadic fire and when it looked like they would be overrun, they would use the escape routes and come out on top of the canyon, leaving Esparza and his men trapped in the canyon below like sitting ducks. Hollister added that once they were on top of the canyon, some of the men should be quickly deployed back to the entrance of the canyon to close the back door and prevent Esparza from escaping.

Kulbane was impressed by Hollister's tactical skills. He remarked how he had chosen the right man to be his second in command. Hollister asked if he could recommend one more thing to the General and was given permission to speak. Hollister suggested they turn loose any of the ranchers and their hands who didn't want to stay. He explained that there were not enough weapons for them all, but most importantly, they would just be in the way, and if they had to be guarded, it would detract from the focus needed to fight Esparza. Hollister paused to let Kulbane think about his proposal. He could see the General was having a hard time with the decision, so Hollister added that after they took care of Esparza, they could always go back and conscript the ranchers and their men.

Kulbane didn't say anything for the longest time. He looked Hollister in the eyes as if he thought he could find the right answer there, and then he agreed it would be the right thing to do, for the time being.

CHAPTER TWENTY TWO

THE BANDIT GANG rode hard for a short time and had covered about a mile when Esparza called a sudden halt. The men nearest Esparza moved in closer to their leader to hear what he had to say. "Enrique Esparza runs from no man!" he announced with conviction. Pausing briefly, in a softer tone, he added, "We will rest here for a few hours, and at first light we will go and finish this business with that loco General."

Fredrico Benito Jamirez was very weary. It seemed he was tired most of the time, lately. Esparza was riding them hard, and they never had time to rest or to drink a little mescal, but most importantly, they weren't getting any sleep. Freddy, as his compadres called him, picked out a nice spot under a Joshua tree where the windblown sand had collected. It provided a nice soft bed to lie on and a few two-handed scoops of loose sand piled where he wanted his head to be, served as a pillow. Freddy took off his sombrero, laying it on the ground within easy reach, and removing his serape, he covered the pillow mound with it. He was deep asleep a few seconds after he closed his eyes, so a short time later he never felt someone gently lift his head just enough to remove the serape and that same someone remove the pistol from his sash.

Cass Tingley was agitated as he sat on a small boulder and rolled a smoke. He was not happy to be here. When the opportunity to quit Esparza and stick with Kulbane had presented itself, Cass had backed down. He didn't want to deal with Esparza's rage, if something had gone wrong. His guilt caused him angst. He felt Esparza knew what he had been thinking and at any moment was going to confront him with it. As he smoked, he glanced in all directions, and that's when he noticed Freddy Jamirez heading towards a small knoll, a short distance away from the main body of men. Cass waved to his friend, but Freddy didn't return the gesture. Cass watched intently as Freddy sat down. With his arms wrapped around his knees and his head down, it appeared Freddy was going to grab some shut eye. Cass thought this was odd, as Freddy usually found a spot away from the camp to sleep, and he usually stretched out on the ground. Cass chided himself for acting so paranoid and went about the business of finishing his cigarette.

When the man mistaken for Freddy was sure the smoking Cass was no longer paying any attention to him, he rose slowly, took the time to stretch, and made his way to a large group of men who couldn't or wouldn't sleep and had gathered around a fire they had built for warmth. He kept his head down and stood just on the outside of the group, listening to the many conversations. It was all small talk about the men's desires for a break where they could spend a few days in some village cantina with a few beautiful girls and lots of mescal.

Jake walked around the outside of the group listening and observing. Juan Jesus Casta was admiring a nickel plated .44 pistol he had secretly taken from one of the ranchers when Esparza had given the order to disarm them. Juan caressed the weapon and then tucked it into his waistband. He didn't think anything of it when one of the other men bumped into him. Neither did Hector Hierra, when the same man bumped into him a few minutes later. Hector thought the man was either drunk or half asleep. It wasn't like the man couldn't see him standing there.

A few seconds passed and Hector felt some pressure against his abdomen. Looking down, he was surprised to see a nickel plated pistol sticking out of his waistband. He gingerly took it out with both hands and slowly looked around as if searching for some answer as to how the pistol might have gotten there. At almost the same moment, Juan got an urge to check his new weapon again. His eyes went wide when he realized the pistol was gone. His sense of wonder changed to rage when he saw Hector Hierra with his prized possession.

Juan charged Hector, knocking him to the ground. Sitting on top of Hector, Juan snatched the pistol out of his hand, tucked it into his own waistband, and then be began pummeling the bewildered Hector with both fists, cursing the man and shouting "Ladron! Ladron!"

Esparza interrupted the beating by grabbing Juan by the shirt collar and pulling him off the beleaguered Hector, who began shouting he was not a thief, and he did not know where the gun had come from.

While Esparza and most of his men were focused on the altercation, the man who looked like Freddy, made his way to where the horses were tethered. The lone sentry did not hear a sound as a shadowy figure came up behind him, grabbed him around the neck with one arm, and tapped him twice on the temple with the handle of his large knife. Once all the horses were loosened from the line, the man took a snake rattle from a medicine bag and began shaking it in rhythm. To the horses it sounded exactly like a rattle snake, and they bolted in fear and panic, taking the path of least resistance, which happen to be right through the open area where most of the bandits were gathered. Chaos ensued. Men scattered in all directions, some running, others diving behind convenient bushes or logs, and a few climbing atop boulders. Esparza stood his ground, and drawing his pistol, he shot the lead horse between the eyes. As the animal went down, Esparza holstered his pistol and dove behind the carcass for cover just as half a dozen other panicked horses jumped over their dead companion. It would take the better part of four hours to round up all the spooked mounts.

Just as the morning sunlight brought the promise of a new day, Kulbane, Hollister, and company entered the Valley of the Hawk. An uneasy feeling came over Pat; not a feeling of impending doom or misfortune, but an unexplained sense of mystery. He felt as though they were trespassing, as if there were those about who didn't want them in the valley. As his horse plodded along, its hooves making clicking sounds as they bounced off of fist size rocks that had rolled down the moraine and unto the canyon floor, Pat felt somewhat claustrophobic, as if the canyon walls were closing in on them. He kept glancing from side to side and would occasionally turn in the saddle and look at their back trail. Mex noticed Pat's nervousness, and approaching his friend, he asked, "Everything okay, amigo?"

Pat shot Mex a quick glance and the look on Pat's face indicated he might have been deep in thought and had been rudely interrupted. He cleared his throat, and after one last look around, he glanced back at Mex and said, "I don't know, pard, this place gives me the willies. I don't have a good feelin' 'bout this."

"Not to worry, my friend. As I have said to the General, we can climb out at the other end of the canyon and get behind Esparza," replied Mex, trying hard to be reassuring.

Pat seemed more at ease and smiled back at Mex. "Okay pard, if you say so," Pat said as he spat a big brown gob and then added, "I hope we get somewheres soon. I'm just 'bout outta chewin' tobacco."

Sinclair Thornsbury was not faring well. He had a slight concussion and four fairly deep scalp lacerations still oozing blood. No one had bothered to pick up the man's hat, so here he was, barely conscious, riding in the hot desert sun with no head cover and the deer flies constantly seeking a meal from his wounds. The flies would gather and Thornsbury would wave his arm half-heartedly, which caused the flies to vacate only to return a few seconds later. Patrick Dunnigan wasn't doing any better than his portly friend, Thornsbury. He was in his early sixties, and the lashing had taken his aged body to the brink of death. One of his men rode beside Dunnigan and kept talking to him, encouraging his boss to stay awake. He would stop every so often and make sure Dunnigan took water.

A short time later, traveling at a very slow pace, the troop came to a dead end. It appeared to the naked eye that the canyon had closed in on itself, and there was no way out but return the way they had come in. Kulbane called a halt and hollered for Mex to come front and center. As soon as Mex arrived, Kulbane said in rather sarcastic tone, "Well, here we are soldier! As you can see by the terrain around us, we have nowhere to go! I am beginning to think you have led us into a trap, and we are caught like hens in a chicken cage."

Hollister saw where Kulbane was headed, and he intervened when he said, "May I remind the General that Mex is not one of Esparza's Men? He rides with me, so why would he lead us into a trap? I suggest, if it pleases the General, we let Mex explain."

Kulbane's silence convinced Mex the General had accepted Hollister's explanation, so he responded, "Si! If you two gentlemen would dismount and follow me, por favor?" Mex dismounted, followed by Hollister, Pat, and Jim. Kulbane waited briefly, as if deciding whether or not to trust these men. He glanced around the canyon walls once and then slowly lowered himself from the saddle and onto the ground. He glanced back at the rest of his men and the ranchers and ordered them to dismount, but to stay put, then he gestured to Mex to lead the way.

Just before the end of the canyon there were two protrusions of sandstone that jutted out perpendicular to the canyon walls. Thirty yards beyond them another wall of rock formed the back end of the canyon. The jutting two walls combined with the back wall created an alcove, a natural corral, so to speak. The only thing missing was a gate. Mex walked swiftly until he was in the middle of the alcove, where he stopped, turned and waited for everybody else to catch up.

As the four men drew closer to Mex, he turned and disappeared behind a huge pile of loose rock and boulders that had accumulated over thousands of years from wind and rain erosion. Kulbane quickened his pace and followed Mex behind the mound. Not expecting to see anything except a wall of sandstone and shale, Kulbane was quite surprised when Mex pointed to his right and he saw a crevice in the canyon wall. Millions of years ago, the crevice had run all the way down to the canyon floor, but centuries of flash floods, frost heaves, and scorching summer suns had slowly filled the gap with a loose moraine of fine sand and broken shale. Kulbane, after careful inspection, concluded someone on foot could climb up the inclined spill-way and reach the top of the canyon, quite easily. He doubted if their horses, mounted or not, could make the climb.

Hollister had seen the terrain a split second after Kulbane, and he had already formulated a plan of action in his head. He conveyed his idea to Kulbane, when he said, "This is perfect! Esparza will follow us into the canyon. We will climb out and circle behind him, leaving a few men at the top there to stop them from escaping up this gap. We will have both ends covered and he will be trapped in the canyon."

Hollister expected Kulbane to give his plan the full stamp of approval. He even thought the self-proclaimed General would show some enthusiasm for the strategy. Instead, Kulbane thought for a long moment and then said, "Yes Colonel, it is a good idea, as far as you have taken it. However, I cannot, in good conscience, trust these ranchers and the men who work for them, but we can use them to our advantage. We shall leave them here, at the mouth of the alcove to engage Esparza while the rest of us make our way out of the canyon and put your strategy into effect."

Hollister protested vehemently, "That's like a death sentence to those men. Esparza and his bandits will cut them to pieces!"

"Ah, such are the sacrifices of war, Colonel," said Kulbane, then he added, rather condescendingly, "Good men sometimes die for the good of a cause."

If he had been armed, Hollister would have surely drawn his weapon and shot Kulbane right between the eyes. Kulbane began issuing orders, telling his men to dole out weapons to the ranchers and their hands, but to keep them covered in case they decided to try something foolish. He positioned one of the ranch bosses, DeLarosa, behind a large boulder just in front of the entrance to the alcove. He stationed John Ballard in a similar position on the other side of the canyon. There were about a dozen hands who Kulbane instructed to take up any cover they could find in front of the Alcove.

Sinclair Thornsbury stumbled as he climbed down from his horse, ending up on his backside. While he was on the ground, he spied a large boulder that Morley Gruber was using for cover. Thornsbury called to Morley for some help, but Morley ignored him. As far as Morley was concerned, it was every man for himself. Patrick Dunnigan was barley conscious, so he ignored Kulbane's command. Hollister, seeing the man was in jeopardy, dismounted and assisted the severely injured rancher down from his mount. He helped Dunnigan to the nearest cover, a Joshua tree near the boulder where Thornsbury and Morley Gruber were hiding. Hollister laid Dunnigan behind the vegetation, so he could not be seen. He covered the man's lower legs with sand, and after making him comfortable, he tried to convince Dunnigan that if he kept perfectly still and very quiet, he would not be seen or heard, and he just might survive.

As Hollister walked back to his mount, passing Thornsbury's position, he noticed the rancher hadn't picked up a weapon when he had headed for cover. Hollister remarked that he should arm himself, but Thornsbury gave him a woeful look and then hung his head in his lap. "Suit yourself," said Hollister as he continued on to his horse, where he climbed into the saddle and looking straight at Kulbane he remarked, "Thornsbury and Dunnigan are both unarmed, and they won't stand a chance! You know that! You can't put them in that position."

Kulbane sat motionless while he stared at Hollister for a moment before answering. "I know exactly what I am doing, Colonel!" he stated emphatically. "Now, stop questioning my orders, or you could find yourself cannon fodder, as well." He paused briefly and then added, "You and your three cohorts best get to the top of the canyon, before I lose my good mood."

A few minutes later, everyone was in place, waiting for Esparza and his bandits to arrive. Kulbane had supervised while DeLarosa and Ballard positioned their ranch hands behind what sparse cover there was. Satisfied, Kulbane ordered a couple of his men to bring the horses into the alcove and hobble them, or tie them to big rocks or strong bushes. Since Thornsbury and Dunnigan were both incapacitated, Ballard took it upon himself to organize their men. Morley Gruber was huddled down in the fetal position behind a large boulder, whimpering like a scolded puppy and was not going to be any help. As soon as the crazy General and his men disappeared from sight into the alcove, Connor Muldoon, Sandy Russell, and four other men took off running back up the canyon the way they had come. Ballard raised his pistol and took aim, but he could not pull the trigger. Looking back, he could see the fear in Joseph DeLarosa's eyes. Ballard lowered his weapon, let out a deep breath, and said to DeLarosa, "Go on, get out of here and take the rest of these men with you!"

As soon as the five remaining cowpunchers heard Ballard, they got up and sprinted up the canyon. Before DeLarosa left, he asked, "Are you not coming with us, Senor?"

Ballard replied, "No, my friend, I will stay and look after Mr. Thornsbury and Mr. Dunnigan." DeLarosa took off running while Ballard prodded Morley Gruber, urging him to leave, but Morley had crawled deep inside his fear and didn't understand or even care what this man wanted from him.

With all the horses safely secured in the alcove out of sight from anyone who was in the canyon, Kulbane, most of his men, Hollister and his three amigos, quickly made their way up the moraine filled gap to the top of the gorge. Kulbane directed Hollister, Pat Wilkens, Mex, and Jim to a sheltered area a few yards back of the canyon rim. He assigned Chatter Tolliver to guard them, giving the man strict instructions that if any of them tried anything, to shoot them without hesitation. Upon hearing the order, Tolliver grinned from ear to ear and gave Hollister a look which seemed to indicate that Tolliver was hoping they would try something.

Kulbane assigned five men, which included John Curtis, Mathew Allen, Norbert Bigelow, Harley Dunn, and Stanley Hawkins to cover the gap they all had recently climbed up. The gap was very narrow and if Esparza's men tried to climb out, they would have to do it in single file, easy pickings for a few men at the top of the gap. The remaining dozen men, he split into two groups and ordered them to run as fast as they could along the canyon rims, back to the entrance. Kulbane instructed his men not to fire too soon. The plan was to let Esparza and his gang enter the canyon and to move forward. Once the ranch hands opened fire, Kulbane's men would follow suit by firing on Esparza from the rear. They would have the bandits in a crossfire, and the battle would not last very long.

Kulbane stood on the canyon rim, one foot on the very edge. He felt contented, for this was the first time since the war that he felt the adrenalin rush, the anticipation of an upcoming battle. "Yes," he said to no one in particular, "this is, indeed, a glorious day."

CHAPTER TWENTY THREE

GENERAL GEORGE KULBANE had one outstanding fault; his constant penchant for underestimating his opposition, whether it was in the form of a card game with a friend or an arch enemy on the battle field. He was especially ignorant when it came to assessing the intelligence level of those he commanded. His belief was that the smartest man was always the one in charge, so it never occurred to him that the low-life, Mexican bandit would be able to figure out that he was riding into a trap.

Kulbane was forced, out of necessity, to do business with Enrique Esparza, and the bandit leader, in his symbiotic relationship with Kulbane, let the self-proclaimed commander have his ground. He had never shown any disrespect for the General's orders and did whatever Kulbane asked when there was something in it for him and his men, and for the most part the raids and robberies, which Esparza and his cohorts carried out, satisfied their mutual needs. Kulbane's half of the profits went directly into his coffers towards his dream of financing a new army to continue the Civil War, and Esparza and his men spent their share on tequila, women, and cards, which they could do at Kulbane's rancho without fear of any type of law enforcement disturbing them. Kulbane supplied the liquor and the women, and he usually got most of the money back from the banditos, who, unwittingly, were doing all the dirty work for him. In short, he had the best of both worlds. Kulbane thought he had outsmarted Esparza, but the bandit leader knew what Kulbane was up to. He didn't seem to care as long as there was more money to be made.

Late afternoon found Esparza a hundred yards from the entrance to the dead-end canyon where he had ordered everyone to stop. He didn't know why; he just had an uneasy feeling. Using his right hand pressed down on the saddle horn for leverage, he raised his body up and turned as far as he could, first in one direction and then the other, all the while scanning both sides of the canyon. Cass Tingley, taking advantage of the stop, approached Esparza and explained to him that he knew this area well, having done some prospecting in the vicinity a few years ago. Tingley went on to describe the canyon, the alcove, and the climbable chute at the far end.

Esparza gathered the men together and when they were all within earshot, he explained their situation. He described how General Kulbane's trap was supposed to work and concluded by saying since it was late in the afternoon they would make camp for the night and in the morning they would determine if the General was still waiting, or if he had given up and departed across the mesa towards Mexico and home.

If anyone had paid any attention to Juan Jesus Casta as he meandered about the camp, not stopping to talk to anyone, but momentarily pausing near groups of men to listen to the conversations, they would have noticed that although Juan was wearing his oversized sombrero and the sheepskin vest he always wore to keep warm in the cold desert nights, the man was not Juan. If they had looked a little closer and seen the knee-high rawhide moccasins, they would certainly have detained the man and asked him what he had done with Juan. They would have found out that a short distance on the back trail the man wearing Juan's attire had tapped poor Juan a couple of times in the temple with the butt end of a knife handle and had left him unconscious and nearly naked, laying out in the desert. Not far from Juan, staked to a small tree were two horses; a mustang pony and a big black stallion. Leaning against the tree was a Sharp's .50 with a leather pouch full of ammunition on the ground next to the rifle.

For the first few hours after sunset, events unfolded as they usually did when the gang stopped somewhere for the night. The bandits broke up into four smaller units. In each group there were a couple of men who started a night fire, cooked a meal, cleaned up afterward and generally saw to the needs of the others. After the meal, goatskin wine flasks was passed around, although they seldom contained wine, but rather some rotgut whiskey or more than likely, some home-brewed tequila. Most of the men got a lot drunker and a whole lot louder, and on this particular night strange things began to happen.

An entourage of rattle snakes, scorpions, and tarantulas suddenly appeared and just as suddenly disappeared. Punch Hamner was exceedingly inebriated and was waltzing with some imaginary senorita, when a huge rattlesnake reared up. It stood as tall as Punch and it had these short little arms that beckoned to Punch to come closer so they could slow-dance. Punch stared at the snake, closed his eyes, and shook his head and when he opened his eyes again, the snake was gone, but there were hundreds of scorpions covering his boots. Punch changed from a waltz to a rather lively Irish jig. To Punch's eyes there were scorpions flying in every direction as he kicked one foot and then the other in the air. To everyone else, Punch was a drunk, dancing fool.

Hector Hierra didn't drink, not because he felt any religious or moral obligation to abstain, but rather because he just didn't like the taste of alcohol. Imagine his surprise when he tried to sit on a large rock to eat his plate of beans and tortillas and saw a Gila monster suddenly appear on the boulder. Hector stood and stared in wonderment at the sudden appearance of the creature, but he threw his plate to the ground, turned, and ran when the monster said, "Buenas noches, Senor."

Several fist fights and one knife fight broke out. It seemed two men were making small talk while eating some supper. One of the men casually brushed some crumbs from his shirt in the direction of the other man, who didn't see crumbs but wriggling, squirmy, smelly maggots. He took offence and pulled his knife and slashed the first man across the cheek and the fight was on. The fist fights started in a similar manner. As one man removed his sombrero, a small lizard sitting on his head leapt at another man close by who removed the reptile from his shirt and threw it at the first man and fisticuffs ensued.

Five men were standing in a circle, trying to calm one distraught individual, Stephan Alberto Baca. Stephan was not the most pleasant looking man. He was a very large man, extremely overweight, caused by his love of food. The man was constantly eating. While the rest of the bandits spent their money on liquor and women, Stephan could be found at the nearest eating establishment. A childhood bout with acne had left his face covered in divots which were filled with his oily sweat mixed with the dust of the desert. Stephan seldom washed any part of his body, let alone his face. His clothes were as filthy as the rest of him. Stephan usually ate with his hands and all the grease and other juices found their way to his shirt front, which he used for a hand towel. When asleep at night all the night creatures would be drawn to him because of the odor of rotting food. Many times he was awakened by a coyote, licking his face or shirt.

Not only his appearance, but his odor caused everyone to avoid him. Consequently, he was given tasks that took him far from camp and contact with others, such as gathering wood for the night fires, or keeping watch over the horses. Tonight it was guarding the mounts. Shortly after watching Punch finish his dancing, Stephan thought he heard voices coming from near the horses. He moved closer and after careful inspection on all sides of the long line of tethered mounts, Stephan saw nothing out of the ordinary. Thinking it was his imagination, he turned his back on the horses and headed for the spot he'd found to spend the night. Then he heard someone say, "Whew, man needs a bath."

Stephan turned sharply, fully expecting someone to be right behind him when he said, "You want to say that to my face?" He scanned the entire area and seeing nothing, he called out, "Who's there? Show yourself or I'll start shooting."

A mangy, scrawny looking pinto, second horse in line from the end nearest Stephan, turned its head in Stephan's direction and looked him squarely in the eyes. To this day, Stephan will swear on a stack of Bibles the horse spoke to him and said, "Yeah you, fat man, we are talking about you!"

Stephan pulled his pistol and taking careful aim, shot the horse right between the eyes. As the pinto was going down, Stephan shot it a couple more times, just for spite. Pandemonium ensued: all the horses panicked at once and began snorting and rearing, trying to pull themselves free from the picket line, while a dozen men came running and shouting with guns drawn expecting to do battle. Once they had the horses calmed and quiet, they asked Stephan why he'd shot the pinto. Stephan, thinking quickly, made up some story that he'd seen a man atop the horse and was trying to shoot him but missed and killed the horse instead. Not many of the men believed Stephan's claim, but because of the scowl on his face, no one challenged him on it.

Esparza thought he knew the cause of all the mayhem in his camp. He took out his pistol and fired a couple of rounds into the air. This action still didn't get everyone's attention, so he fired a couple of more shots and shouted at the top of his lungs. Everything went deathly quiet and all eyes were on the bandit leader. Esparza stood silent for a moment, scanning the group gathered before him, back and forth from side to the other, as if he were looking for someone in particular.

He took a deep breath and after sighing he shouted, "Senor Apache, whatever your name is, I know you are among these men somewhere. You think you can fool us with your magic? You think you can make us see things that are not there? What did you do, put some peyote in the chili?" Esparza waited for a response and he didn't have to wait long as a small rattler flew through the air from the back of the crowd and landed at Esparza's feet. The bandit leader kicked at the snake and it vanished into thin air.

The second snake landed on Esparza's shoulder. Again, he casually brushed it off. Esparza's eyes went wide when he realized the snake was real. His second swipe at the reptile wasn't quick enough and the rattler sank its fangs deep into his right hand. Esparza pulled the snake free with his left hand and flung it into the crowd. The men spread out like a drop of oil on water, and the snake landed harmlessly in the sand and crawled away to the nearest cover.

Punch Hamner with knife drawn, and a crazed look in his eyes, approached Esparza. Not knowing Punch was going to use the knife to lance the wound and draw out the poison, Esparza, fearing for his life, drew his pistol and shot Punch with the two remaining rounds in his pistol. He hastily loaded the pistol from his ammo belt in case anyone else had any ideas of a leadership coup. He paused momentarily and a thought came to him that perhaps he should cut the wound and drain the snake venom. Then he realized what Punch had in mind. He cut an "X" over the puncture marks and sucked hard, spitting out the blood and venom. As he wiped his mouth with the back of his sleeve, he looked down at the still body of Punch Hamner and said, "I am so sorry, amigo. I thought you were trying to kill me." He shook his head and shouted out to the darkness, "Lipan, you truly are a devil and I curse you. You see what you made me do? He was a good man who wanted to help me and I shot him!"

As if in answer, a puma screamed back out of the darkness and a wolf howled on the canyon rim above them. That was the proverbial straw. Over two dozen men turned in unison and sprinted for their horses. In a matter of minutes, the rumble of pounding hooves died out and Esparza was left standing at the mouth of the canyon with the three of his men who had remained loyal.

Esparza stood still for the longest time before he took out the makings and rolled a smoke, lit it, took a couple of pulls, slowly blowing the smoke out, while he searched the canyon rims on both sides of the gorge, as if he intended to find some answers there. One could say he was in a state of minor shock. A few minutes ago he was in command of a gang of vicious killers and thieves, and now he stood alone with three men, one of whom was his retarded nephew and the other two were not the sharpest knives in the drawer, either. In other words, if they had been any smarter they would have left with the others. Esparza turned to his nephew and asked, "Pedro, what has happened?" He hadn't expected an answer and when Pedro began to say something, Esparza said, "Ah, shut up!"

While Esparza was trying to decide what his next move was going to be, a faint, muffled sound, coming from inside the canyon, caught his attention. He hushed the three men with him and turned his head slightly to the left, listening intently for the sound to repeat itself. After several seconds Esparza could hear the sounds again. Once more, he concentrated, trying to identify the sound and from whence it came. There was nothing for a long while and then Esparza could hear voices and it sounded as if they were shouting.

Patrick Dunnigan had regained consciousness and was moaning and groaning from the intense pain he was enduring. Harold Ballard had made his way in the darkness to Dunnigan's position and getting his attention, Ballard explained where they were and their situation. After a couple of sips of water and a pull on Ballard's cigarette, Dunnigan felt better and closing his eyes, he drifted off into much needed sleep.

Sinclair Thornsbury, on the other hand, wasn't so easy to placate. Although he was not nearly in as rough shape as his friend Dunnigan, he moaned and groaned even louder. After Ballard settled Dunnigan down, he made his way to Thornsbury's position to see if he could be of assistance.

"What the devil is going on here? Why did you all leave me here? I want some answers!" ranted Thornsbury. He paused his tirade long enough to sit up and look around. Seeing nothing or nobody but John Ballard, he change his tone and asked Ballard politely what the situation was.

Ballard told him the whole story, which only infuriated Thornsbury. With Ballard's help, he struggled to his feet and shouted in Esparza's direction. "You filthy reverberate! Do you know who you are dealing with? I will see you hang, if it's the last thing I do!"

If it was one thing Esparza detested more than anything else, it was a loud mouth Gringo. He was just about to turn around and leave, calling it a day, but Thornsbury's condescending arrogance wouldn't let him. He shouted back as he began to walk forward, "Is that so, my fat, little friend? I shall come to you so you can hang me, but look around, amigo. There are no trees!" He chuckled at his own attempt at humor as he chambered a shell into his rifle.

A large chunk of lead ricocheted off the small boulder beside Esparza, followed closely by the boom of the .50 and a moment later by the sound of Jake's voice emanated from the darkness. "Hey Bandito, I will not let you kill this man. Walk away and I will not shoot you, today."

Esparza stopped and partially turned in the direction he thought Jake's voice had originated. He asked, "What is this gringo to you, Apache?"

"He owes me forty dollars."

Esparza laughed out loud and answered, "You amuse me, Apache. The man is a pig. I believe you would enjoy skinning him over an open fire and yet you want to save him because he owes you some pesos? Aye cramaba, I will give you fifty dollars if you let me kill him, por favor, amigo."

"It is not the money," replied Jake.

There was a very long pause and then Esparza shouted into the canyon. "Gringo, you live to see another day because the Apache believes in honor. He does not know that you are not an honorable man. I would not wait too long to settle the debt, Gringo. Even the Lipan can grow impatient."

He turned and headed back toward the mouth of the canyon and as he walked he said loud enough for Jake to hear, "I will do as you ask, Apache. The loco General may not be so generous." He had made up his mind. He'd had enough of delusional generals and witch doctors who liked to play with snakes. There had to be an easier way to make a dishonest living. He beckoned to his three cronies and the four of them turned and half running, half walking, they headed out into the darkness, without so much as a glance backwards.

CHAPTER TWENTY FOUR

"WHAT THE HELL was that?" asked Jim Clemfeld.

"Sounds like the canon, ole Jake is carryin'," replied Pat Wilkens.

"Who's he shootin' at?"

Pat spat and wiped his moustache with his sleeve and then said, "Don't rightly know, Jim. Don't rightly know."

A short time after the shot, Hollister lowered the field glasses and turned to face Kulbane. "Interesting," was all he said.

Kulbane expected more and was annoyed that he had to prod his subordinate for further information. "Pray tell us all, Colonel, what has captivated your interest so," he asked, sarcastically.

As if to annoy Kulbane further, Hollister replied, "Esparza."

Kulbane played the game and asked, "What is our fearless bandit leader doing?"

Hollister answered quickly, "Nothing. It appears his men have left, whether on his orders or through fear, I cannot determine. There isn't enough light to see clearly, but it appears Esparza and three of his men are at the mouth of the canyon. It sounds as if Esparza and Sinclair Thornsbury were yelling at each other."

Hollister gave Kulbane a chance to digest the information and then continued his narration, "Now, it sounds as if Esparza is talking to the shooter. I am guessing that would be Jake." There was a long pause before Hollister spoke again. As he lowered the field glasses, he said, "Mr. Kulbane, it would appear Esparza is no longer a problem for you." Without waiting for a reply from Kulbane, Hollister turned to Pat and said, "Pat, take Mex and Jim back down in the canyon and see to Mr. Dunnigan and Mr. Thornsbury." He issued the order for two reasons: one, he was sure the ranchers could use the help and secondly, he wasn't sure what the unstable Kulbane was going to do next, but he had a feeling it wasn't going to be good, so he thought he could get his three friends out of harm's way.

Kulbane added, "Yes, it is almost daylight. Why don't we all head back down into the canyon and assess our situation?"

Hollister, Pat, Mex, and Jim waited while Kulbane's men made their way past them and down the trail that led to the chute and the moraine. Once everyone was down on level ground in the alcove, Kulbane began issuing orders, instructing three of his men to round up the rancher's and their men. He ordered a group of others to bind Hollister and his three friends, with their hands behind their backs. It appeared Mex was about to do something stupid, but a glance at Hollister, who shook his slightly in a *'no-not-now'* gesture, convinced him to wait it out.

The men who had been sent to retrieve the ranchers came back to the alcove with two of them dragging the near-dead Patrick Dunnigan between them and the other man was prodding and shoving Ballard and Thornsbury's hand, Morley Gruber, with the barrel end of his Winchester. Sinclair Thornsbury, moaning and groaning with every step, stumbled and fell several times. No one stopped to help him back to his feet, but they merely paused where they were and waited while the portly ranchman made it back to his feet, and then the entourage continued on its way.

Hollister was amused to see there were only four men left of the ranchers and their hands. He surmised that, given the opportunity, the rest of the group had escaped. Kulbane's reaction, however, surprised Hollister. Instead of going off on a tirade, Kulbane simply sighed, looked around, and said, "Let us get a nice warm fire built and some food and coffee brewing. We will rest the horses and the men for the day, and then we will make some decisions."

The long, hot day passed without any incidents. No one slept very much that night; George Kulbane, least of all. Kulbane's world and his mind were both unraveling. The events of the last few weeks had broadsided him. A month ago, he was well immersed in his goal to create an army and rekindle the conflict with the Yankees. He had a base of operation, and a small army of men to procure the resources they would need, albeit it was all illegal activities that involved robbery, rustling and anything else that would bring in some revenue. To George Kulbane the end justified the means.

His dreams were torn asunder by a bunch of cowpunchers concerned about a few lousy head of cattle. Some old renegade white man, who thought he was an Apache, killed his son and burned his headquarters to the ground. And now his main fighting force had deserted along with his second in command. In Kulbane's rattled brain, someone had to pay for these transgressions. He needed to think a way to draw out that cursed Apache and get the savage in his sights. He smiled slightly as a thought came to him. He would use Hollister and his three friends as bait and once he had the Apache in his clutches, all of them would die a slow agonizing death.

Unlike Esparza's group, Kulbane's men all knew one another by looks and by name, which would make it difficult for Jake to mix and mingle without being spotted. That night as most of the men were just drifting off to sleep, a wolf howl, echoing through the canyon, brought them back to full conscious. There would be no sound for a short time and then the scream of a puma would get everyone's attention. Several men, on different occasions, leapt to their feet and when asked what the trouble was, they replied that they could have sworn they had heard a rattlesnake in close proximity. And so it went for most of the night, a symphony of animal sounds that sounded, at times, as if they were right beside the men.

It was the darkest part of the night, a couple hours before dawn, when already jumpy men began to receive unwelcome company. John Curtis had just nicely dozed off when he felt tightness around his neck. When full consciousness returned, he realized that his own bullwhip was wrapped around his throat and someone behind him was pulling the loose ends tighter and tighter. The tension stopped just short of cutting John's wind off. He raised his hands to his throat, tugging at the coils of the whip. Someone, whose mouth was next to John's ear, whispered, "Be quiet! I am not going to kill you this time, but if you are still here the next time we meet, you will die."

It was a full two minutes before John realized there was no longer anyone in his vicinity. He leapt to his feet, pulling at the whip around his throat. Knowing the horses would be guarded, he simply took off sprinting back up the canyon and out into the desert. In the next couple of hours, most of the other men had a knife put to their put to their throats and the wielder whispered in their ear that it would be best for their health and peace of mind if they left the camp as quickly as possible. They all took the offered advice.

Just before dawn, the two men watching the horses were rendered unconscious by a tap to the temple with the butt end of a big Bowie knife and then the perpetrator cut the tether lines. The odor of Azul and the distinct sound of rattlesnakes at their feet created a stampede of wild-eyed, terror filled horses, all headed for the perceived safety of the open desert, which was very unfortunate for the men who had bedded down in their path. Several of them were trampled, while the rest of them, including George Kulbane, scrambled to the safety of the boulders scattered about. Hollister, Pat, Mex, and Jim were still tied up, but they had been positioned under the shelter of an outcrop of shale and thus they were out of the path of the bone crushing stampede. Thornsbury, Dunnigan, Ballard and Morley Gruber, were unbound, but out of harm's way, as well.

As the sun came up, the morning light illuminated a despondent and angry George Kulbane. He stood in the middle of the alcove with a cocked pistol in his right hand which hung at his side. Only two of his men, Mathew Allen and Norbert Bigelow, who hadn't been persuaded to leave by the whispering, shadowy figure of the night, remained with the General. Kulbane raised the pistol into the air and fire two rounds and then shouted at the top of his lungs, "Apache!" He waited a full minute and then shot twice more into the air. He lowered the pistol and said as he began to reload the gun, "Apache, show yourself! Show yourself or I will begin shooting your friends, one by one, starting with Colonel Hollister."

"They are not my friends," came a muffled reply from somewhere out in the canyon.

Kulbane walked to the opening between the alcove and the canyon and using one of the perpendicular walls for cover, he shouted, "If you are not here to rescue them, then what do you want?"

"The one called Thornsbury owes me forty dollars."

Kulbane was taken aback. His mind was reeling as he tried to make sense of what he had just heard. *'Could it be that simple,'* he thought. *'All this trouble because some greedy carpetbagger didn't pay some old Apache?'* Kulbane's blood pressure went through the roof. As he strode towards Thornsbury, he couldn't recall a time when he had been this angry.

Hollister was paying close attention to the proceedings and he had a fair idea of what Kulbane was about to do, so he shouted in protest, "Kulbane, you can't do it! It's just plain murder! Kulbane, you are insane!"

The General stopped in front of Hollister and said in a cold calculating tone, "If you know any short prayers, you better get to saying them, because you are next!" Then he finished his deliberate walk to where Thornsbury and Dunnigan sat propped up against a boulder. He bent down and lifted Thornsbury by his shirt front and began dragging him to the opening between the canyon and the alcove. He was moving so fast that Thornsbury could barely keep up and several times he lost his balance. He never fell to the ground, as Kulbane, bolstered by angry adrenalin, lifted him to his feet and continued on. When he got to the partition between the alcove and the canyon, he shoved Thornsbury with all his strength into the canyon area. The force of the push caused Thornsbury to stumble and eventually fall to the ground.

"Is this the man you want, Apache?" hollered Kulbane. He didn't wait for an answer. Instead, he took careful aim and shot Sinclair Thornsbury in the center of the forehead. He started to laugh, like he had just heard a very funny joke. He even began do dance a little jig as he continued to cackle. He stopped laughing as abruptly as he had started and asked, "What now, my savage friend?" and then he cackled again.

"Now, you have taken on the dead man's debt. I shall collect what is owed to me, from you," Jake replied." It wasn't the answer Kulbane was expecting. His rage returned. He did an abrupt about face and headed back into the alcove to select another victim.

While Kulbane was engaged in the murder of Sinclair Thornsbury, John Ballard had made his way unnoticed to Hollister's positioned where he nervously but quickly undid the ropes binding Hollister. Allen and Bigelow were both standing a few feet away, but their attention was entirely on Kulbane as he dragged Thornsbury to his doom.

Hollister, while still seated, searched the ground around him and found a solid, fist sized rock. He carefully and quietly rose to his feet and stood for a moment to let the blood return to his cramped leg muscles, before making his move. He sprinted with rock in hand and coming up behind Mathew Allen, Hollister hit him as hard as he could in the back of the head with the rock. Bigelow, hearing the commotion, drew his pistol just as Hollister's rock came straight for his head, causing him to duck and avoid the flying stone, which gave Hollister enough time to cover the short distance between them and place a well aimed fist between Bigelow's eyes. Bigelow went down like a sack of sand and Hollister was on him, stomping on his gun hand, forcing him to let go of the pistol. Hollister was picking up the gun just as the shot that killed Thornsbury rang out. He turned towards the sound, which gave Bigelow an opportunity to get to his feet. He charged Hollister, but the Colonel sensed him coming and swung the pistol in a wide arc behind him catching Bigelow right across his already broken nose.

Hollister turned to face Kulbane, cocking and raising his pistol at the same time. Kulbane was stomping towards Hollister, but he was so intent on his mission that he hadn't noticed Hollister was there until the Colonel said, "That's far enough."

Kulbane stopped dead in his tracks and instinctively raised his cocked pistol to a shooting position. The two men were about twenty feet apart, pistols centered on each other's chests. Kulbane spoke, "Well, here we are Colonel. What now? Are you going to kill me and take command? Is this what this is, a mutiny?"

It was Hollister's turn to see red. He replied with frustration in his voice. "You poor sick bastard, do you actually believe I would have anything to do with your delusion? I have never wanted any part of you or what you stand for. Can't you understand that?"

Kulbane looked like he had just been slapped in the face. He regained his composure and retorted, "That's insubordination, Colonel! I will have you flogged! Curtis, give this man twenty five lashes!" Not hearing or seeing any response, he diverted his attention away from Hollister and looked around. Curtis was nowhere to be seen. In fact, the two of his men who hadn't run off into the night were lying prone on the ground.

Realization infuriated Kulbane, but before he could pull the trigger, Pat Wilkens, who had been untied by Ballard, cupped his hands together and drove his fists as hard as he could into the middle of Kulbane's back, driving him forward with a lurch that almost broke his neck. Kulbane couldn't maintain his balance and after stumbling for a few feet, he fell to the ground. Pat was upon him immediately, kicking the gun out of his hand. He then put one foot on Kulbane's throat and before he could deliver the other boot to the General's skull, Hollister asked him to stop. Pat looked at Hollister, back at Kulbane, back at Hollister once more, and then he spat a brown wad into Kulbane's face and said, "Whatever you say, Colonel. You're the boss."

In the ensuing three months, Hollister bought out Thornsbury's mortgage as well as Patrick Dunnigan's, who had succumbed to his injuries and died on the way back from the canyon. Hollister made Pat Wilkens the foreman of what was now one of the biggest ranches in the territory. Pat convinced the Colonel that both Mex and Jim should be made "*deputy*" foreman, as Pat called the position and Hollister gladly complied.

One early evening, Hollister and Pat had just finished their supper and were out on the veranda having some tobacco; Hollister in the form of a cigarette and Pat the chewing variety. A line rider appeared in the distance, and as he drew closer, Hollister and Pat could see that he was leading a big black stallion, which caught Hollister's immediate attention. He stood and walked to the top of the stairs leading to the veranda with Pat Wilkens close behind.

When the rider was within speaking distance, he stopped and before he could say anything, Hollister asked, "Where did you find him?"

The cowboy replied, "I was checkin' the tree line for strays over by Burnt Timber, and I come out in this here meadow. There was this old Apache on a pinto, sittin' there still as all get out. He was holdin' the reins to this big black, here. When I ride closer, he starts towards me. Well Sir, I wasn't sure what he wanted and when I was about to pull my rifle, he stopped. He held out the rope to the big black, like he wanted me to take it. When I took the rope from him, he told me to bring the horse to you, Colonel. He said it was a gift."

There was a momentary pause and when it looked like the cowboy wasn't going to say anything more, Hollister asked, "What's your name, Son?"

"Most folks call Dave, Sir"

"Well Dave, tell me exactly what the Apache said and use his words," said Hollister.

"Yes Sir, he said a few things that I thought were a little strange."

The cowboy paused like he was trying to recall the conversation, scratched his chin, then spoke, "He told me to tell you that it took some convincin', but finally some General paid him for the stallion, and then told him to keep the horse because he didn't want anythin' to do with it." After a short pause the cowboy added, "That there's got me right confused. What kind of a man buys a horse and then gives it back?"

Pat spit a big brown wad onto the first step, wiped his mustache with his sleeve and asked the man, "Did he say how much he got for the horse?"

"Yep," replied the cowboy, *"Forty Dollars."*

THE END